W9-CKU-982

Photo by Colleen Harvey

NINA KILLHAM lives in London with her husband and two children. *Believe Me* is her third novel.

Praise for *How to Cook a Tart*

"A devilish delight . . . smart, sexy, hilarious and not to be missed."
— *The Washington Post*

"A delicate, wicked comedy that made me want to throw out my margarine and luxuriate in butter. I can relate to a book that celebrates eating and laughs at diets."
—Tracy Chevalier, author of *Burning Bright*

"Wickedly funny."
— *The New York Times Book Review*

"*How to Cook a Tart* is gastro-porn—as if Julia Child and William Burroughs had a bastard child. Filled with magnificent descriptions of the best of food, the novel's dark subtext left me questioning whether I should cook less and have more sex—or cook more, just with more butter."
—Anthony Bourdain, author of *Kitchen Confidential*

Believe Me

A Novel

Nina Killham

A PLUME BOOK

PLUME
Published by the Penguin Group
Penguin Group (USA) Inc., 375 Hudson Street, New York, New York 10014, U.S.A. •
Penguin Group (Canada), 90 Eglinton Avenue East, Suite 700, Toronto, Ontario,
Canada M4P 2Y3 (a division of Pearson Penguin Canada Inc.) • Penguin Books Ltd.,
80 Strand, London WC2R 0RL, England • Penguin Ireland, 25 St. Stephen's Green,
Dublin 2, Ireland (a division of Penguin Books Ltd.) • Penguin Group (Australia),
250 Camberwell Road, Camberwell, Victoria 3124, Australia (a division of Pearson
Australia Group Pty. Ltd.) • Penguin Books India Pvt. Ltd., 11 Community Centre,
Panchsheel Park, New Delhi – 110 017, India • Penguin Group (NZ), 67 Apollo
Drive, Rosedale, North Shore 0632, New Zealand (a division of Pearson New Zealand
Ltd) • Penguin Books (South Africa) (Pty.) Ltd., 24 Sturdee Avenue, Rosebank,
Johannesburg 2196, South Africa

Penguin Books Ltd., Registered Offices: 80 Strand, London WC2R 0RL, England

First published by Plume, a member of Penguin Group (USA) Inc.

First Printing, February 2009
10 9 8 7 6 5 4 3 2 1

 REGISTERED TRADEMARK—MARCA REGISTRADA

LIBRARY OF CONGRESS CATALOGING-IN-PUBLICATION DATA

Killham, Nina.
  Believe me : a novel / Nina Killham.
    p. cm.
  ISBN 978-0-452-28976-5
  1. Teenage boys—Fiction. 2. Mothers and sons—Fiction. 3. Faith—Fiction.
  4. Maryland—Fiction. 5. Domestic fiction. I. Title.
  PS3611.I45B35 2009
  813'.6—dc22   2008022065

Printed in the United States of America
Set in Adobe Garamond

BOOKS ARE AVAILABLE AT QUANTITY DISCOUNTS WHEN USED TO PROMOTE PRODUCTS OR
SERVICES. FOR INFORMATION PLEASE WRITE TO PREMIUM MARKETING DIVISION, PENGUIN
GROUP (USA) INC., 375 HUDSON STREET, NEW YORK, NEW YORK 10014.

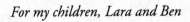

For my children, Lara and Ben

Acknowledgments

A big thank-you to Elise Laird, Amy C. Fredericks, Stuart Vogel, Tanner Parsons, Jonathan Drori, Lisa Hogg, Isobel Dixon, and Stuart Krichevsky. Special thanks go to my sister, Amanda Davis, for tirelessly reading my drafts, and to Sarah Fortna for reminding me I wanted to write this. And, as always, endless gratitude to Andrew, for making it all possible.

Believe Me

Chapter One

What is the point of life? I mean, why do I have eight kinds of crunchy peanut butter to choose from, and this kid in Pakistan whose house just fell on his head doesn't even have a word for peanut butter? Why does Darryl Green have five broken bones and I've never even sprained my ankle? Why do people die of stupid things all the time?

And I know what you're thinking. Duh, you moron, you just noticed this now? And no, not just now, but I guess I've been thinking more about it because I'm thirteen. Mom calls it the "cusp" of manhood. She says the cusp used to be thirteen forty years ago, though now she says it doesn't seem to arrive until a guy is at least thirty-five. So I'm thinking, okay, I've been born and, eventually, I'll die, so now what? Am I supposed to do some living? But how? And if I don't do it on reality TV, does it count?

"Nic, it's a quarter to eight. You've got to go."

"I'm busy here."

"You're *still* in the bathroom?"

"Can't rush these things."

"You're going to miss the bus."

"Any minute now . . ."

Mom keeps telling me she wants me to find my passion. She says she's found hers: *stars*. She's this big professor of astrophysics at the University of Maryland. Says she's lucky because she found her passion early and she wants me to find mine too. She's pretty intense. Dad says it's her red hair, and she always frowns and says that's a cliché. But everyone knows clichés are usually true. My dad now lives in Williamsburg, Virginia. He's a professor too. He got a job down there, but Mom had just gotten her job here and so she wasn't budging. They were pretty calm about it. This town isn't big enough for the both of us, he joked, when he stuffed all his clothes and a billion books into his Volvo and drove off.

It's not like I don't see him. I see him lots on the weekends and vacations. It's been two years now. They're not divorced; they're not anything. I'm not sure what their point is. Maybe they'll let me know.

So I'm living with Mom alone now and every morning she hassles me.

"Got everything?"

"Yeah."

"You sure?"

"Yeah."

"Great. See you later."

I'm halfway out the door when I remember. "Oh, we're supposed to do an oral history project interviewing two generations older than us and turn it in this morning."

"I'm going to kill you."

*   *   *

Even when Mom comes home from work wiped out, she doesn't chill. When she comes home she starts her second job: tormenting me. She's determined to teach me everything she knows. She keeps a humongous stack of books on the kitchen table. If a question comes up that I don't know—and I mean any question, like What is the composition of a second generation star? or What era is a trilobite fossil from? or How many sperm does your average chimp have?—she considers it her duty to find out the rational answer then and there. It's as though, if she doesn't tell me right away I might break out in a bad case of ignorance and end up believing in astrology or superstitions or, worst of all, God.

She's got a lot of opinions, my mom. And she's not shy about telling you. Our car is the National Gallery of Bumper Stickers: FREETHINKER, ATHEISTS BELIEVE IN PEOPLE, PEACE IS PATRIOTIC, and the latest: ASTRONOMERS DO IT FOR THE BIG BANG.

Everything is a debate with her. And she's really smart. Though I got to tell you she sort of wears it on her sleeve. You know, the whole "I'm a brilliant scientist, so what the hell have you done lately?" You know the type. But she's nice. She just gets worked up about things. Like the M74 galaxy. I mean, let's face it, the thing is 30 million light-years away. Like it's really going to affect us. Like it's really going to change my day. But intelligence is a big thing for her. Nothing lamer than a dumb kid. Of course if you really are a dumb kid she'd sympathize and be all for the government paying for you to have tutoring.

She's no ogre. She just doesn't like brains wasted. Says they are "the hallmark of humanity." Lucky for her I'm no slouch in that department. I'm a class-one brain.

At school, Mrs. Brickman sees it differently.

"Nic, I see you've neglected the assignment again."

"I told my mom, but she didn't have time to drive me around."

"This is the third time this month."

"I told her."

"I'm going to have to send a note home."

"Maybe that'll help. I don't know."

When I get back that day from science club, Mom's where she always is. In her souped-up home office. She's got more wires in there than Barnum and Bailey. She spends most of her nights designing computer programs to measure how far away the stars are and what might be circulating around them. She's a planet hunter. Which means she's looking for a star that has a planet the same distance away from it as the earth is from the sun. She's trying to prove that we are not the only life in the universe. That our world is way more complicated than we morons can imagine.

"What's this?" she says when I come in and hand over the note.

"It's from my teacher. She says you're really letting the team down."

"But . . ."

"Sign here and you can consider yourself formally warned."

"Nicolas . . ."

Nicolas. Can you believe it? She named me after Nicolas Copernicus. You know, the guy who figured out that the earth revolved around the sun, not the other way around? Can't decide if that's pretty cool or the geekiest thing ever. I change my mind a couple of times a day. So I'm Nic. Without the *k*, which is a real pain sometimes. The popular kids call me Nicotine. Otherwise it's fine. Short and sweet. The name. Not me. I'm pretty tall for a thirteen-year-old. I just wish I'd bulk up. I'd ask Mom for some muscles for my birthday, but I don't think she can deliver. Not that kind of scientist.

Luckily she clicks off like a blinker at 9 PM.

"Is there anything I need to know about your education before you turn in?"

"I'm flunking math."

"Very funny."

"Later."

"I love you."

"Yeah, yeah."

Mom likes to tell me she believes in the universe. She believes in its wonder. In its ability to confound us. Which is why she says she wants me to know everything. Why the leaves on the trees change colors. Why the sky is blue. How the wings of a bird make it fly.

So I asked her once: "Why do I have to know it all?"

"Because it will save you."

I said, "How? What difference does it make if I know that bullets made from iron and copper are less toxic than lead? That sulphur dioxide and nitrogen oxide are key components of smog? How will that save me?"

"It will help you to do something about it," she said.

"Why haven't you done something about it?"

Then I got to play Nintendo. Which is what I get to do when she doesn't like where the conversation is going.

I mean, don't you think life is a funny thing? It's supposed to be right there, laid out before you, but it's not really. For example, do you know how time works? It's really funky. We all have our own personal time clocks. So time for me is going to be different than time for you. There's this famous test they did, where they showed that time on the watch of someone traveling in a train was different than that of the person standing on the platform when the train swooshed by. Pretty cool. I mean, it wasn't by a lot but enough, you know, in science, to get those tails wagging. You'd think it would be the same everywhere. Time, that is. The same for me and same for Mom and same for Layla.

Layla's my babysitter. I know, what the hell am I still doing with a babysitter at thirteen? Talk to my mom. Anyway, she's been coming over for eons when Mom works real late. Then, three Tuesdays ago I looked up from doing my homework and there she was on the couch with her legs up and crossed and they were really long and tan-looking. She's from Egypt, or at least her dad is. Well, I don't know, I think I stared at them for a zillion minutes until she said something like "What's your problem?" and I said, "Nothing." So she's looking at me and I'm looking at her. Finally, I had to look down at my books and not move for at least five minutes until I could tell she had gone back to reading her *Girl Power* magazine. And it's been like that ever since. I'm always looking at her. All the time. It's like she was a babysitter one day and the next, well, she's Layla. Layla with the long legs. Can't tell Mom. She'd research "physiology of a hard-on" and read it out to me at dinner.

What I'm getting at is, Layla's time is different than mine. Time has its own laws. Its own thing going on. And no matter what we do, we don't have much to say about it. Sometimes I think, how can we live in a world like that?

Basically, Mom's upset that we don't do as many things together as we used to. We used to do a lot of things. We used to play Monopoly during dinner and just keep the game running for days on end.

"Want me to set up a game?" she says all the time now like a broken record.

"Nah."

"Come on, it'll be fun."

"I don't feel like it."

We used to go for walks along Rock Creek. She taught me how to ride a bike along there. I nearly fell in. I don't think I've seen her laugh that much before or since.

At bedtime, when I was a kid, I used to grab her hand when she tried to get up from my bed and leave. I'd grab both her hands and pin them under me so she couldn't get away. Can't believe I used to do that. Now I just wave to her from the hallway and do the whole wash/brush teeth/shower drill by myself. Sometimes I don't feel like taking a shower, so I sit on the edge of the tub reading comics with the water on, pouring down the drain. I know, earth killer. But getting undressed and getting all wet and having to dry off again. It's too much of a hassle. She gets so pissed off when she catches me. Once she gave me one measly knock of a warning before she opened the door. Now I keep it locked. A dude needs some privacy.

Because Mom acts like she knows everything that goes on inside my head, but there is so much she doesn't know about me. She doesn't even know I want to try out for basketball this year. If I tell her she'll be all "Rah-Rah, you can do it. I believe in you!" Which is a crock because when I should have been going to basketball camp to practice she had me interred in Brilliant Minds of the Future. So I've been shooting hoops in the driveway. *Thunk, thunk.* The tryouts are in a month. I'm going to walk in and be the man from nowhere. Their mouths are gonna drop open. Coach Milton is going to pour his Big Gulp Pepsi down his front. I'm gonna be their big hope for the next season. And after the championships they're gonna carry me out on their shoulders.

I can see it. I'm gonna leave my mind behind. I'm going to be part of the popular group. I'm gonna walk down the hall like I own it. I'm going to graduate Totally Cool Dude. And I'm going to get the girls to do whatever I want. Well, some of them. Like Alice Campbell. And then I'm going to pretend not to know her because, really, you don't want to stick around afterward. She's kind of weird.

Mom thinks I'm going to be a rapist when I grow up.

She's always talking about how bad the statistics are. "I hope you realize that these poor girls have feelings. And I hope you speak up if you see anything bad happen."

"Like what?"

"Like someone being taken advantage of. It must be so hard for them being mauled in the hallways."

I think of Gina Kosta, who sent me a photo of her right boob.

Mom keeps going on about how it's a man's world out there. But I don't know. Have you noticed how many girls there are? They're everywhere. Even when they're not there they're there. On posters all over the place. They sell everything. Cars, iPods, beer. Lots of beer. Which is weird because most girls I know don't like beer. They're into alcopops. They suck on them like candy and then get bombed. Their dads have to come pick them up from parties and scrape them off the floor.

I can't see Layla being like that. She's too . . . I don't know, too . . . I can't imagine her not being in control. She's so totally, "Yes, Mrs. Delano. No, Mrs. Delano, I won't let him watch TV until his homework is done." Like I'm some poodle that's pissed on the carpet again. And then she hangs up and walks really straight and sits back down in front of *A Simple Life*. She's such a liar. Liar with the long legs. I dreamed about her last night and boy, what a mess. I was stuffing the sheets down the laundry basket pretending I poured Gatorade all over the bed. If Mom knew the stuff I dream about she'd bust a pancreas.

And yes, we've had "the talk." It started with Mom leaving

sex pamphlets around everywhere she thought I'd be: back of the toilet, in cereal boxes, tucked under my place mat. But she didn't say anything. She just left them there. When she'd clean the table she wiped around them. I don't know what she was expecting me to do—say, "Gee, thanks, Mom, I was wondering where everything goes. I've been sticking it in the dog's ear but boy, did you set me straight"—so I just left them there. She finally gets Dad to come up from Williamsburg and they call me in and sit me down.

"So, Nic . . . you're probably wondering about sexual intercourse," she says.

I look at Dad, who is staring hard at one of the pamphlets like he's never really understood all the stuff he's been doing.

I decide I'd much rather choke than answer.

The secret to a good choke is to fall forward and bang at your throat so it looks like you've got a marble down your windpipe. Don't make a choking sound because people who can't breathe can't make a sound. And clawing is good too. I like to claw with one hand and bang with the other. If you want to put on a really good show flop your legs around and don't let anyone get behind you because if they do they'll try to Heimlich you.

Later, before Dad leaves to go back to Williamsburg, he comes up to my room and hands me a box of condoms. "Learn how to use them and don't ever think of going without. You don't want to ruin your life."

I don't know who they think I'm having sex with. It's like they think there's all these girls in school who drape themselves in the hallways and just pull down their panties and let you in. All my parents have got on their minds is "Hold on there, son, before you go zooming in be sure to cover up." It's not like my dick is in great demand.

And no. No way. I can't think of them doing it. Every once in a while Mom'll kiss my dad on the lips quickly and I want to go yuck. She calls him her lusty elf. Quadruple yuck. Just thinking of them doing it thirteen years ago grosses me out.

So, lately there's been all these books lying around the house with titles like, *Dynamics of Effective Parenting During Adolescence, Literacy and Learning: Strategies for Middle School, Readings on Emerging Adulthood,* and my particular favorite, *You and Your Adolescent: A User's Guide.* I've been taking a peek when she's not looking and did you know that from age nine to thirteen a guy's testosterone levels go up five times. How cool is that?

The other day I found this gargantuan book called *21st Century Culture and Teenage Depression.* A few days later, when Mom got home she made me turn off *The X-Files* and asked if everything was okay and I said sure.

"No, but really. You can talk to me, Nic, I'm here."

"Yeah."

"To listen, if you need it."

"I know."

"But do you? Do you really?"

"Sure."

She checked me out for a long time until I finally said, "So, what's for dinner?"

She stood up, poured herself a glass of wine, and said, "Yeah, I'm fine too, thanks." Then walked off to the kitchen.

I think she thinks I think a lot more about stuff than I do. You know, as in, I don't know, interesting stuff. Like he said/she said kind of stuff. To tell you the truth, most of the time I'm not catching myself thinking anything.

Chapter Two

"Nic! There's no hot water left."

"Really? There was plenty when I had a shower."

"You're a dead man!"

Every weekend Mom likes to get together with her atheist friends. They've pulled together a local group and plan to take over the world. Her best friend, Carla, is president. My mom is vice president and does all the hard work, like getting rally permits and keeping the mailing list. Carla, Mom says, is busy getting haircuts so she looks good at the podium. They're always having big discussions about who to let in: hard-core atheists only or some agnostics too. Mom says, "We should welcome everybody, we're lucky to have them," but Carla gets pissed off about the agnostics who she says are like people on airplanes who can't decide beef or chicken.

Mostly they meet in our backyard but sometimes, when it's a real big wingding, like today, their anniversary, they meet at Takoma Park and hope it doesn't rain. Mom makes jerk chicken and Carla makes her gross tofu salad. A few meetings ago they finally got a lawyer to join and Mom and Carla drank themselves into a celebration mess. Carla left her tofu salad out all night in the backyard. Even the rats wouldn't eat it.

So when Mom finally comes down she's wearing her I-don't-believe-in-God outfit: green J. Crew dress, Birkenstocks, and knee socks. Me, I'm wearing my POPE BENEDICT FOR SHERIFF T-shirt. A real conversation starter.

By the time we get to the park they've already set up the little podium with the atheist flag spread across the front. The flag's got a picture of the planet and an interrupted black chain, which is supposed to signify we're not locked up by ignorance and superstitions. There are a couple of tables selling literature and bumper stickers—the usual ATHEISM IS MYTH-UNDERSTOOD; FINE . . . I EVOLVED, YOU DIDN'T; HAVE YOU HUGGED AN ATHEIST TODAY?

"Nic, good to see ya." It's Mr. Phillips. He's third-generation atheist and damn proud of it. "Not a mumbo jumbo gene in my body," he likes to say. I'm supposed to be second generation. There aren't that many second or third generations. Most in the group are newly AWOL from religion, like my mom. People so freaked out by a religious upbringing they'll spend a Saturday afternoon choking down organic coleslaw with soy mayo. And most are old people. Old men. Mr. Phillips is always going, "Where are all the young women?" like he thought atheism was a dating service and he wants his money back.

He's been eating one of the granola/carob muffins. I know this because half of it is still roosting in his mustache. "How's school?" he says.

"Good," I say, like I'm really going to go into it with him.

"They teaching you creationism yet?"

"Not yet."

"Just a matter of time," he says, and chugs his wine.

And we stand there a while like the baboons we're two degrees from, just staring at the grass, not saying anything. All around us people are talking up a storm. Mom is weaving in and out gathering signatures. Carla is reading over her notes for her speech.

"How 'bout them Redskins," Mr. Phillips finally says.

"I root for Green Bay. My dad went to UW."

And he shakes his head. "An atheist *and* a Packer fan. Now that's just making life hard for yourself."

And then we see them. The cops. Two of them getting out of their car and making their way toward us. Carla goes into a panic. "Where's the permit? Where's the permit? Lucy, you got the permit, didn't you?"

And Mom drops her files and riffles frantically through her bag. "Here it is." You can see everybody sighing with relief.

The cop just torpedoes, belly first, through the party and stops in front of Mom.

"Afternoon, ma'am," he says.

"Hello," she says and hands him the permit.

He takes a good look at it, placing his hand on his noisy walkie-talkie, which is going on about some "situation" they've got going down on D street and 23rd, and then hands it back to her. "Looks all right."

Mom nods.

"Nice day for this," he says, looking around, checking out

the flag, the bumper stickers, Carla trying to hide the OSAMA BIN LADEN TALKS TO GOD TOO poster with her skirt.

Mom peers up at him. "Yes. It is."

"What's in the big jugs?"

Mom glances back at the collection of wine boxes that have been covered with white paper to hide their labels. "Would you believe it if I said Kool-Aid?"

He looks over at his fellow cop who turns out to be a woman. She doesn't move a muscle.

"Make sure it's all cleaned up afterward," he says.

"Yes, we certainly will. Thank you."

"You have a good day now." And he sort of touches his helmet like he's tipping it. "And God bless."

Later on, I can see Mom talking to some guy I've never seen before, some geek in chinos doing the "Just thought I'd come by, see what you were about, 'cause I've been thinking lately . . . blah, blah, blah." Mom's looking around like crazy and I know she's looking for me. She wants me to make him feel comfortable. To talk the talk, to be young and cool with him. Luckily I'm saved by my IM.

Kevin: UR L8.

Deadman: B thr in 5.

Kevin: Latr.

Deadman: In yr dreams.

Kevin: LOL!

So I go and tell her that I'm out of here. I'm meeting my friend Kevin. She says, "Just say hello to Jason here. He's a Web designer. He's reexamining his beliefs . . ."

"Nice to meet you," I say. See ya later. Got to go. Have a nice God-free life. And I run toward the end of the park.

I've been hanging a lot with Kevin Porter lately. Total text maniac. He's new in my class this year. His family just moved from Pennsylvania. He hasn't found his crowd yet so he's been hanging with me. Which is okay, I guess. I'm not one of the popular crowd. Which is okay too. I'm what you call a geek with a small *g*, which means I get through the day all right. I'm a whiz at physics, and in my school, if you're pretty good at something and not too lame, like wearing corduroys or something, kids will leave you alone. Maybe they think some teacher will help you if they try anything because you're the only one keeping up the averages. The real geeks are left out in the open like sitting ducks. I try to fly under the radar. Maybe if I was Jim Butts, Mr. Varsity Football dude, I'd take the chance and try and save their asses, but I'm so not. If you see them being cornered in the hallway you avoid them, you never catch their eyes, they're too pleading. You just pretend you've got something really interesting in your pocket as you go by and put your head down as you scramble to get it out. You can spend a whole passing period wrestling with it until you get into a classroom with a teacher present and you straighten up again. I know. Pathetic.

But Kevin's cool. He's into a lot of stuff I didn't even know about. Mom would freak. And he talks about things. Things like how all that stuff kids have been fed is mostly a load of crap. How there's an answer out there if we can just stop all the noise and figure it out. We just sit around. Chill. And I've made a lot more friends. Didn't even have to change out of my Converse Customs. When Kevin told them I was into it, they just nodded and I was in. Even Jim Butts is into it. Which surprised me. So I'm really glad I met Kevin because the next thing I know I'm sitting next to Jim the other night like I belong there and he was really cool. And so was I.

"You with us?" he said.

"Totally," I said.

But I can't tell Mom. She'd tell me it was a slippery slope with nothing but misery at the end. You know, the usual stuff. Especially if she got a look at Dele. Dele's a big friend of Kevin and Jim's. We call Dele our facilitator. It's our joke. Before I knew what he was I used to see him around at the mall. He's just like an ordinary guy. I think he's from Africa somewhere. He likes to wear nice suits. He's pretty happy clappy.

I know Mom's starting to really hate it that I'm with Kevin all the time. I think she's getting suspicious. I've been telling her he needs help with algebra. Sometimes when I come back late, I try to walk by her office real quiet but she always calls to me. Then she comes out and I swear to God she's sniffing me.

"Did you have fun?" she says.

"Fun?"

"Good study?"

"Uh, yeah."

"Your eyes are red."

And I back up the stairs and leave her standing at the bottom all alone.

" 'Night," she says.

I know I'm pushing it but I just can't help it. I know it's gonna be fine. I can handle it.

But tonight when I get back from Kevin's all hell breaks loose. It looks like Mom ran into Jim Butts's mom who said it was so nice to see upstanding boys taking their place at the table of God. Well, once she worked her head around that one I think she figured out that I wasn't going to Kevin's every night and teaching him about the wacky world of variables.

She's waiting for me when I come in and she really grills me.

"Where the hell have you been?"

"What do you mean?"

"How do you know Mrs. Butts?"

I tell her there must have been a mistake, that Mrs. Butts must have seen some other kid who looked just like me. I mean, what am I supposed to do? I don't want to tell her the truth. That would really piss her off.

She's calmed down by dinnertime and is poking the microwave like it's some voodoo pincushion when suddenly there's a knock at the door. Somehow I know it's no good. I think about ignoring it but whoever it is has found the doorbell and begins ringing it like their life depends on it. So she comes out, wiping her hands, and sees me hovering in the hallway and snaps, "Can't you get the door?" and I want to say something like "It's a sixth-sense sort of thing," but she would say, "That's not quantifiable," and before I can figure out what I could say to that she has opened the door and oh, my God, it's Dele.

"Hello?" she says.

"Hello, Mrs. Delano. I am Dele." And he waits as if that was introduction enough. But she stands there, probably waiting for the punch line or an identification card or something. He sees me and says, "Hello, Nic." Only he says it like it rhymes with "reek." "Hello, Neek." She looks back at me with an eyebrow that's an isosceles triangle. And I say, "Hello, Dele" and hope that if I don't go any closer he might get the vibes and fade back into the dark and never come back again. But he's too happy. I've seen it before. He's bursting with something on his mind and it's gonna come out and I can't stop it. And then I see what it is. It's in his hand. I begin to sweat.

"Mrs. Delano," he says, "Neek left this with us and I wanted to return it." And he hands her my Bible.

"I see," she says, holding the book with two fingers like it's the tail of a rat. "Thanks very much, Mr. . . . ."

"Reverend. Reverend Dele Ombatu. Very nice to meet you." And he gives her the biggest happiest shake of his hand.

Chapter Three

Okay, okay, I should have said something, but I just didn't want anyone to get stupid about it. Everyone is so touchy these days. So, yeah, I'm going to Bible class. Kevin goes and his mother drives us. I suppose she thinks I'm some refugee or something because she doesn't rat me out—unlike most mothers, who are on the telephone the second there's a sniff of anything that your mom might not know about.

Mrs. Porter, though, she looked me up and down and said. "Nic, are you a Christian?"

And I had to say, "I'm a nothing."

Well, you'd think I was some orphan or something the way she opened her arms and gave me a big hug, which was kind of nice because Kevin's mom is really nice-looking, you know, blonde and fit with long legs too. I guess I'm a leg man. Anyway, we go and read this book, this Bible, and talk about it. I mean, it's no big deal. Is it?

Well, Mom seems to think so. When Dele is here she's polite. She invites him in, offers him a glass of wine. When he says no, I find him a glass of Gatorade. He takes up a lot of space in our living room. He's not what you expect in a minister. He's young, for one thing. And you can tell he works out. Talk about muscles. He isn't wearing one of his suits. He's wearing khakis and a nice ironed white shirt that really shows off his dark skin. He looks like he is straight out of a video. He sits on the couch really close to my mom and grins at her like he's known her for a hundred years. Like I've been on and on about her and he knows everything. I can tell she's getting really annoyed.

She stands up. "Well, it was nice of you to return his book."

"Bible. The Word of God."

"Hmmm."

"You must come to Bible class. Join in the Scriptures with us. Other parents do."

"I don't believe in it."

"Ah."

He lets this hang in the air where it curls itself into clear writing, *Oh, I've got your number.* He just sits there, grinning at her, looking at her from top to toe.

"Do you make a habit of indoctrinating children behind their parents' backs?" she says.

"When Jesus sends us someone we don't ask questions."

"Ah," she says back.

And he smiles like they're having a rip-roaring time together.

"Reverend Ombatu," she says, "where are you from?"

"Nigeria."

"Do you miss it?"

"I do. Someday I will return. God willing."

"Well, travel safely."

He finally gets the hint and stands up. He takes both her hands in his and says, "Until we meet again."

I can tell she's trying to get her hands back, but he won't let go.

"The Bible is a love letter," he says. "It is not to be feared."

"We have enough love right here," she says.

He peers into her eyes. "Do you?"

She's getting really pissed off. "Yes."

He finally opens his hands, releasing her. "Everyone is a child of God. Some know it. Some do not."

Then he gives us both another killer of a handshake and leaves.

Afterward, Mom pours herself a whopper of a glass of wine and slumps at the kitchen table.

"You want me to set the table?" I ask.

She shakes her head. "I don't understand. I raised you right."

"You want me to nuke dinner?" I'm trying to be helpful. Red wine and angst is not a good mix for her. But obviously this isn't very smooth because she throws up her head and stares at me with those neon eyes of hers. "So you want to talk about it?"

"Not really."

"Well, I do."

She zeroes in on me with her eyes narrowed the way she does when she's trying to navigate through what she calls my "territorial waters." She leans forward, putting on her reasonable voice.

"We all have questions at your age. I did."

I head for the silverware drawer. Two forks, one knife.

"It's just that I don't want you to get in above your head. There's a lot about this that you don't understand."

"I know. That's what the Bible class is for."

"No, I mean, the whole thing. It's . . . it's . . . seductive. You think it's got all the answers . . . and then it lets you down and you're worse off than before."

I open the microwave oven. "You want the garlic chicken pasta or the five-cheese pizza?"

She sighs and empties the rest of the bottle into her glass.

I don't know why my mom is so freaky about God. She let me believe in Santa Claus for years. I had to find out the truth from Bert Krauss, who laughed so hard when I told him Santa Claus was bringing me a GameCube that I couldn't look him in the eye for a whole year.

And the tooth fairy. I wrote notes to her for years. Really sappy stuff like, "Hi, Tooth Fairy, it's me, Nic. Here's my tooth. I love you." I mean, how could she let me do that? Turns out the whole time I was sticking my tooth under my pillow Mom was waiting for me to go to sleep to slip it out and slip in a dollar bill. Then one night she slipped out the note I'd written that read: "Sorry, I don't have a tooth because I swallowed it but please, please just this once give me my money. Here's a little something for you." The something was Mom's antique pearl necklace that I had stolen from her jewelery box.

"Everyone learns sooner or later there's no Santa Claus or

tooth fairy," Mom answered. "They might not learn there is no God until they die."

Grandma Rose comes over the next day. After dinner, she and my mom wash the dishes, Mom banging the pots and pans real hard. I listen at the door and hear Grandma Rose say, "I think you're overreacting."

I knew she'd say that. She's pretty cool. She's Catholic. But she doesn't really talk about it much. Just makes the sign of the cross when an ambulance goes by.

"What's a little Bible class?" she says.

"They're fundamentalists," Mom replies.

"Ooo," Grandma Rose says. "They *are* crazy."

She's not what you expect in a grandmother, I guess. She's not the Little Red Riding Hood type with an apron and a big basket of biscuits. No, she's more a Dora the Explorer type but with wrinkly skin between her shorts and her hiking boots. And she's got this thing for orange lipstick. And it's got a thing for her teeth. She's from Ireland and still has an accent, even after all these years. But she's been kind of slowing down lately. She's starting to put Post-it notes on what she wants to leave everyone in her will. I'm down for her computer, which is so old it takes about a century to start up. I'm gonna have to pay someone to haul it away.

So Grandma Rose tells Mom it's because she didn't take me to church when I was younger. Didn't inoculate me. "Of course he's going to grow up and join some weird cult. What did you expect? You've got to give him a bit in the beginning so he can grow antibodies to the real crazy stuff. You should have done it when he was young."

And I remember having a heaven stage back when I was about six. Mainly I was worried about dying. I don't know. I just got really wound up about it. I used to lie in bed at night and think about what it meant and it seemed to mean a lot of nothing. Just a big black hole. Sucking you in and never letting you out. I imagined just twirling around in this black blackness. It scared the hell out of me. Well, my mom was no help. I once grabbed at her, yelling "I don't want to die!" and all she could come up with was, "Well, hopefully it won't hurt."

I said, "Wait a minute, what about heaven?"

She rolled her eyes. "Oh, heaven."

I said, "Yeah, heaven. If I'm good I'll go there."

She looked at me sadly, like my dog had died but I didn't know yet. "There is no heaven."

"What do you mean there is no heaven? Everybody is always talking about heaven all the time."

"It's a figure of speech."

"What? Like 'Nice to meet you'?"

"Sort of."

Well, that's when the real tears started and I began howling and getting louder and louder until Grandma Rose, who luckily was visiting, rushed in and sat down by me on the bed, practically pushing my mom off. She held me close and stroked my really wet cheeks and said, "Of course there's a heaven."

I said, "Are you sure?"

She said, "Yes, I'm really, really sure."

"What does it look like?"

"It's green, your favorite color and it's cloudy and there's lots of computer games, a huge boxful for each person."

I said, "Will Hunter go?" (He was my best friend then. He moved last year.)

She said, "Of course Hunter will go. And you'll be able to stay up all night and drink root beer and eat bags and bags of Doritos just like a big sleepover."

Well, that was nice and comforting, and my mom, she sort of slunk out of the room, after kissing my wet face and stroking my wet hair. Later, when I was supposed to be asleep, I heard Grandma Rose downstairs, reading the riot act to Mom.

"For God's sake, girl, you can't deny heaven to a six-year-old child."

And so my mom was a little less mouthy after that. Didn't bring it up. Laid low for a couple of months. Even started nodding if I talked about heaven, what it looks like, who'll be there, what they'll be serving: Doritos extra spicy or Ranch. Until one night, she thought for a second and said, "Why don't we think how beautiful it can be on earth?"

"But there's lots of war and disease here."

"Yes, that is unfortunate."

"Probably not in heaven, though."

She bit her lip and I could see her fighting, fighting . . .

"Mom?"

"Hmm."

"When we die do you really think that's all there is."

She held her breath then let it out. "...Yes."

"There's nothing after that?"

"I don't think so."

"Nothing left?"

"Well, there's our tissue, which decomposes."

"And turns into maggots . . ."

"Maggots hasten the decomposition of the body tissues into . . ."

"Mom?"

"Yes, Nic?"

"Why can't you be like Hunter's mom? She's got great stories about kingdoms and gates and beautiful angels in designer jeans."

"Would you like me to lie to you?"

"No. But you could make it sound nicer."

She kissed me. "Good night, Nic."

"Mom," I said, "don't you get scared?"

"Of what?"

"Of dying."

And she thought a moment and said, "Not of dying itself, but of leaving you."

"Mom?"

"Yes?"

"I love you."

"I love you too."

"That stays, doesn't it?"

"Yes, Nic, that stays forever."

Chapter Four

"Oh, holy one, can you remember to take out the garbage?"

"In a minute."

So I've been watching television and this G. W. guy comes on. I'm not allowed to say his name in the house because it makes my mom so angry, but I think you know who I mean. You know, the president. Which is funny because, at Kevin's house, he's like their best friend. Mrs. Porter is always saying to the TV, "You tell 'em, George." But Mom, really, I think if she found him lying in the street hurt somewhere, like if someone had run him over and no one was looking, she'd probably finish him off with a rock or something. And she'd think she was doing her country a service. When he comes on the television she starts drinking her wine really fast and spitting. She does. She starts stabbing her finger at the TV, saying things like, "He can't even speak the goddamn language!" Excuse her French.

I asked Mrs. Porter about that once.

I said, "Do you think he talks funny?"

She said, "He's a man of the people, Nic. He tells it like it is."

It's like she and Mom are on different football teams and they're gonna root for their team no matter what. They practically do that wave thing when the other team goes down. Like remember when he won the second time? You could see the one team waving in the streets. And Mom and her friends, they sat around the house the day after and moped into their bagels. One guy was actually crying. He kept sniffling and snorting and I finally had enough so I went over to Kevin's house. You'd think it was the Fourth of July. It might have been November, but it had that barbecue feeling. Fried chicken and Mrs. Porter's special red, white, and blue brownies. We had a great time.

Mom gets so worked up but I think life is going to be okay. Though sometimes, real bad things happen. All those earthquakes and hurricanes and people having to ask for money. Sometimes it seems every day somebody else has bought it. My mom, she's handing out checks like no one's business. She and the Red Cross relief effort appeals are like this. She just about tosses them a hundred bucks every time she logs on. I think that's all well and good, but what about my college fund?

Funny thing is, Mom is a class-A weeny. She always turns off the news when there's kids involved. She can't hack it. They were showing these kids getting bones set without painkillers because the emergency aid hadn't arrived yet and she ran from the room. I kept watching. I mean, if they're from the middle of nowhere and they've managed to get on TV, having their fifteen seconds, the least someone can do is watch.

And I think, Why is that kid born there and I'm born here? Is there a lottery somewhere before we're born? Are they handing out pieces of paper and you open them up and either it says, "Lucky you" or "Man, are you totally screwed"? And who makes these decisions? And why? And I think of all those starving kids in India and I figure it makes sense that they believe in reincarnation because most of them are probably not too thrilled with their lottery number.

Dele says "It is God's will" and "We are not to question" and "It will all make sense in the end." He seems so sure about it too. Even if his accent is radical. He seems to sit on all the wrong syllables. Sometimes it's hard to understand him. But once you get used to it he gets real clear. And boy, does he love Jesus. He's just walking through life with J. right by his side. He doesn't make a move without Him. Dele says it's like having this best friend that never lets you down. Never rats you out. Never bullies you. Or disses your hair.

I asked him once, if he got married who he'd love more, Jesus or his wife, and Dele said, "Jesus will not make me choose. My wife will love Jesus as well. We will all be in it together." I thought, Well, that could get funky.

Then he said, "My wife, she might die, she might leave. But Jesus will never leave me. It is a great comfort to me."

I thought of Mom and how she might be less lonely if she believed in somebody like Jesus. I brought it up once.

"No thanks," she said.

"It doesn't have to be Jesus, maybe his sister or something."

"I don't think he had a sister."

"Maybe his mom."

She smiled and said, "Catholics love praying to Mary."

"Perfect, then. I mean, because you were born a Catholic, even though you don't do it anymore."

"I sure don't."

"What do you have to do to be Catholic anyway?"

"Suspend my disbelief."

"Well, that's not so difficult, is it?"

"Apparently not."

Now the British are pretty smart. Well, they sound it at least. This guy at Mom's work is British. His name is Nigel. He's really tall and says things like, "That's not quantifiable." Which my mom says, too, but it doesn't sound so destroying when she says it. When Nigel says it, it's like "No more discussion, go kill yourself quickly and turn your sword in at the counter." He told me that the British are world-class astronomers.

I told him the Italians had done pretty well too. He nodded and said yes, for a collection of practicing chaos theorists they manage to churn out a decent stargazer now and then. Problem is, he said, they're creating all these Ph.D.s and they don't have enough universities to give them jobs. They're leaving Italy and trying to take all the teaching positions. I asked why they don't just build more universities in Italy and he said light pollution. Wow, a little thing like light pollution can be so far-reaching.

Mom invites him over every once in a while and he comes over and they drink Dos Equis in the backyard and talk shop. Sometimes she lets him stay for dinner, fires up our little hibachi, and tosses on a couple of steaks. Nigel always says, "That's very American, isn't it?" But he says it like there's something wrong with it, like we're creating a turbine of global warming right in our backyard, like we're decimating the entire stockpile of protein for the twenty-first century. He says it about our automatic ice maker too, as if it's the most decadent example of a dying empire he's ever witnessed. Mom used to just smile and nod. Now she's started saying yes, that's very American. And she turns it into a good thing. Like, damn yes, it's American, you got a problem with that? I think his days are numbered.

I mean, what's wrong with being an American? We've got cool guns and tanks and rockets and stuff. And we've got eight kinds of crunchy peanut butter in our supermarkets. Nigel says that in Britain there's only two. How can you run a country on just two kinds of peanut butter? A nation needs choice. That's the democratic process. He keeps telling me that I really need to travel and see how the other half lives. I want to say, Hello? I got YouTube twenty-four friggin' hours a day.

I can tell he likes my mom. But he likes her in this sneaky way. So he just looks at her a lot when she's not looking and then when she comes over and smiles at him, he gets all serious and starts talking about stuff like he's trying to impress her with everything he knows. You can tell that sometimes she just wants him to shut up.

I suppose my mom is kinda pretty. She's got short hair and

she's really pale. She's got crow's feet around her eyes. They look like starbursts when she smiles. She seems to worry a lot about them because she rubs whole jars of cream into them. I swear my college education fund is going into those jars. I looked at the price tag on one of them the other night and just about fell into the tub.

It's hard to think of her doing girly things. She's soooo scientific. She's dying for me to be a scientist. She taught me the names of the planets when I was two. By four I could have told you how a lightbulb worked. By five we were tackling the theory of evolution. She even made up a little ditty:

Fishy to monkey to Nicky.
Took a long long time,
Took a lotta lotta steps.
But we got there in the end.

Okay, so it doesn't trip off the tongue. But it worked. It's amazing what a kid will do for an animal cracker.

The good thing is that now that Mom knows I'm going to Bible class, I don't have to sneak around anymore. It makes life easier. Mrs. Porter can pick me up right at my house. I'm starting to think Mom's being unbelievably cool about the whole thing until I hear her talking to Carla on the phone.

"It's just a phase," she says. "I suppose it could be worse. It could be drugs." She laughs like it is the funniest thing. My life.

I'm standing right next to her when she hangs up.

"It's not a phase."

"You shouldn't listen in on my conversations."

"Fine. But it's not a phase."

"Fine."

She gets up and starts walking up the stairs. It just pisses me off the way she's so certain about everything.

So I yell, "You think you know everything!"

She turns around with that smile of hers. "I don't know everything. But at least I'm willing to admit it. . . . Don't you roll your eyes at me."

"What if you're wrong?"

She cocks her head. "Listen. The way I see it there's this fine line that some people cross. They go from "Hey, this is what I believe and it helps me" to "This is what I believe and if you don't believe it, you're stupid."

"Sort of like what you do."

Silence.

She hands me her *Skeptic* magazine. "Read it. And learn. Some of those people you're hanging out with actually believe the earth is six thousand years old."

"So?"

"So? It's crazy."

"You don't know that for sure."

"Don't go there, sweetheart. The next thing you'll be telling me is that dinosaurs roamed the earth at the same time as humans."

"You know, most of the founders of modern science were creationists."

"Like?"

"Newton, Pascal, Galileo."

She snorts. "Those were different times. Luckily we've learned a thing or two since then."

"Why is it so hard for you to recognize that we live in a universe designed by a superior being? Do you really expect me to believe the universe started in a random explosion?"

She looks so surprised I think she's going to slip down the stairs. But luckily I hear the beep of Mrs. Porter's car and run outside.

Chapter Five

"Nic, do you love me?" Mom always asks me.

"Sure."

"Do you love pizza?"

"I *love* pizza."

"Hmmm."

"Why?"

"Just gauging my worth to you."

"Pepperoni and sausage? To D.I.E. for."

Mom says that life probably came from a comet that rammed into earth about 3.9 billion years ago and it sparked life in our oceans. Talk about wishful thinking. She really had me going there. Sounded good to me until Kevin and I sat down and really started talking about it. Like, Who sent the comet? he asked. Who put the life on the comet? I saw he had a point. I mean, it's a question you can keep on asking. Who did that? Who did that? Until you're so far back down the line there's only one answer: God. You know, I'm starting to think my mom doesn't know what she's talking about, I'm starting to think she should just stick to stars.

Maybe if she just keeps studying and looking into that telescope of hers she'll see Him. Wouldn't that be cool? She's looking up and He winks at her. Because it's not like it's a question anyone can answer for sure unless they die, which personally I'm not willing to do. I'm willing to wait and see and hedge my bets.

Plus, why would anybody be good if there wasn't a God? If they weren't scared they were going to piss him off why would they do the right thing? Why not rob everyone blind because you can get away with it? Survival of the fittest. Kevin and I talked about that. We've been thinking that it wouldn't be such a bad idea if there was a law saying you have to believe in God. Because that way everyone would try to be good. And that wouldn't be so bad. I mean, that's what we want everyone to be in the end, right? Good.

The question is, Kevin says, does Mom believe in anything besides herself? I look around her room and what do I see: a computer, pictures of us, the papier-mâché of Einstein's brain that I made her when I was seven. And I think, wow, this is it. This is her life. This room. The glow of the computer screen and the little halogen light on her desk. Pretty damn sad.

And I remembered what my mom told me about the lonely hypothesis. Have you heard of it? It's pretty lonely. It says there's no good God and most likely no God at all. That we're just specks of insignificance in a pointless cold universe. That's my mom all over. When I tell her that's a shitty thing to think, she says, "But Nic, don't you see the splendor in it? The honor. The inspiration." And I've got to say no, not really. All I see is a lot of nothing. Which is how we always get to talking about human achievements, creativity, and love. She calls them her Holy Trinity. I call them straws. As in clutching.

We have to be different, right? I mean, does a spider go, "Look, I just want to be creative and love my zillion eggs? I just want to make the best damn web I can make and then check out, knowing I've contributed my little bit of love to this stinking world." I mean, what is he thinking every time I open the back gate and destroy his legacy. Is there a place where spiders jump from? Saying, "Good-bye, cruel world, I can't take it any more"?

So that makes us different, doesn't it? The fact that we care so much?

So I corner Mom late one night and I ask her, "Do you have proof that God doesn't exist?"

She looks up from her computer, leans back, and rubs her eyes. "No one has proof about God's existence so my reasoning is that we shouldn't spend so much time fighting about him. We should get on and save humanity."

"Mrs. Porter visits old people and heads the soup drive."

"Mrs. Porter sounds like a saint."

"You?"

She smiles. "I stare at the stars and love you. You are my gift to humanity."

"That's one hell of a burden."

"Well, my beast of burden, it's time for bed."

"Don't you think there's something different about us?"

"Like?"

"Don't you believe in spirit?"

"You don't have to believe in God to believe in human spirit."

"Then where did it come from? Why do we think we have it and animals don't? All this staring into space, looking for stars, downloading jpeg files into your computer, you think a mole could do that?"

"No."

"So why us?"

She stares at me a second. "I just don't know."

"I don't know. I don't know. How can you live like that? You've got to know something."

"I know I love you."

"Well, coming from someone who doesn't know much, that's not very helpful." And I left her there in front of her stupid computer.

So I can't believe it the next day when I catch her reading my Bible. I'm looking for it everywhere and it turns out she's reading it in her office.

"What are you doing?"

She looks up guiltily. "I'd forgotten how . . . intense this is."

I put my hand out and she gives it back.

That's when she drops the bomb on me.

"I'm coming with you," she says.

"Where?"

"Your Bible class."

I stare at her. "Why?"

"Because I'm curious."

"But you don't believe in it."

She smiles. "I'd like to know what they're teaching you."

Well, you can tell what I'm thinking. I'm thinking, Oh, shit, she's gonna mouth off. I call Mrs. Porter to tell her Mom's driving me to Bible class. And she says, after a second of silence, "Really? Isn't that nice."

There's about twelve of us that go on Thursday nights and we all sit around on gray plastic chairs under fluorescent lights. Kevin says it used to be just kids but since Dele's been doing it, more moms have shown up. So it's Jim Butts and his mom, me and Kevin and his mom, June Ann and her sister, Ruby, and their mom. Plus there's the twins, Jill and Jane and their stepmom. There's also Mrs. Milla, who's kind of crazy, but Dele lets her sit in because she's old and she doesn't really have anywhere else to go. She doesn't hear very well so she spends a lot of the time staring out the window. In the next room there's a "50s & Better" group and you can hear them laughing and carrying on while we're trying to ponder Jesus' sacrifice on the cross.

The church isn't very fancy. It looks like a warehouse. Inside it's industrial business: blond wood, light blue carpeting, metal exits. Behind the altar there's a plain cross. Not like the one at Grandma Rose's church where you can see the blood trickling down Jesus' side and the holes gouged out of his hands and feet. Grandma Rose says I should get a load of the beautiful churches in Europe where you can visit the foreskins of Christ.

On Sundays the church is packed. People jump up and

down, and the pastor holds his hands to their head and prays, and we all pray and everybody's yelling Jesus, Jesus, Jesus! It's pretty over the top but hey, everybody gets pretty riled up. It's not like my grandma's church, which is pretty droning. Everybody shuffling up for their piece of bread with no enthusiasm whatsoever. They look like they're in line to be executed. Kevin's church, man, they're practically dancing in the aisles. Even the fancy soccer moms, *especially* the soccer moms. They're swinging away and clapping. And everybody slaps each other on the back and hugs. In Grandma's church they seem to work up all their courage just to give each other the Peace Be with You sign.

Tonight, when we get to Kevin's church everybody is already standing around, waiting. They all stop talking when we come in. Mom walks up to Dele and shakes his hand. He gives her a big hug, which takes her by surprise. Then he waves to the whole group calling out, "This is Nic's mother!" like she's been lost at sea for a couple of months and has just been found clutching a buoy. "We are happy to have you with us." And everybody smiles while staring at her real hard.

Mrs. Porter comes up and gives her a hug and says, "It's so nice to meet you." Mrs. Porter looks great. She always dresses nice. And Mom, I got to admit, looks a little sloppy next to her. Mrs. Porter has on a skirt and blouse that obviously were bought together because the colors match. And her hair is brushed. Mom's is all over the place. It's the style, she tells me. But next to someone like Mrs. Porter it just looks messy. Mom's wearing a T-shirt and some long skirt she fished out from the back of her closet. I wouldn't let her wear jeans.

When it's time to go into the room and sit down, Mom sits next to me at the long fold-up table even though, usually, the kids sit next to each other at one end of the table and the parents sit at the other end. But Mom, she just plunks herself right down between me and Jim Butts. I can see Jim Butts eyeing me like I'm the saddest dork he's ever seen.

"So," Dele says when he sits down at the far end with the parents, "let us see what the Bible has for us tonight." He asks for June Ann to read a passage. She begins, "Therefore Jesus said again, 'I tell you the truth, I am the gate for the sheep. . . .' " Usually this is the part I like, hearing the words because it's pretty writing and everything. But with Mom around it sounds weird, and I am embarrassed listening to June Ann even though she's a good reader and doesn't make too many mistakes.

"I am the good shepherd; I know my sheep and my sheep know me . . ."

Mom has her I'm-not-going-to-make-a-fuss smile on. It's plastered over her face like a Mickey Mouse Band-Aid. Her eyes are open wide and she's sitting really tall like a nerd.

When June Ann finishes Dele puts his fingers together and lets the silence sit on us a bit. This is the time when we're supposed to think about the passage and about what God might have meant to say. Dele nods to my mom.

"Would you like to try?"

"Me?"

She looks around the table. We're all looking at her.

"I'm unfamiliar with this passage. Please"—she sort of waves her hand around the table—"why doesn't someone else jump in?"

Mrs. Porter must take pity on her because she bails her out, saying, "The more you get to know Christ the more you recognize his voice."

Mom nods her head but I could see inside it's going the exact opposite way.

Dele jumps in with "And God speaks to you when you pray, doesn't he?" And everybody nods a couple of times.

"How?" he asks.

Everyone stares at their pages. Usually they're pretty chatty but I think my mom being there really clams them up.

Dele jumps in again. "He gives us good thoughts and feelings, doesn't he?"

And everyone nods.

"What else?"

Everyone stares at their pages.

"He gives us the will to act according to his good purpose, doesn't he?"

And everybody nods.

And then there's silence again. Mom raises her hand and points to a passage in the Bible. "It says here Adam lived for nine hundred thirty years."

Dele looks over at her. "They lived longer then, didn't they?"

And everyone nods.

Mom says, "Really? Why?"

Dele leans back comfortably in his chair. "Because God created Adam perfect. He did not have the health problems we have today. Like stress and cancer and mutant genes."

Mom opens her mouth.

"All those early people lived long lives," Dele continues. "Methuselah lived even longer than Adam. Nine hundred sixty-nine years. The life spans, they decreased as more illnesses arrived."

Mom closes her mouth.

"And remember," he adds, "the temperature of the world was subtropical. Better for your health."

I swallow real hard. But Mom glances at me and smiles. And I think, cool, she's going to let it go. I smile back. But then she addresses Dele.

"And evolution?"

Oh, shit.

"Pardon?" he says.

"Evolution. Darwin's theory of evolution. What does the Bible say about that?"

Mrs. Porter jumps in. "It doesn't say anything. It was written before Darwin's time."

"But you do believe in the concept, don't you?"

"It is not consistent with Bible teachings," says Dele.

And they all shake their heads. Dele puts his hand over his Bible. "This is our truth."

Mom says, "I see."

That's when Mrs. Milla wakes up from her daydreaming out

the window. "Well," she says, "my boy asked the same thing and I told him, 'George, have you seen an ape turn into a man lately?' That answered that one."

Mom takes a deep breath.

"Mom . . ."

"No, Nic. This is crazy."

Dele raises his hands. "Is it wrong to believe in miracles?"

Mom shakes her head. "No. It's not wrong to believe in miracles. Life is a miracle. The miracle is that we evolved at all. That you and I are here at all. Ninety-nine percent of the species on earth have become extinct. Think of all those insects, birds, animals that have died out. We have survived. We are here breathing this rarefied air, reveling in the most gorgeous form in the universe, water. This is what to me is glorious. Do you still need a god after that? What more spectacular miracle could he or she create?"

And they all look at her like she's sprouted a couple of antennae.

Dele smiles. "I do not have all the answers. I do not even know many of the questions."

"You know what I hate?"

And we turn toward Mrs. Porter. She's looking at Mom and speaking slowly. "I hate intellectual arrogance."

"Arrogance?"

"Yes, arrogance. Coming in here thinking you're smarter than anyone else. Trying to make us look stupid. It has no place here."

Mom runs her eyes over Mrs. Porter then says, "Yes, I can see that."

"This has nothing to do with how smart you are," says Mrs. Porter. "This has everything to do with faith. I am choosing to believe in the Bible because Jesus has asked me to."

Mom looks over at Dele who holds up his hand and says, "Perhaps you are not ready for this yet."

Mom stands up from her chair. "I think you're right. Come on, Nic."

But I just sit there. I mean, I'm thirteen years old. I don't come when my mom whistles. Especially in front of Jim Butts.

The thing is, Mom is smart. She swings her eyes around the table, sees what she's up against and doesn't insist. She nods to me like a captain to a mutineer.

"I'll see you at home then," she says, and walks out.

Chapter Six

When I get home Mom is in her armchair in the living room reading *Dysfunctional Families for Dummies.*

I stand in the doorway. "Hey."

She looks up briefly, then looks down again. She is silent, which is really unlike her, so I think I better say something just to make it normal. "It's cold out."

"Is it?"

She keeps reading.

". . . Yeah."

Silence.

"Well, I'm gonna . . ."

"So what's it going to be next?" She swings her head up and glares at me. "Aliens abducted you?"

"It's not that bad," I say.

"You're right it's not that bad. It's worse! At least an alien would have been interesting. It's verifiable. We could have said, 'Okay, have you seen this alien?' Right now it's 'No, but I've got faith.' "

"Oh, come on!"

"Nic, you are gifted. You are beyond gifted. You have an IQ of 148. How can you believe this stuff?"

I shrug.

She shakes her head. "Look, I'm not going to forbid you from going."

"That's a smart move."

"Excuse me?"

I glare right back at her. I'm pretty pissed off too. She can think what she wants. But it's a free country. She can't tell me what to do. She's the one who's always going on about free-thinker stuff. And here she is, trying to tell me what to think.

She stares at me for a second, then decides to continue. "I just want you to be careful. We've all had our experimenting phases. I just want you to not be stupid about it. Know your limits."

"Fine."

"Fine."

I have to ask her. "Why are you so angry?"

She laughs like that is the stupidest thing she's heard in a long time. Stupider even than shepherds and voices of God. "I'm not angry."

It's my turn to laugh but I don't feel like it. "You are."

Then she whacks her chair with her book.

"You're right. I *am* angry! I'm furious. I'm furious because this is crazy. I don't mind people believing in God, it's none of my business. But Nic, you, of all people. After all we've taught you. And I know what went wrong. It is so obvious. If I hadn't stayed here, you would have had your father and you wouldn't have needed someone like Dele. This is all my fault. And I'm furious with myself."

When I go to bed she's still downstairs. Probably staring at the spot where I disappeared out the door.

I wish I lived at Kevin's. They're really fun at his house. It's less lonely there. It's so quiet at my house. Just me and Mom. The Porters always have people from their church dropping by. Mrs. Porter is always counseling someone in their living room, sitting in her oversized chair with a mug of java in her hand. You see them crying and praying together. Sometimes they'll get down on their knees and hold hands. Then they'll pop up again, dry their tears, and tuck into some nachos and dip.

One time Mrs. Porter asked me how I felt about my mom not believing in God and I said it was okay. She nodded. "I just hate to see a kid not be let in on the glorious truth of life." She placed her hand on my arm. "You know you can always talk to me." And then her cell phone rang and she was gone. You really feel like you could talk to her about anything. She's just so positive. Nothing seems to faze her.

Both Mr. and Mrs. Porter are great with teenagers. You don't feel like such a freak around them. They treat you like you're a friend. Mom tries hard but she's always a bit off, especially when Kevin's around. She sort of looks at him strangely and tries to make jokes but they come out lame and I just want to go straight to my bedroom.

The Porters' house is more comfortable too. Ours is full of books and funky things from my parents' travels. It's like a museum. It's like "Here, look at this, ask me about it, and I'll tell you all about my cool trip to Borneo." Or "Hey, check this one out. Okay, twist my arm, I picked up that little number in Florence when I was on a conference." I've had to be careful all my life in that room. Sometimes I just want to go AHHHH and attack it like a kamikaze.

But at the Porters', man, they even have a pinball machine. And a jukebox. And a pool table. They're a catalogue's dream. And they don't do art. They just put up school pix of their kids. So everywhere you go the kids are smiling down at you. My mom never likes my school pix. She always says it doesn't do me justice. She prefers action shots of the three of us doing something expensive. And photos in frames you place on tables. The walls, they're for tastefully framed obscure pencil drawings of someone on the verge of being famous.

And our furniture. It's called Mission furniture. Mom thinks she's some sort of Shaker. All that simple going-back-to-basics business. But it costs a fortune. You think a Shaker would spend a thousand dollars on a chair? Mom says, "Just look at that grain, that dovetail joint." I tell you, some Shaker is laughing all the way to the barn dance.

From: Dad
To: Nic
Subject: life

Hey Nic. Sorry it's taken so long to get back to you. Woke Monday and had a ton of e-mails to wade through. So tell me what's up. How are you?

How am I? I don't know. Different than when I sent the e-mail two days ago. I stare at his words and then decide it's stupid I have to e-mail my own dad. So I delete his message.

I still need to write that oral history of someone who's old and related to me. My dad's parents are dead. My mom's dad lives in a home. He's got Alzheimer's. He can't remember what he had for breakfast, much less his life history. Mom used to make me go visit him but he got scared of me so I stopped. I felt bad. An old man in pajamas crying at the sight of me. Now I send him pictures of ducks that I see around. For some reason he likes ducks. Nobody knows why. I brought him over a stuffed toy duck once—bright yellow with a big orange beak. Mom said he never lets it go. The nurses have to wash around it when they clean him up.

So all that's left is Grandma Rose. Lucky for me, she's a talker. When I go over to her apartment in Bowie, she's ready for me. She's got the Coke and the chocolate-covered donuts. By four o'clock we're flying.

I sit down on her black-and-white checked sofa that used to be in the corner of her bedroom in her old house but which now takes up most of the room in her small apartment. When she moved she gave my mom boxes full of stuff, like doilies and crystal candy dishes and old satin nighties. They all sit now in a stack in the corner of our basement.

Grandma Rose puts another donut on my plate. "Ready?" she asks.

I flick on my tape recorder and check to make sure the spools are moving.

"Shoot."

And off she goes. All I have to do is sit back and try and munch quietly. She tells me how Granddad had to leave Ireland because he got caught up in the IRA. How he killed some guy in self-defense. How the cops were coming for him, so his parents sold their three cows to put him on a boat to New York.

I stop the tape recorder. "Three cows," I say. "Really?"

She looks at me steadily. "Something like that. This is the story of my life, Nic. You're going to have to believe me."

I nod and flick it back on. She tells me how she met Granddad in Baltimore, where he was working in a dry cleaners, smelling of acid. He wooed her with a bottle of French perfume he stole from a shopping bag left on a bus. She'd come over to the States with the help of her big sister and she went from factory worker to elementary-school teacher in seven years. She says a country that lets you do that is worth praying for, a dig at my mom, who she still can't believe doesn't go to church anymore.

"Though I understand her questioning," Grandma Rose says, reaching for another donut. "When Johnny died, I questioned everything."

Johnny was her first child. He died at birth forty-five years ago and she still talks about him like he's in the next room, just taking a nap.

"You know, when I was a young girl, I used to think of God as my best friend. Someone I could always talk to. But when Johnny died I couldn't believe for a while. The more I thought about it, the more I couldn't believe a friend would do that to me. And then one day I realized I missed Him. I missed God. I wanted nothing more than to believe. I wanted it all to make sense again. Because I liked that. That feeling that it all hung together. I missed it."

I scoop up the last chocolate sprinkle. "So do you believe in God now?

"I must."

"Why?"

"He is the only chance I'll see my son again."

Mr. Branden at school thinks God created our country, which is why we're a Christian country. Anybody who's anybody, he says, was a Christian. He likes to sit at the front of the class on the desk. He brought a Bible to class one day. Made this big show of sneaking it out of the drawer. He first looked out the door to make sure no one was coming and then pulled it out of the drawer and put his fingers to his mouth and said, "Shhhh." Everybody laughed. You're not supposed to talk about God in our school, he says, so he's gonna call Him Bert.

Now, Bert is responsible for a lot of things. Mainly for making our country the best damn country in the world. Bar none. And anyone with a brain can tell that Bert wanted the country to be a Christian one because he sent Christians to populate it and give it a democracy. In God we trust, he says, pulling out a quarter from his pocket and holding it up for all to see. "It doesn't say in Allah we trust, or Buddha, or God forbid, Krishna."

"Do you think we should take this off our coin?" he asks Emir. Emir is from Pakistan. He's been in the country only a couple of years. He stares at Mr. Branden with his big brown eyes and slowly shakes his head.

"You sure? Because if you got a problem with it, we could always take it off."

And Emir shakes his head again. Real slow.

"Of course, if you have a problem with it, you know what else you can do?" And he leaves it hanging there. And everybody laughs because we all know the answer to that one. Emir laughs too. Slowly.

One day, Ms. White, our principal, came in and sat at the back of the class taking notes. Mr. Branden didn't mention Bert once. A couple of days later, some other people came in. Same thing. No Bert. Jim Butts raised his hand once to a question—I think it was, Who was the architect of our constitution? Jim said Bert. Everybody laughed and Mr. Branden grinned at him and said, "Your guess is as good as mine." But he quickly went on to something else.

He doesn't have to worry about me talking. I've learned my lesson. I never tell Mom anything about what they teach in my school. I did once when I was in the fourth grade and she made a big stink and Frank Harris punched me in the mouth the next week and called me a Jew.

But Mr. Branden knows about me. And my mom. He stopped me once when I was walking out of class and said, "So, Nic, you doing all right?"

"Yeah, good."

He nodded. " 'Cause I wouldn't want to offend you in any way."

"Why would you offend me?"

He laughed. "You're doing good, kid. Keep it up."

I mean, I see where he's coming from. It seems like a lot of people did things because they were religious. Like all those pilgrims. I don't know if they could have done all the stuff they did, if they didn't believe in God. Survived those boats, built those houses in the middle of nowhere, made it through those first winters. God seems to have acted like some sort of an energy pill. When you think about it, do you think Michelangelo would have made all that effort, chipping away at those statues, if he wasn't trying to impress the big guy in the sky? Think of all those cathedrals that were built. That's a lot of manpower.

One day in Mr. Branden's class, Kevin comes in wearing this T-shirt. It says BERT BELIEVER. Well, that just about guarantees him straight A's for the rest of the year.

It's not fair. Kevin's got excellent hair too. It's straight and streaky blond. And he's a flicker. He's always jerking his head to flick it out of his eyes. Girls love it. Mine's brown and screwed up. I'm hoping they'll come up with drive-through hair transplants in the future. Just drive up, pick your poison, and drive away looking like a new you. Maybe in heaven you get to have the head you should have been born with: perfect cut, surfer blond, flicked from your face in perpetuity.

Every week Mom makes me wash my hair. And every week we fight.

"You know the rules, Nic."

I slam the bathroom door. She won't give me my allowance unless I take an industrial shower and wash my hair. But my hair only looks good when it's dirty. Only time it stays down in place. Otherwise it sticks out at the sides and I want to kill myself. Even Kevin notices.

"Dude, your hair."

I mean, it's so obvious but Mom acts like I've got some sort of mental disease.

"I don't know what you're talking about," she says.

"Look at it. Just look at it!"

"It's fine."

"Oh, God, you are so dumb!"

"Nic."

It's true. I slam the door again for extra effect. How can she do this to me? On a Friday. Gina Kosta is having a party. And I'm now supposed to go as Bozo the Clown? I try everything. Masses of gel but it looks like some sort of goo helmet. If I wash it again it'll look worse. I try parting it on the other side to see if that helps. I can't tell. I'd ask Mom but she'd be, like, what's the difference? How can she be so obtuse? When I was in her office last night I was looking at all these photos of me on her bulletin board and the only hair I like is when we were sailing in Chincoteague. Good cut and it sort of blew back away from my face. It looked really good. Wouldn't it be cool if you could have a fan attached to your face, blowing your hair back all the time? Maybe I should look into it.

I finally went to a real barbershop for the first time last year.

No more Mom cuts for me. But the guy, I don't know, he had a vendetta or something because once he started he just wouldn't stop and he took off all my hair. I should have said something but he looked so pissed off, like the whole world was sitting right on his head. When he was done it looked like I'd been scalped. I wouldn't go to school for three days. I just lay on my bed. Mom danced around and yelled, then finally had to go to work. There was nothing she could do about it. She said, "So what are you going to do, call in bad hair?"

But hair, I don't know, it sets you up. It's like the canvas everything else is painted on. It's the first thing you notice. It's the difference between acceptable and deviant behavior.

Dad wears a ponytail. Dull dishwasher, graying. But then, he's forty. I guess you just let yourself go. He teaches comparative religions. He calls the Bible the original blog. He speaks Greek, Hebrew, Latin, and Aramaic. Aramaic, though, he just reads, he really doesn't have big long conversations in it. I think he's a good teacher. I've sat in on a couple of his classes. He really fires up his students. He brings them to different churches and synagogues and even channelers. He has a whole class where his students can make up their own religion. He's invented his own too. It's called Robertism. It worships a god called, yup, you guessed it, Robert. And every third Thursday of the month you have to sacrifice a pint of Rocky Road ice cream to him.

Because Dad doesn't drink but he can put away ice cream like no one's business. It's not like he won't drink, or had a problem before or anything. He just doesn't see what the fun is. He'll have a glass of wine if someone puts it in his hand but he sort of leaves it half empty. Never really needs it. Not like Mom, who comes home from work and says, "If I don't have a drink immediately, I'm going to castrate the dog."

But every night he has to have that bowl of ice cream. Like some ritual. Out comes the bowl. The spoon. The ice cream. He always has about three cartons in the fridge. And the best. Not the crap. We're talking Ben and Jerry's, Haägen-Dazs, or this English cream one. And since he only allows himself two scoops he makes them massive. He digs down really far and just about brings up the whole carton and then goes back in because, hey, that's just the first scoop. And then he takes a mouthful, closes his eyes, and goes "Ahhhh."

If I do that when I'm forty-three, shoot me.

He says he's most tempted by Buddhism, which teaches that reality is good and that bad things are just clouds that pass in front of it. Because nothing really exists, nothing can really hurt you. You're supposed to let the good and the bad wash over you and not get too freaked out by it all. It's called unattachment. I think it must take a lot of practice because Dad's not there yet. You should have seen him lose it when I left his ice cream out on the counter all night.

But he's not bad. I've only seen him seriously pissed off one or two times. Once it was when a guy he sold his car to didn't pay up. The guy drove up, handed Dad a bad check, and drove away in Dad's old VW bus. Dad was mostly angry at himself but he really let loose. Like he'd been personally assaulted. Mom wasn't a huge help. She just raised her eyebrows and shook her head.

The other time was when I called Mom a bitch.

It just sort of came out. I don't know. She was on me for not cleaning my room. And I'd just gotten up and she wouldn't let me eat anything, not even have a glass of milk, until I went back up and cleaned my room. I just said it and Dad jumped up and pushed me against the wall. He spoke real slow: "Don't you ever call her that again."

I said okay.

And that was that.

Now Mrs. Hansen in English class wants us to keep a diary. So I've been trying to write. To tell the truth, like she says. To tell the truth as I know it. The problem is, I'm not sure what the truth is. I've got mine. But maybe it's like time. Maybe everybody's truth is different depending on where they are.

I ask her, "Can you be a little more specific?"

She says, "Write about your family."

"I live with my mom."

"Fine, write about your mom."

I don't know what to say. I guess the first thing I'd say is Mom thinks she's a real serious person. She passes herself off as such an intellectual but she doesn't even know who Iago is.

"Sure I do," she says.

"Okay, who is he?"

"He's the kind of elfin one, right?"

"Unbelievable."

"I get them mixed up. I can't know everything."

And she's not a big smiler like Mrs. Porter who must sleep with a huge grin plastered on her face. Come to think of it, the only times I've seen Mom get good excited (as opposed to bad excited, which is what she is always getting) is when she watches the Discovery channel. The other night we were watching this program about spiders and one of them was using a string of silk to lasso his prey. Mom just about jumped up and down.

"That's incredible," she said. "Look, he's using it as a tool. Isn't that incredible? Don't you think that's incredible? I think that's incredible." And she stared at the screen like it was the second coming.

She's into that stuff—animals, science, the planet earth. It's funny, at school you'd think science was all about facts, about all those things that you learn that are true. Mom says, though, that science is really all about what you don't know. She remembers being in a class when the teacher said, "Who knows how many states of matter there are?" And everybody said three: gas, liquid, solid. He said, "Well, I'm going to let you in on a secret. There's more. A lot more. There's crystal and plasma, and that's just for starters." Mom says it was the most exciting day. Because that was the day she realized that science was the greatest mystery of all.

She's also a big recycler. But because they don't recycle plastic bags in our neighborhood, she saves them and stuffs them into this closet until it's overflowing and then suddenly she'll just grab them, stuff all of them into the trash can outside, and moan about how they're going to end up in some whale's body and how she's going to be personally responsible for this whale's death by choking. When she's really feeling guilty she starts naming the whale and giving it an age. Little three-year-old Ishmael floating down the California Current with his blue-whale mom. I tell her, "Why don't you buy one of those reusable bags?" and she glares at me and says, "You ever try to do a weekly shopping with one reusable bag?"

In the end, I wrote about how I've been playing this game called *The Sims* where you create your own family and move everybody around like you want. I had Mom be a rock star and we traveled around to her gigs and stayed in hotels with room service. Dad was an insurance salesman and had to stay home. I thought about making up brothers and sisters, but they were taking up too much of Mom's time so I killed them.

I wonder what Kevin wrote about. Mrs. Porter used to be a lawyer. She did corporate stuff where she helped companies buy other companies. Then she had Kevin and his sister and brother and she decided to stay home with them. She's excited that they've moved here because she has lots of things to do. She was really involved with their school back in Pennsylvania. She got them to put stickers on the biology books saying that evolution is just a theory. And now she wants to do that in our schools. She's really excited about it. She's getting all these signatures.

"But it's harder here than it was in Pennsylvania," she says. "People are being really resistant to the truth. I can't believe the hooey Kevin comes home with."

"Look at this." She starts reading one of our school biology books. "Humans are fundamentally not exceptional because we came from the same evolutionary source as every other species." She tosses it on the table. "I mean, that's just ridiculous. That just offends me. I mean, that has no business being in a science book. That's religion."

She looks over. "Right, Kevin?"

Kevin yawns. "Yes, ma'am."

"You know they're going on all the time about keeping religion out of schools and then they go and put it in the science textbooks. And I for one have had just enough. Look, look right here, they say that human knees and spines have been borrowed from four-legged ancestors. That's why we get all those sprains and injuries. Well, that's just false. Not only false. It's slamming God. And that's what I object to."

"It is?" I say.

"Why, of course it is. It's saying we weren't perfectly designed for our tasks. And we are. My body is perfect. How about yours, Nic. Isn't yours?"

"I don't know."

"You don't know? Of course it is. It's in God's image. And you can't get better than that."

"Yours is from a rib," I say.

"Yes, that's right." She smiles. I don't know if she's joking or if she's pleased about it. "God didn't want you boys to get lonely so he made us women. He thought of everything."

Now, I must look a little unconvinced because she leans

close. "I don't know what people have been telling you, but it's time you started thinking for yourself."

She pats me on the back. "We are a people who question, Nic. It's what makes us great. We don't swallow what our government tells us. We think about it. I'm going to believe the earth is six thousand years old until you can prove it otherwise. To my satisfaction. And you know what? You'll never be able to do that because science is fallible. It's been proven wrong so many times I've lost count. So it might be fashionable now in science to say the earth's a couple of million years old—"

"Four and half billion."

"But what are they going to say tomorrow? Scientists are not something to place your faith in. God is."

"Yes, ma'am."

"Four and a half billion. That's just ridiculous."

Chapter Seven

Today there's this big story in the newspaper about a guy losing his job because he wouldn't say something the government wanted him to say. His bosses wanted him to say that these panthers down in Florida weren't all that endangered after all, but he wouldn't. His research showed that it was those gated golf communities they were putting up that were killing them off. So they fired him.

"I don't know what the world is coming to," Mom says, shaking her head.

"Well, maybe I shouldn't be a scientist after all."

"Why not?"

"I might get fired."

She pours herself yet another cup of coffee. "You tell the truth as best you know it."

"But what if I lost my benefits? I wouldn't have health insurance."

"You leave your health insurance to me."

"But what about my 401K plan?"

"Aren't you a little young to be worrying about that?"

"I'm just thinking maybe there are other avenues."

"Like what?"

"Like starting up a teen pornography site."

I'd like to say she nods as if I have a point. But she doesn't.

I want a computer in my room but Mom won't let me. She thinks I'll watch porn all night. Jerry Haggerty showed me a site that was pretty gross, with dogs and stuff. But the girls seemed to like it. So I don't know.

Pretty soon you won't have to go outside anymore. You can just live in MySpace. I talk to people there more than I do in person. I talk to Jen Winton all the time but wouldn't be seen dead in the hallway with her. She's goth. Well, borderline goth. More like dark gray. But she's got great taste in music. She's really into metal. Mom says heavy metal. Yeah, maybe back in the twentieth century it was called heavy metal. Anyway, Jen helped me figure out the whole cursor thing. Now I've got a bright purple question mark for an arrow. She's got a hatchet. Mom asked to see my site and I said no. She said, Why not? I said, Hello? It's private. And she said, The whole world can see it and I can't? I said, If you can find it, knock yourself out. She said, Don't write anything stupid on it. You don't want to get arrested. I said . . . I forget.

Gina Kosta has a site. It's kinda gross. She talks about herself like it's someone else. Like it's this babe called Gina who's got big boobs and who'll do anything you want or think of. And then, when you see her in real life, in the hall, she's just normal. It's weird.

Mrs. Porter won't let Kevin have a MySpace page, so he's

totally undercover. He signs on when he's at the library, when his mom thinks he's working on his Abe-Lincoln-Was-a-Cool-Dude project. His first link is to Tila Tequila. I think Mrs. Porter would fall down dead if she knew. Though I don't see what the big deal is. Jesus was heavily into Mary Magdalene and if she lived today you can be sure she'd be linked to MySpace. Every self-respecting hooker is. No offense or anything. I'm just saying.

I found my dad's page. There he was: Shaman360. It's got all this Gaia stuff on it. He talks about what a great dad he is. He posted a picture of the two of us fishing in Glacier Park. I'm holding a bass and he's putting his hands apart wider like it's the biggest fish ever landed. Funnee, Dad. Oh, so funnee! It looks like he's advertising for a girlfriend.

I had a girlfriend once. For about forty-five minutes. It was at Adam Clark's Halloween party last year. She was dressed as a bunch of grapes. She had on a light green leotard with light green balloons stuck to it. She kept running around yelling, "I'm Chardonnay! Get it? Get it? Wine. I'm wine. Chardonnay!" Her name is Kay. She was really drunk by the time I ran into her outside the bathroom and she just grabbed my shoulders and hung on. We kind of stumbled around like that for the rest of the party. Every time I went to kiss her she took a slug from her bottle. She kept telling me how she thought I was so cool even if nobody else did. Then her friends came and dragged her away. The next week she wouldn't look at me in Social Studies class. Acted like there was no way in hell she'd let a lowlife like me stick his tongue down her throat.

When Dad doesn't come up this weekend, Mom says she'll take me out to lunch. She adds, "I never see you anymore."

We go to Hard Rock Café, which is awesome because they've got Eric Clapton's guitar. Though I don't know what it's doing in a restaurant. It should be in a museum. Talk about a prime example of evolution. They've also got Joan Jett's leather pants. Which I think is pretty weird.

After we order and our waitress goes off to get our drinks and appetizers, Mom leans forward and says, "Well."

Now, I know what "Well" means. It means she's got something big to tell me and I don't want to hear it. Because "Well" is always bad. It's never been good. It's never been, "Well, I think we should move to Tahiti." Or "Well, your teachers think you are so smart you can skip the rest of your education" or "Well, we've betrothed you to Layla and you may begin your marital duties immediately." So I try to avoid her "Wells." The last "Well" was "Well, your father and I have decided it's best if he goes to Williamsburg and we stay here." And that has sucked.

But I skip the choking option and go instead for the attack. I tell her she's being an unfit mother. I tell her I'm way behind in assignments and that she has to do something about it.

She leans back so the waitress can set down her chili-cheese-and-bacon potato skins in front of her. "Is it that bad?"

"It's that bad."

"But your grades are fine."

"Is that all you care about, *grades?*"

"I'm sorry, I didn't realize. I guess I just haven't had time . . ."

"You *always* say that."

"Alright. You're right. We'll talk to the teacher. I'll get on it." Then she smiles and leans forward again. "Well . . ."

I tell her a mother should be with her husband for the child's sake.

"What?"

I tell her she made a decision and got married and had me and that she has to make some sacrifices.

"You mean give up my job?"

"He will take care of you."

"Who?"

I don't want to say God because she would laugh. So I say Dad.

She smiles. "Ya think?"

"Of course."

She takes a humongous bite out of her potato skin and chews awhile before she asks, "So when could I go back to work?"

I think about it and say, "Maybe when I graduate. From college." But then I think she should be around to help out with the grandchildren, so I add, "Or after I'm married awhile."

"You planning on getting married soon?"

"Maybe. I wouldn't want to be led astray by impure thoughts."

"You really like this Bible stuff."

And I shrug. There are three girls at a table behind her. I

can tell they think I'm a geek for sitting with my mom. They keep looking over and giggling. One has long blonde hair. She's wearing a pale blue shirt that opens out and you can see the tops of her tits. I think *she'd* make a good wife.

Mom says, "The thing is, Jesus doesn't seem to have much for me."

"He'll keep you safe."

"I don't think that's enough."

"Maybe it should be." I dig into my Texas tostados and let her ponder that for a while. The thing is, it works. She forgets to say "Well" again.

Afterward we go over to the Museum of Natural History and mooch around. I know that place like the back of my hand. We've been coming here ever since I was in one of those baby slings. Usually we stand in front of the FossiLab's window like it's some altar. All those dinosaur skeletons they have hanging around? They're like family. The fossil section is our church. We go and pay our respects to Mr. Darwin.

Mom'll say, "Look, isn't that amazing? Dolphins evolved from a wolflike animal. I wonder why."

And I'll say, "Seventy percent of the earth is covered in water. Maybe they wanted the real estate."

And she'll say, "Hmmm, interesting idea. I wonder what we'll evolve into." Because she likes to do that. Encourage me and then ask more penetrating questions.

"Bad motherfuckers," I'll say.

Not.

But today I have something else in mind.

"Mrs. Porter gave me some books. They haven't found all those fossils I always thought they'd found. The ones that connect us to the apes."

"Sure they have."

"No, they haven't. Everybody goes on about it like they exist, but they don't. Not the ones that would be conclusive."

She stares at me. "Well, that's because fossilization is relatively rare, especially for land-dwelling animals. The main fossils we have are animals that lived in the sea."

"The missing links are still missing."

She crosses her arms. "Evolution is not a theory."

"It is."

"Well, it's a hell of a lot better theory than they've got. It's the best one. The most complete. The most possible."

"But still a theory."

"I can't believe we're having this conversation."

"I'm just asking questions. You shouldn't get so defensive."

She waves her hand around. "Look at these numbers: 340 million years, 260 million years, 118 million . . ."

"McDonald's writes Good for Your Heart on their Cobb salad, doesn't mean I have to believe them."

"This is insane."

"I've been looking into it. Using my brain, like you wanted. And you know what? I think they're right. I think dinosaurs did live with man down through the thousands of years of our existence."

"That's impossible."

"Yeah, well, where did all these legends of monsters and dragons come from?"

"What legends?"

"Think about it. There have been legends of reptilian creatures and dragons passed down to us from our ancestors for ages. From across Europe, China, America. What these people remember seeing are the dinosaurs. Why should they be ignored because they don't fit in with evolution?"

Mom stands there, gaping like a fish, with her hands at her side.

"Listen to this." I take out my Bible. I've been carrying it around in my knapsack. It doesn't take long to find the place. "Listen to this: 'Look at the behemoth, which I made along with you and which feeds on grass like an ox. What strength he has in his loins, what power in the muscles of his belly. His tail sways like a cedar . . .'"

"Stop."

So I stop.

She pulls her coat close around her. "Is this how it's going to be? God said it, I believe it, that settles it."

"What about you? You think 'Scientists said it, I believe it, that settles it.' What if they change their minds again?"

She puts her hand to her head.

So I keep on. "I'm just saying, humans and lions live on earth at the same time today. So why couldn't humans and dinosaurs have lived at the same time? There are at least two places known today with human and dinosaur tracks in the same sedimentary layer. One is in eastern Turkmenistan. The other is in Paluxy, Texas."

Finally Mom stalks off and I have to race after her.

I have to follow her all the way to the Native American museum. I knew that's where she'd go. She likes all the bead-work. But I have to tell you it's weird looking around at all these shoes and pipes made by people who don't exist any-more. Backed the wrong horse, Mr. Branden in Social Studies would probably say. Meaning they didn't wake up and smell the coffee and read their Bible. They were too busy talking to those fake gods floating in the wind and rivers. I wonder sometimes if that's why God's so pissed off at the Africans and Indonesians, because they really seem to get it in the neck. Famines, wars, AIDS. Maybe they're not reading the right book. That's probably why Mary Allen from church is work-ing so hard on her African missions. To make sure they got the right book.

Though I still don't know why God doesn't like Mrs. Vogler. She was reading the right book and her kid got killed. Five years old and smashed by a deadbeat in a pickup truck. She's put up a whole shrine on the side of the road where his body landed. Lots of flowers and his picture in one of those clear folders so it doesn't get wet in the rain. She still goes to church, but I don't know what she's saying when she bows her head to pray. Maybe she doesn't say much, just listens to God trying to explain.

You know who God must really like? Sandra Miller. She's in

my school and she's got it all: Long blonde hair. A stay-at-home mom. A brother who drives a Ford Mustang GT. A summer condo at Dewey Beach. She even does modelling after school. She did a shampoo ad where they made her hair look like gold. I tell you, God is into her.

Chapter Eight

I worry. I worry all the time. I worry that my grades won't be good enough for my first-choice college. I worry I won't get a good job. I worry about being mugged or jumped. I worry about waking up dead. Getting kidnapped, getting arrested for something I didn't do. Dying in a house fire. Dying in a car crash. Being drowned in a hurricane. Being blown up in a terrorist bomb and losing my legs. I worry I might accidentally commit suicide.

Mostly, I worry that Dad is getting to like it in Williamsburg. That he might not come back. He keeps going on about all the space down there. And the history. He drove me to this condo he's thinking of buying.

"But I thought you weren't going to stay that long."

"It's the prices, Nic. I'd be crazy not to. The way they're going, in a couple of years I could make a killing. I'm just throwing away money renting."

But I don't know. It makes it more permanent than I thought it would be.

He says, "Don't worry. When I come back, I'll rent it out.

And then, if you come down here, you can stay in it. So take a look, what do you think?"

What do I think? It's a condo. It's got a living room, a kitchen, a couple of bedrooms. Not much of a yard.

"Less to take care of," he says.

"I was hoping you'd be closer to Dog Street."

You see, I know the place. Mom and I go down to Williamsburg a lot to visit Dad and we go to D.O.G. Street for dinner where they have these inns where the waiters wear old costumes and put *e* on the ends of words. I'm really into Sally Lunn bread. I've been up and down D.O.G. Street—it stands for Duke of Gloucester—so many times I probably could live in one of those houses that have been there since 1600 and not blink an eye. I could probably churn my own butter too. Give it a good stir and slap it on some Sally Lunn.

Dad's been talking to Mom about me going to his college, but to get the in-state tuition we'd have to move to Virginia soon and Mom's not convinced the local high school's science department is good enough. It's one of the things they like to talk about at dinner when we're together. It's like pulling out a favorite CD and using it as background noise. But there is no way Mom is moving. They both know that. It's just something fun to talk about because it's got a lot of tangents off of it, like university costs, the state of their football team, what I'm gonna be when I grow up—and before we know it, we're trying to decide what to have, ye olde colonial cobbler or the Duke of Gloucester mince pie.

"Dog Street?" Dad says. "Are you kidding? Too rich for my blood. You can grab the bus shuttle. It goes right by the end of the street."

"I thought it was for students only."

"For you they'll make an exception."

Mom's not too thrilled, either. "Can we afford this?" she asks him.

"Can we afford not to?"

"It's the top of the market."

"That's what they said three years ago and look."

"I don't know, Robert . . ."

"I just need your signature. I'll handle the rest."

I think it will be kind of cool to be land owners. To say we have properties in Maryland and Virginia. Like the olden times when people had shitloads of land and servants. But I can tell Mom's not sure and is not putting down her Jane Hancock. And it's getting to be a thing.

"Jesus, Lucy, will you just trust me on this."

"I think it's insane. We've got a house already."

"You've got the house. I'm living like a bum."

"It's a nice place . . ."

"Fine, you live in it."

"Now, come on . . ."

"How long are we going to do this?"

She sighs. "I don't know."

"Do you think this is good for . . . ?"

And she looks at him. I know it's me he's talking about.

"Nic," she says, "don't you have some homework to do?"

So I walk out. At the stairs, I'm straining my ears but they get quieter. I give up.

Kevin says I come from a broken home. He said it in front of his mom once and she shrugged, which makes me mad. It's not broken. It's just sort of bent a little. Mom says she's worked too hard for her position and why should she be the one to give it up just because my dad's in Virginia. Loving her work, she says, doesn't mean she loves us any less.

Kevin told me once that he asked his dad if he loved him and his dad said, "Sure. But remember, God loves you. That's what really matters." I couldn't tell you why but I didn't like that answer. And I don't think Kevin did, either.

Which might explain why Kevin is called a terror. Though to tell you the truth I'm not sure what it is that he does that's so terrible, but his mother says she's praying for him all the time. And she does too. She gets together with other moms and they pray for kids at the school. Kevin says he saw them once when he stayed home sick and she made him stay downstairs in the rec room while all these women gathered in his kitchen and drank French vanilla coffee and clutched hands and closed their eyes and prayed that Mary Ellen Ramsey wouldn't get pregnant. Which she didn't, so I guess it worked.

'Course with my mom working and not being able to come to these get-togethers I don't get any prayers and, yeah, I feel bad about it. I told Mom once and she just about bit my head off.

She said, "How is God going to help Mary Ellen keep her

legs closed when He doesn't seem to care that young children get raped every day of the year? How is He going to make sure Charlene Porter gets an A in English when He can't seem to keep Darryl Green from being beaten up by his stepdad again? If you can tell me that I'll eat a raw egg."

So I guess that's one more thing I'll just have to go without. Add it to the list: iPod, a resident dad, and prayers.

Though it's probably a good thing my mom doesn't pray for me. If she did it would mean even more questions like: What are you doing? Who did you talk to? What are you thinking? Who are you thinking about? Where are you going?

Kevin's mom doesn't ask so many questions. Mrs. Porter's more of a statement kind of person. She's very concerned about excellence. It comes up a lot in conversation. She talks about being excellent in parenting. She reminds us she's an excellent parent because she cares and she's helped in her job by Jesus. With a supervisor like that you can't go wrong. She will not tolerate slouches or bad manners. It's "yes, ma'am" and "no, ma'am." She's nice to me about it when I forget but she makes no secret that that's how it's gonna be. So you find yourself "yes, ma'aming" and "no, ma'aming" with the best of them. It tends to make conversations a little longer than usual.

"Yes, ma'am, Mrs. Porter, if you please, that would suit me just fine." And so on.

"Yup" and "nope" in her house are not an option.

One time Kevin was talking about how cool my mom had been about showing us her telescope and Mrs. Porter said, "Lucy? Lucy? What are you calling her Lucy for?" And I didn't get it but Kevin did, and he started stammering but he got confused because he didn't know my mom's last name and he said, "I mean Mrs. Delano-Coen." But that's *my* last name. My dad's name is Coen. My mom's last name is Delano. So she's Ms. Delano. And Mrs. Porter just rolled her eyes and said, "Why do some people have to make things so complicated?" But Mom's told me plenty of times that it's easier to keep your name than to change it. You don't have to do anything. But Mrs. Porter didn't seem to like that answer and pretty soon afterward she told me it was time for me to be getting home.

She thinks I'm a bad influence.

But Kevin's lucky. He gets to spend every Sunday with his dad. They're part of their church baseball team. They said I could join if I want, and I want to. It's fun. Dele plays and he's really good. When he runs around the bases he yells "Hallelu-jah!" the whole way and everybody laughs. Jim Butts plays too. They're top of their church league. We're playing Christ Is Lord next week and we're gonna kick their ass.

When Dad does come up we always do the same thing. Museum or a movie. Which is okay. Mom's always pushing us together. She's always going, "Okay, you two, run along," like we're kids or something. She likes us to go off and get really hungry while she fiddles with a complicated recipe for dinner. But she always screws it up and nothing comes out at the same time so we're eating the meat first then maybe the vegetables and then maybe the potatoes. And "Oh, yeah, here's the gravy," she'll say, and put it down next to our empty plates.

Every time Dad says to her, "Come with us," and she says, "No, no, it's father/son time. Shoo."

Shoo?

So we go outside and she closes the door and sometimes we just stand there and Dad says, "The usual?" I think they should have had more kids. That way it would feel more like a family. More like a team. I said this once to my mom and she laughed and said, "Oh, God, one's killing me as it is."

Layla says my problem is that I don't have a tradition. "A man who doesn't know what to die for doesn't know what to live for."

I don't know how we got on the subject. One minute we're drinking Mountain Dew and the next she's lecturing me on Modern Life 101. I said, "Do you know what you want to die for?"

And she said, "I am a woman now. I die a little every day."

Huh? She has gotten so weird. If she didn't have such long legs I wouldn't listen to her. She says I need to find something to fight for. And the Green Bay Packers aren't gonna do it. A cause, a passion, she says, her eyes dark and wounded-looking.

And I look at her boobs in that tight shirt of hers and think, those'll do.

But she shakes her head. "A cause, moron. Or a culture." Then she swings her eyes around to me and says, "Oh, I forgot, you don't have a culture."

"Sure I do."

"Yeah? What is it?"

"I'm American."

"That's your nationality. What's your culture? Where did your parents' parents come from?"

"Mom's are from Ireland. And Dad's . . . um, from Lithuania. I think. Or is it Latvia? I forget."

She rolls her eyes. "So you're a mutt. You're not even Anglo-Saxon or a full Russian. Russian would be cool. They're poets."

"I thought they were communists."

"Not anymore. They're the biggest corporate raiders around. But they do it with soul."

"Lithuania is sort of Russian, isn't it?"

"I guess."

"Anyway, it doesn't matter. I live in Maryland now."

"Maryland!" She starts laughing. "What's the culture here?"

"It's . . ." And I think maybe she's right. At least Virginia had Thomas Jefferson. "It's got a lot of seafood. And . . . and anyway, not everyone needs a culture."

"It helps define who you are."

"So what are you?"

"I'm a Muslim of Egyptian descent."

"On your dad's side."

"It's enough."

"Well, I'm Nic, pleased to meet you." I shake her hand.

She laughs and switches on the TV. She says "Jackie Chan's on, you want to get the Doritos and salsa?" And I don't know about you but that's enough culture for me.

*   *   *

Then out of the blue Sandra Miller talks to me. Sandra Miller of the gold hair. I couldn't believe it. I'm sitting at the football game on Friday night and she comes up the aisle and stops in front of me and talks to me. *To me.* I don't hear a word she says. I'm just staring at her perfect lips, wondering what they must feel like. But then they stop moving. And I can see she's waiting. But I keep looking at her, thinking, Wow, Sandra Miller is talking to me. Then she looks annoyed. She's frowning. And I want her to stop. I panic. I stand up. I say, "What!?" She jumps back and almost falls back down the steps. "Whoa!" I put my hand out to grab her. But she jerks away before I can touch her, looking at me now like I'm a terrorist on crack or something.

"What are you, a freak?"

"I didn't hear you."

"I *said,* could you move? I want to sit there."

I look down at the row of seats and, sure enough, her friends are all sitting there next to me in a line, looking at me now like I'm something the cat dragged in, and I'm still making dying gurgling noises out of my ass. How could I have missed them all? I must have been on cloud-cuckoo when I sat down. So I say, "Sure." And I move out of her way and she sits down. But I keep standing there, staring at all that blonde hair she's flicking, and she looks up at me and does that breathing-out thing girls do when they are so annoyed they can't even believe it. So I go home.

Chapter Nine

"Hey, Nic, I'm dropping by Safeway on the way home. Need anything?"

"Lip balm."

"Already?"

"And moisturizer."

"I just got some."

"I've used it. And get the kind in the tub, not the bottle. The bottle is for the body. The tub is for faces."

"Jesus, Nic, you're the girl I never had."

Mom has been going on about the horror of advertising from the very beginning. I remember how she used to give me pop quizzes. We'd walk past a poster and she'd ask, Okay, what are they trying to sell? Sometimes it's not so easy. I'd have to really concentrate to figure it out. But I've gotten pretty good. She wants to me to be aware of the mind-bending going on, of what they're trying to do. Which is rip my hard-earned money from my fist. But, you know, I don't earn any money yet so I think she's talking about *her* hard-earned money. She really loses it when she sees more billboards around. She calls her congressman and makes a stink. Nothing ever happens. She's discovered that a lot of the billboards are illegal but even then nobody does anything about it. She and some friends of hers tried to take one down and nearly got arrested.

Her real worry, though, is that they're going to start putting billboards up in space. She read about it once in a magazine and screamed her head off. "Can you imagine? Looking up at the stars, the most primal human urge there is, and you find yourself looking at an ad for Nike? They'll do it too. If they can get their asses up there they will." You know it always amazes me her bad language. I'm supposed to be squeaky-clean and she's got garbage mouth. I've given up correcting her. She always says sorry but then does it again two seconds later.

Did you know that shooting stars have nothing to do with stars? They're just dust from comets in space. The dust burns up when it falls into earth's atmosphere, and that's what causes the streak. Sometimes it's more than dust. It's a chunk of rock and it survives the entry and turns into a fireball that smashes into earth. Mom says the thought of comets smashing into the earth keeps her up at night. Like she doesn't have better things to worry about.

So I find myself talking to Mrs. Porter about Time again. I don't know why I spend so much time talking to her, but I think it might have to do with her chest because I've never seen two more perfect round mounds. And she always looks like she's just taken a shower. She's got this squeaky-clean look to her like if you looked behind her ears you might find a dollop of Palmolive. Anyway, I'm explaining about Time being the fourth dimension.

And she says, But the world is in 3D. Which is true spacewise but it's also got this fourth dimension. (Some say seven, maybe even ten, but that's a different story and she looks enough put out about the idea of four.) Anyway, she says, What, like a sixth sense? I say No, Time. And she glances at me through the rearview mirror like I might be telling a joke but she doesn't get it. So I try to explain it to her. I tell her that space and time are measured differently. Time is measured as if a tape measure is being unrolled and you make a note of each marker as it's passed. "So you've got one foot, two feet, three feet, and so on. But neither end of the measure can be seen, only the passing of the markers. The only choice is how big an interval to take."

"An interval," she says.

"You know, a space in between."

"Oh, an interval."

"Space is different because both ends of a spacial measurement can be seen at the same time and you can measure it from one end to the other. But a length of time can't be carried around like a length of string. Which is why we use clocks, which are sort of always in the middle of things."

There's a bit of silence in the car after that. Finally she says, "My, you are persistent." Which I look up in the dictionary, thinking it means something like "really smart," but it says "continuing to exist in spite of interference or treatment" so I'm now going to have to go back to her and tell her she got it wrong. I mean, it's kind of embarrassing when grownups use the wrong words.

When I get back, Mom is sitting at the kitchen table entering receipts into her laptop. Her glass of wine is empty.

"You're late tonight," she says.

I don't say anything, just head for the refrigerator. The pickings are slim. I settle for a half-eaten wheat germ–topped vanilla yogurt. I can feel her sitting there staring at me while I carefully spoon the wheat germ over to one side. If I lived at Kevin's house Mrs. Porter'd probably jump up and offer to make me a sandwich. But Mom doesn't do that. No way. The last time Mom offered to make me a sandwich was when I was three, in bed with chicken pox, too weak to lift the mayo jar.

"I talked to your father today."

My eyes flick over.

"He says he's sent you many e-mails but you're not responding."

I dunk a huge scoop of germ into the garbage.

She lets fifteen seconds go by (I count them by the ticking of the kitchen clock) before she asks, "Are you angry with him?"

I dig into what's left of the yogurt.

"Are you angry with me?" she says.

I crush the carton with an ear-blistering crunch.

"Nic, I don't know how to talk to you anymore."

"Well, that's too bad."

"You can't just ignore your father forever."

"Sure I can. He's just my earthly father. Not really anyone to depend on." I walk out of the kitchen, up to my room, and let the silence settle on the house like a bad smell.

Dele's been stressing. Turns out the ministry housing he's been staying in needs remodeling and he has to find somewhere else to stay for a while. He's asked around but no one seems to have a place for him. He's got one week. When he asks at Bible class if anyone knows of anyone he could stay with, I'm surprised that no one raises their hand. They all look real concerned but keep their hands in their laps. "Don't I wish," I hear Mrs. Butts murmur to Kevin's mom. And I think, hey, we've got an extra bedroom. So I say he can stay with us and he laughs.

I don't see what's so funny.

"Maybe you should ask your mother first," he says.

"She'll say yes."

He nods, but I don't think he believes me.

Later, when I get home and I ask Mom about Dele, she laughs too.

"What's so funny about letting a guy stay here when he doesn't have anywhere else to go?"

"I'm sure he'll find somewhere," she says.

"Well, he hasn't. And he needs someplace and you're the one who's going on all the time about how you don't have to be religious to be nice to people."

She looks over at me and says, "Okay."

"Okay?"

"Yeah. Okay."

And that was that. I think, Wow, I didn't think it was going to be so easy. I look at her, trying to figure out what she's up to.

And she looks back at me all innocently. "What?" she says.

So, a week later, right before dinner, Dele comes to stay. He puts his suitcase and big backpack in the guest room and says thank-you a million times. He keeps washing his hands. I think the fancy soap we've put in the bathroom for him, the clear green one in the shape of an octopus, has already lost its legs and is heading for extinction. I gotta say, having Mr. Clean staying in our house really shows up all the warts. It's been looking pretty fuzzy ever since Juanita quit to help her daughter with her new baby. Mom hasn't gotten anybody else yet. Says—wait for it—she hasn't had *time*.

She's not exactly a happy homemaker. When a study came out that claimed cleaning too much was actually bad for you— that it killed off too many bugs, so your immune system wasn't working properly—Mom acted like she knew it all along. She said, "You know, I always thought all those cleaning products couldn't be good for you." And that's BS because she and I both know she was just too lazy to clean up properly. "Domestic goddess I'm not," she always says. Before, she used to be apologetic. Now she says it like it's some badge or something. Like she's won the purple heart of household chores.

Mom's eyes become Frisbees when Dele pulls out four Bibles from his suitcase. Different translations, he explains. When he starts opening one to show me, Mom backs off and mumbles

something about getting dinner ready, which I know is an excuse because all you have to do is take it out of the freezer,
pull off the packaging, and set it in the microwave. But if she's
gonna be weird, that's just fine. I'll be the normal one for both
of us.

At dinner she's okay. She calls up the stairs and we come
down to pasta with carburetor sauce already spooned into our
bowls and juice already in our glasses. So we sit down and are
just about to dive in when Dele says, "Shall we say grace?"

Mom looks up and says in a really high-pitched voice,
"Sure."

Dele says, "Would you like to lead us?"

She stares at him a second and says, "Sure," again, twice as
high. And this is what she says: "Thanks for the big bang and
thanks for evolution, thanks for our big brains, and may we in
this house continue to use them."

Then she smiles at Dele and he smiles back and I smile at
them both. The pasta is pretty good.

When I come down to breakfast the next morning the place is
sparkling. Mom stands in the middle of the kitchen panting
and sweating up a storm.

"What's all this?"

"What's all what?"

"This." I wave at the gleaming counters that usually have a
bacterial buildup thick enough to slice off and sell to labs. "You
trying to show him that the godless are clean too?"

She gives me the look.

"Mmmm," I say, scooping up a chunk of fresh raisin bread.

"Don't you dare drop those crumbs on my clean floor!"

I'm not allowed to sit on her puffed-up cushions, walk on her freshly vacuumed stairs, or even brush my teeth in the clean sink. She tells me to lean over and use the tub instead.

When Dele comes down, all dressed and more scrubbed than the kitchen floor, she sits at the table reading the newspaper like she has nothing to do with the transformation. Like some supersonic maid flew in during the night and made it perfect. The only problem is she looks like she's run a marathon to Jupiter and back. Her hair is all stuck down to her head.

"Anything special you would like for breakfast?" she asks. Like Jeeves the butler is gonna appear from behind the refrigerator and whip it right up.

"Oh, no. Anything is fine."

So I show him where the cereals are. We've got a whole bunch: Wheaties, Cocoa Puffs, Froot Loops, Natural Swiss Muesli, and this brown sawdust Mom buys for herself but never eats. He looks at them all and says, "Now, this is nice." He shakes a bit of all of them into the same bowl and stirs.

I watch to see if he'll say grace over breakfast. And he does. Not a big thing, just a quick dunk of the head and clasp of the hands before diving into his cereal. I think he'd probably linger longer with God but he has my mom staring at him. She has old mascara smudged under her eyes and is breathing like she's inhaled too much dust and might keel over. It's morning and she looks like she should turn in. I hope he's remembered to pray for her.

He polishes off the cereal in no time.

"Coffee?" Mom asks.

"No, thank you. A bit of caffeine and I fly through the sky all by myself."

Well, Mom raises an eyebrow to that. She can't even open her eyes without mainlining espresso straight into her jugular.

"Cold crystal water. That is all a body needs." He drinks his glass down in one gulp.

"I think I'll get dressed," Mom says and shuffles out.

Dele winks at me. "Your mother is not a morning person."

She's not really an afternoon or an evening person either, but I let it slide.

He stands up and rubs his hands. "I go off to do the Lord's work. You?"

"I'm, um, going to go to school."

"Excellent."

"How are you getting to church?"

"I will take the bus."

"There's a bus here?"

"Yes. The J7 goes to 43 and then I change and take the D6.

"How long does that take?"

"As long as it takes."

I nod my head.

"Shall we say a little prayer?"

I shrug. "Sure."

And what can I say. It feels good having a little prayer sitting on your shoulder to start the day.

Mom, as you can probably guess by now, isn't a prayer person. Instead of prayers, I remember when I was a kid she had me crawl into bed and think about all the things I was grateful for.

"Like what?" I'd ask every night.

"Like your mommy and daddy who love you."

"Oh, yeah."

"Can you think of anything else?"

"Hunter took my dump truck. I'm not grateful for that."

"That's fine. But what are you grateful for?"

I'd think and I swear to God I could never think of anything. I could only think of the bad stuff that happened that day. Like who was a jerk at recess or how Mom still hadn't got me a PlayStation.

"How about food on the table?"

"Oh, yeah." Boring.

"A nice clean bed."

"Yeah." Wasn't that in some kids' bill of rights?

"Anything else?"

"No, that's it."

And she'd tuck me in with a blanket and kiss my nose and look deep into my eyes and say, "I'm grateful for you."

"And Daddy," I'd have to remind her.

"And Daddy, of course."

I guess being grateful was sort of like praying. But you didn't really talk to anyone. You just said what you were grateful for that day. You didn't expect an answer.

Dele prays when things are bad and he remembers to pray when things are good. He prays when people are sick, he prays when he doesn't know how to make a decision. He says it's like taking your hands off the steering wheel and letting God be the driver. You just relax and be the passenger. And start looking for signs from God.

So I'm looking for a sign. A tree winking. A duck nodding hello. Anything. Dele says I'll start seeing Him everywhere. Little things in my life will start to make sense. And I start thinking about the time when Mom said she didn't have a four-cheese pizza and I really, really wanted it, and then she dug a little deeper in the freezer and there it was. Four-cheese pizza. It was like Jesus heard my plea and coughed it up.

It works again today. I pray really hard that Dad will call. Because I am tired of e-mails. I want him to make the effort of a real phone call. And he does. It's amazing. Just like dialing up and getting through. Dele says that I'll start noticing all sorts of things like that. Special messages to me. He told me once how, when he was back in Nigeria and he wanted to know if he should come to America, his Bible kept falling open to this one passage: "May He give you the desire of your heart and make all your plans succeed."

Then his friend came over and said, Look I've got to show you something and read him the *same* passage. The clincher was when his dad came over and said, Son, you'll never guess but last night I was reading the Book and I ran into this passage. There it was, the same one, good ol' Psalm 20. That's God talking, Dele says. Loud and clear.

So I've been asking God a lot of questions. Like, When will Dad come back? Or, When will Mom and I move down to live with him? I haven't heard anything yet, unless I'm just not picking up the signals. But it's cool. In the morning I say, Hey, Jesus, and I can hear him in my brain saying, Hey, Nic, whazzup? And I'll say, Not sure what to have for breakfast. He'll ask, What are the choices? (Being polite, I guess, because of course He knows.) And I'll say, Bagel, Cheerios. Or if I'm feeling really healthy, Bacon and eggs. And he'll go, Hmmm, sounds like a bacon-and-egg day to me. It's great. Just to have that extra pair of eyes, that extra opinion. Of course I wouldn't tell my mom about it. She'd be, like, children are starving in Africa and He's helping you with breakfast?

Chapter Ten

After dinner Mom shows Dele star pictures on her computer. Dele really gets off on the beautiful colors of the supernovas. I think Mom's got a real convert in him. He checks out the clouds of stardust. This man who thinks the world began six thousand years ago is gaping at the remains of a two-billion-year-old explosion. But he isn't conceding anything. He says, "God works in mysterious ways. I don't question."

Mom rolls those eyes of hers but weirdly doesn't say anything. When I ask her about it later, she says she thinks the only reason fundamentalists admit that the earth revolves around the sun is because they can see it. But something like biology and evolution, which they can't see, they can ignore. Which is ironic, she says, because biologists believe that eventually everything will be reducible, while many astrophysicists believe that in the end our universe could be unknowable.

Well, that's just the kind of thing she would say, wouldn't she?

Still, she's doing her best to teach Dele the things she knows. It's like she has him by the lapels and isn't going to let go until he grasps the idea of an infinitely complex universe.

"See that?" She points at her screen where it looks like a massive neon blue bear is on fire. "That's the crab nebula. The remains of a supernova."

Dele leans forward. He puts his hand to his heart. "Beautiful," he says. People get very weird when they check out Mom's nebula photos on the computer. I remember when Carla first saw the photo of the Veil, which looks sort of like a one-eyed pink-and-purple eagle flying straight at you. She just stood there speechless until she whispered, "Damn, it's enough to make you believe in God, isn't it?"

Mom's got her university professor voice on. "Supernovae occur when a massive star ends its life in an amazing blaze of glory. For a few days a supernova emits as much energy as a whole galaxy. When it's over, a large fraction of the star is blown into space as a supernova remnant. Which is what this is. Crab nebula. It was observed exploding in 1054 by the Chinese."

"Incredible," Dele says.

She shows him the Horsehead nebula, my personal favourite. It looks like a rose-colored horse galloping out from billowing pink clouds.

"Wondrous," he says.

"Supernovae are responsible for creating many of the elements that you come into contact with in your everyday life. Gold, titanium, mercury, and iodine all lived part of their lives as supernova remnants before they settled and condensed into the planet earth."

"Amazing," he says.

"It wasn't until 1993 that Walter Baade and Fritz Swicky

suggested that the light emitted by a supernova didn't indicate the birth of a new star but the death of a star similar to our own sun. Its hydrogen core completely burns out and it ejects its atmosphere to create a planetary nebula. Stars live and die, just like we do."

"Extraordinary," he says.

"The farther one peers into space, the further back in time one is seeing. We've managed to discern supernovae over nine billion years old."

Dele shakes his head, having run out of things to say.

"But you know what's really interesting about the supernovae?

Dele looks at her warily.

"They've showed us that the universe has been expanding at an accelerated rate during the past six billion years or so. One day our universe could expand so far our galaxies could be torn apart. Our universe could end. We call it the 'big rip.' "

Dele is silent. Then he smiles at her and shrugs philosophically. " 'The heavens declare the glory of God; the skies proclaim the work of his hands.' Psalm 19."

Luckily for him, Dele's not around much. He spends most of his time at the church. He's usually gone by the time we get up. I look in his room and it's like no one lives there. His bed's made up, his clothes all put away. I don't know where he puts his dirty laundry. Mom says he tiptoes down at night and runs a load.

I went in once and went through his suitcase in the corner. I felt a little weird doing it but I figured he's so open about everything he wouldn't mind. I found some letters: Dearest Son . . . Dearest Brother . . . I started to read them but I thought that was pushing it, so I put them back. All he's got on his nightstand is his Bible and a picture of two people who I figure must be his parents. She's wearing a bright yellow dress covered with blue swirls, with a matching scarf tied big and bold on her head. She's glancing away from the camera and grinning. The man's wearing a dark blue suit and isn't cracking so much as a smile.

Then I sat down on Dele's bed and just listened to the quiet. I thought if I just stayed quiet maybe Jesus would poke His Head out of the closet and say hello. I thought he must be around because Dele talks to him all the time. Though He'd probably be at church with Dele but then maybe Dele kept a home version in his room. To tell you the truth I still have a hard time with the "God is everywhere" idea. It sounds easy until you start really thinking about it. How can He pay attention with so many people talking at Him all the time?

When Dele is home for dinner he insists on doing the dishes. He wraps a dish towel around his waist, unbuttons his sleeves, rolls them up and tosses everything from the table into the sink. Mom keeps reminding him that we have a dishwasher. But he always waves her away like it's stupid to use a dishwasher when you've got a perfectly good sink. She just shrugs and leaves the room.

I like to hang out with him in the kitchen so we can talk. One night I ask about the photo he keeps next to his bed. Dele doesn't seem to mind that I was in his room.

"You ever talk to your parents?" I ask.

"Yes, to my mother. She sends me letters. Sometimes I call."

Dele hasn't been back to Nigeria for three years, mainly because he has to save up to bring back presents. It's the custom. He says there are all these Africans around the world unable to return to visit because they can't afford the presents. And it's not just for his family, it's for everybody. His brother's wife's uncle. His mother's oldest friend. His sister's brother-in-law's boss. They'll all come to his house to say hello and expect a little something, and so Dele is busy saving as much as he can. He's trying to hurry too, because his mom isn't feeling so well. He wants to save up to bring her back an air conditioner.

"And your dad?"

"My father is dead. May God rest his soul."

"Oh. Sorry."

He nods his head.

"Did he get sick or something?"

"No. He was very much a healthy man."

I stare at him, waiting for more but he claps his hands together. "But enough of this. God wants us to rejoice with our blessings. Not dwell on our sorrows. It is past. My father lives with me in my heart."

"You have a lot of people in your heart."

Dele laughs and spreads his arms. "The whole world!"

Some nights he's in the kitchen so long and working so hard, I have to get out of the way. About every other night, he mops the floor. Mom says she's never known a floor could be so clean. And he says it doesn't take so much time. Like she should try it sometime. She just laughs and says, "Probably, but I'd much rather watch TV."

When he's done, he comes in the room where we're collapsed, watching total crap. Laugh sound track, gratuitous sex, commercials to make you weep. Mom's got a dish of ice cream. Me, I'm reading a comic book with my feet over the side of the couch. And Dele sits down in the armchair and reads his Bible, his back straight, eyes looking right down at the Good Book. He doesn't come up for air.

"Is this too loud?" Mom will ask.

Dele will look up and blink, like he's been somewhere else, and say, "Oh, no. It's fine."

Mom'll go back to watching her shows, spooning in the ice cream, and I watch him the whole time to see if he peeks. And you know what? He does. He can ignore *Lost, House,* even *24.* But *Sex and the City* reruns, he's all eyes. And he laughs. He laughs real loud. The first time he laughed Mom and I just about jumped out of our seats. Carrie was going on about cherry-flavored condoms and he barked like a dog.

I asked him once. "Do you think she's cute?"

Dele said, real serious, "She is a very attractive woman." Then both he and Mom laughed.

Layla's been teaching me to say hello in Arabic. *Assalamu alaikum.* Well, it's not actually "hello," it's "Peace be upon you." And then you're supposed to answer, *Wa alaikum assalam,* which means "And on you be peace." It's like a secret handshake in a secret club. I once heard some moms at school say it to each other. I thought they were telling each other where they hid the bombs.

Layla's been teaching me that Islam is a lot like Christianity, at least the believing-in-God part. Where it's different is that they don't think Jesus was the son of God. They just think he was a prophet. A good prophet, full of good ideas, just not able to turn water into wine, like it boasts in the Bible. Muslims say that's a figment of Christians' imagination. When I mentioned this to Mom she said, "That's pretty rich coming from guys who think virgins are draped around heaven like party streamers."

Still, Mohammed sounds pretty cool. He used to wander around the desert every morning waiting for some sort of signal from God. And then finally God spoke to him. Out of the blue. It's like an If-you-build-it-they-will-come sort of thing. If you stand there with your hand cupping your ear long enough, somebody's gonna start talking. Layla says Muhammad's misunderstood. She says he gets a lot of crap.

So I guess I shouldn't be surprised when Layla shows up in a veil today. Well, not a long veil, one of those head scarves. A *hijab* she calls it. She looks very solemn.

"What's up?" I say.

"This is my religion," she replies.

"A head scarf is a religion?" I say. I like to mess with her.

"Islam, you moron."

"Well, hit me with a hockey puck."

"I will not be subject to men's eyes. This retains my dignity."

"Yeah?"

"It means men can look at me and not be so passionate."

I look at this tight scarf hiding all her passionate hair, when her body is pushing out from her tight shirt like it's got another idea.

My mom, of course, tries to talk her out of wearing it when she comes home. She's digging in her purse for Layla's money and shaking her head at the same time.

"I can't believe you're falling for this."

"This is my culture," Layla replies.

"Oh, come on, it's not your culture. It's a culture made by men long ago who couldn't handle women being themselves."

"That's feminist crap."

You would think Layla stuck out her hand and whacked my mom right across the face. She just stands there, her hand lost somewhere in the bowels of her purse, staring at Layla. "What?"

"We're beyond that. Women now take what we want. Now the point is to live together in peace, promote our differences, and work together for the future."

"I see."

"I am treated as a person, not a sex object. Look around you. Our privates plastered all over the walls. We are nothing but body pieces. Like this, with the *hijab*, they see *me*."

Mom doesn't say a word, just hands her the money before walking stiffly up the stairs. Layla lets herself out. I'm sure Mom would like to get a new babysitter but it's hard to get good babysitters who won't rip you off or throw parties in your house when you go out at night. Even if Mom thinks Layla's lost her mind, she knows she can trust Layla with my life.

*   *   *

Dad shows up for Columbus Day. Schools are closed, so Mom asked him to come down. I'm not sure why it's an official holiday. The descendants of the few Native Americans not wiped out by the smallpox Christopher and his pals brought over in 1492 are probably not partying up a storm. Dad arrives around three o'clock. Mom told him to come earlier but he says they got a late start. And then we see her. Skye. She slides out of the car and stands in the driveway with a jug of wine in her hand, staring at the house. She gives Dad a rolled-eye look and then walks up the path like she owns the place.

I've seen her at Dad's house a couple of times. She's okay. Used to be a student at the university but she dropped out a couple of years ago. She's an Earth Firster. She likes to sit in trees when people are trying to cut them down. She's got a silver stud in her tongue and says things like "rad" and "reform." According to Skye, we are species-centric, meaning we don't care what the other species think, we just mow them down when we feel like it. I kind of agree with her. But I still can't resist a good juicy bacon cheeseburger or one of Domino's MeatZZa Feasts. She doesn't eat meat or wear leather. She calls them by-products of the rape of our land. She wears a lot of rubber. She's cool. She was going to let me smoke a joint once until my dad stopped her.

The thing is, Dad didn't tell Mom he was bringing Skye. Mom's only vaguely heard about her. Not from me. No way. But Dad, I guess, slid her into the conversation a couple of times. And now he's brought her. Mom doesn't look too happy about it.

"Skye?" she says, and glances up at the clear blue sky. "How descriptive." She puts her arm around Dele's shoulders and says, "Robert, meet Dele," and acts like Dele's head of the family now. Dele, with that big handshake of his, just about takes Dad's arm off. Skye squeezes her hand open and shut a couple of times when he's done with her.

And so, yeah, what a party: me, Dele, Skye, Mom, and Dad. Good thing Granddad and Grandma couldn't make it. The crazy feelings winging around the room would have just about cracked the walls open. First thing Skye does is disappear into the bathroom and I know what she is doing. I can smell it. I tap on the door lightly, hoping she'll share but she just stays dead silent. Mom is on about her third glass of wine by the time I come down again and has forgotten all about cooking. We were supposed to have a barbecue, but it suddenly started pouring so she left the chicken pieces out on the counter and is now chewing Dad's ear off about all the stuff going on at work. And Dad's holding his beer bottle by the neck and grinning at her like he is really thinking about something else, something he has to say.

Dele, luckily, turns out to be a whiz in the kitchen.

"Nic, you stand in my way. Get out of my way!"

A bit of a dictator, I admit, but he can get chicken fried in no time. He even makes mashed potatoes and a large salad. Then he makes everyone sit in a particular seat like at a big old-fashioned dinner party. I notice he's got Mom and Skye just about as far away from each other as possible without popping Skye out back with the trash cans.

And, oh yeah, grace. Mom is pretty plastered and relying on her teammate Dele, so she doesn't make a peep when he practically barks at us to get our hands out of the butter and rolls and put them together.

He looks around at us sternly, then begins, "God is great, and God is good. God knows things that we do not. He knows our hearts and our souls. We must remember that. We must wash away our sins. We must purify our thoughts. And hearts. We must make peace with Him and with each other. May the Lord truly bless this house and all those who have come today. Amen."

Well, you can just about stuff a whole roll in Dad's mouth after that one. And Skye starts laughing so hard she trips over herself getting up from the table and running back up to the bathroom. Mom, poor Mom, she just starts crying right there over her fried chicken because she knows what's coming and she's probably upset at herself that she isn't ready for it. It's been coming down the track for two years now. He tells her in the kitchen while they're drying the pots and pans. I hear the tail end when I come in mooching for some more coffee ice cream.

"I don't mean to hurt you," Dad says.

"I know. I know."

"I just think it would make things clearer. So we can move on."

"Right."

"Did you think you were going to move down someday?"

"No. No. Not really."

And since he knows what she's thinking, he adds, "Skye's a nice girl. She likes Nic a lot."

For such a smart guy, Dad can be so stupid. Mom just throws down her towel, pushes past me as I'm coming in, and runs upstairs. And I think it's funny what a little piece of paper can do. All those people who say they don't want to get married because, after all, it's just a piece of paper, it's not going to change the way they feel. Well, it turns out it goes the other way too. Might as well not get divorced, either, because, after all, it's just a piece of paper.

That night I lie in my bed and stare at nothing. It has finally happened. Dad isn't moving back and we aren't moving to Williamsburg. God has spoken. It isn't fair. I mean, I've been going to Bible class and everything. But maybe He can tell I don't really buy it. Not all the way yet. Maybe God is testing me. Maybe I have to make a bigger commitment.

Chapter Eleven

The next day, Dad and Skye take off. Dele tries to pick up Mom's spirits. Frankly I think it would have been better if he just left her there, sitting in a lump in front of *Oprah* with a cold chicken leg in her fist. But he's determined that she's going to see the light of day. That she's going to see that life is worth living. I think he thinks that because she was so nice to him the evening before, they're still comrades in arms, but she's demoted him right back to preacher non grata and she isn't making it easy for him.

"Will you please leave me alone?"

Dele stands before her, arms crossed, blocking her view of the TV.

"Why you sit there feeling so sorry for yourself? Don't you take any responsibility? You made a choice. Now you face consequences. Don't you sit there sad. The Lord gives you a new day today. Next time you make another decision."

Whew, boy.

Dele and I have to make ourselves scarce pretty quick after that.

We go and play miniature golf. Turns out that, back in Nigeria, Dele was king of putt-putt. He has moves that would put Tiger Woods to shame. And every time the damn ball drops he sighs real heavy and says, "I am blessed." It gets a bit obnoxious after a while and I tell him so. No fair taking the Lord on your side. He gets serious all of a sudden and says, "But, Nic, the Lord is on everybody's side."

I sometimes envy Dele. He's got this whole world in his head. All these people. Moses, Peter, Paul, the woman at the well, Timothy, Samson, Solomon, Job. It's like they're more real than the people around him. These are the people he hangs out with. He talks about them as if he has really met them. And when he talks to others in the group about them, they know exactly what he's talking about. It took me awhile. I had to read the stories a couple of times before I got the hang of it. But now they're there, in the air, ready to use as examples, to use as a compass. "They will show you the way," he said.

And I think, well, God—no pun intended—it just makes him so happy. I mean, how can a man base his life on something that's not true? It must be true for him or he wouldn't be doing what he does. It's not easy being nice all the time and taking care of the poor and you wouldn't believe the stuff he has to listen to, everybody's aches and pains. Mrs. Smith plucks his ear for fifteen minutes after service, about every bunion on her foot, and he just stands there, grinning like it's the most fascinating thing since relativity. So I think sometimes maybe God is like a happy-pill. He just makes you feel all good and calm inside. The hard part, Mom would say, is swallowing it.

Kevin says his mom used to be a nothing, a Unitarian. She joined the evangelical church when Kevin was a baby.

"I almost died. God let me live. Mom's been thanking him ever since."

"What were you going to die of?"

"Encephalitis."

"Did you go to the hospital?"

"Spent five weeks."

"Do you think God saved you?"

"Doctors said I had twenty percent chance of surviving. What do you think?"

I wonder what my mom would do if something happened to me. Would she begin to believe? Would she bite her tongue and just do it? I'd like to think so. It sounds like a nice thing Mrs. Porter did for Kevin.

But it would have to be pretty serious for Mom to change her mind. I'd have to be dying too, I bet. Not just a broken arm, it would have to be a flat-out tubes-coming-out-of-my-nose situation. Otherwise she'd be like, "The doctors can help you. We won't have to bother God."

When Dele and I get back from putt-putt, Mom is at her computer, drowning her sorrows with a few gamma rays.

I try to slide past her office but she catches me.

"Nic, will you come in here, please?"

Dele and I give each other "the look" before I walk to my doom. She's barricaded in there with an empty wine bottle, an empty glass, and a bowl of cold, garlic-stinking spaghetti.

"Sit down."

I take the chair covered in notes and books. Don't even move them out of the way, just plunk right down on top of them. She leans forward and gazes deeply into my eyes.

"We're going to be fine."

"If you say so."

She scoots her chair forward and leans even closer until my eyes are watering from her garlic breath. She says, "You're not losing a father. We're just becoming an extended family. Distance-wise, not diluted in any way. You know that, don't you?"

"Okay."

"It's going to be fine. Just fine." She pats my knee.

"Then why are you crying?"

"Oh." And she wipes her nose on the back of her hand which, man, if I did I'd be handed my ass on a platter. "It's just that I keep thinking how I used to see us in the future in rocking chairs, gazing up at the stars."

"You and Dad?"

She nods. Another tear skids down her nose.

"I'll watch the stars with you."

"Would you?" Her eyes are droopy and sad like a basset hound's.

"Sure."

She reaches out her hand for mine.

"Seeing as you gave away Dad," I point out, "it looks like I don't have anyone to hang out with, either."

The Hallmark moment is definitely over. She drops my hand. "What?"

"Did you ever think maybe I'd like to watch stars with him? Before you let him go."

"I didn't let him go."

"Are you kidding me? You practically helped carry out his stuff."

"It wasn't supposed to be . . . you can still see him."

"Yeah, if I spend three hours to drive down to Williamsburg I can. Or if I'm lucky, maybe every third weekend he'll show up here. And for how long?"

She doesn't say anything. Just blinks at me.

"Thanks a lot, Mom. Good going." And I pat her knee right back.

She doesn't like that one. She stays in her office the rest of the night. I sit in my room hating her. I mean, how the hell do you "lose" a husband like that? It's so irresponsible. You know, I don't ask much. All she had to do was make some meals, do the laundry, and keep her husband, and she's failed completely. He was so easy. He did his own ironing, he never yelled. He made great lasagna, unlike Mr. Porter who acts like the kitchen is Injun country, totally off-limits. Dad seemed to like her fine. He wasn't punching her out or anything. She's so careless. She's like that with her other stuff too. Her keys. She's always losing her house keys. Every morning it's the same thing. But this time it was "Hey, anybody seen my husband?"

Later, Dele knocks on my door.

"What?"

He opens the door and pokes his head in. "I can hear her crying," he says.

"So?"

"Go to her."

"Why?"

"She is your mother. She is in pain. You go to her and you say something."

"Like what?"

"Like it is going to be okay."

"You mean, lie?"

I take my time. I burn three Superchick songs on to a CD before I wander down the hall. She's still in there, tears leaking. I sit down and watch her cry a bit. Then, since I'm getting hungry, I figure I better say something.

"Dele says human beings will always let you down. But Jesus never will. He says that's the problem with living without God. Human love becomes too important. And no one will ever love you enough."

She snorts into a Kleenex. "That's comforting."

I shrug. "So you want me to make some popcorn?" Because that's all she's getting from me.

"Yes," she says like it's the biggest decision she's made all week. "I'd love you to make some popcorn."

We get up and go down to the kitchen and toss a bag into the microwave. Then we slump at the kitchen table, one of us on each side, and listen to it pop.

I say, "It's a good thing Dele is here."

She holds her head in her hands. "Is it?"

*   *   *

The weird thing is, Mom's turned over a whole new leaf since Dele started living with us. She's started running. She comes back bright red and splotchy and collapses on the couch. Dele nods and says, "That's very good for your heart." But I don't think that's what's she's working on. It's that big butt of hers she's always complaining about. Dele said he'd run with her because he was nervous about her going alone at night in the dark. You should see them. Dele not even breaking a sweat and Mom doing her imitation of a seal with lung cancer. When they're out, if I hear an ambulance wailing down Carroll Avenue I get nervous.

When they come back they're laughing and high-fiving each other. Here I am trying to embrace the righteous and virtuous love of God, and they're acting like teenagers.

"Oh, Dele, that was great."

"Yes, a few more sessions and your thighs will be velvet."

"Velvet?"

"I mean metal. Steel. My English . . ."

Mom's even wearing makeup, bright stuff on her eyes and mouth. She's walking around now, like, this face? It always looks like this. These clothes? I always wear a belt cinched so tight my eyeballs pop. And she's starting to smile. Which is really freaky. There's a lot of giggling going on and Dele is doing most of it. For some reason he thinks my mom not believing in God is hilarious. Like she's some insect he's got under glass.

He acts like he's a perfect boyfriend. He takes out the garbage, gets her drinks of water. He even mowed the lawn without anybody asking. Mom's floating around with a really surprised look on her face. It's getting really old. The other day she asked him to put our old grill out on the front lawn so Goodwill could come pick it up, and when he walked by holding it over his head, his muscles flexing all over the place, she just stared. A whole pack of flies could have flown into her open mouth.

It's all wrong. It was supposed to be me and Dele against Mom and her wrongful thinking. But now it's Dele and Mom against me.

The other day Dele sees me flopped in front of PlayStation. He says, "Have you done your homework?"

"Hello, don't need a dad, got one."

"Jesus does not need unschooled disciples."

And Mom calls out, "Dele's right, Nic."

Unbelievable.

Later, Carla comes over for dinner. After she meets Dele I hear Carla say to Mom, "Oh, my God." And Mom says, "Tell me about it."

Luckily Mom's a meat eater. Not like Carla, who can't even smell the stuff without making a face. We definitely could not have lived together this long if Mom insisted on a vegetarian house. I would have packed my bags and gone in search of steak. Stan Birrell's mom's a veggie and he has to toe the line at home. Then at school he's wolfing down burgers like his internal organs are gonna seize up if he doesn't get them down fast enough. He keeps beef jerky in his locker and bites off a chunk between classes.

When Carla comes for dinner Mom makes both veggie

and hunter food. On the night Carla meets Dele for the first time, Mom serves rice, tomato salad, and a nice slab of flank steak. Carla just stares at Dele. She's looking at him so hard she doesn't pay attention when I put a slice of beef on her plate. She just forks it into her mouth. You should have seen the look on her face when she chewed.

Dele is going on about God's wondrous creation, the moon, and Carla is choking into her napkin.

"Are you all right?" he says.

"I'm fine." She balls up the napkin. Seeing an opening I say, "Isn't it against your religion to be living with a woman who's not your wife?"

Dele looks at me surprised.

"You guys are pretty strict about that, aren't you?" I say.

"Yes, that is true."

"So?"

He looks over at Mom. "Lucy is a married woman. I am sure she got permission from her husband to let me stay."

Mom laughs. "It's my house."

Dele just looks at her.

I dive in again. "So, isn't it against your religion, staying in some other guy's house without his permission?"

"Nic . . ." Mom starts.

Dele holds up his hand. "I believe in the sanctity of marriage. I would rather die than hurt it."

"But God works in mysterious ways, doesn't he?" I say, winking.

"Nic, will you just shut up." By this time Mom is about as red as the tomato salad.

Dele pats Mom's arm. "Do not worry, Nic. I am not interested in your mother's body. It is her soul that attracts me most."

Carla glances at Mom who now looks like she's swallowed a toad. "Ouch," she says.

Chapter Twelve

When I get home from school the next day, Mom is standing at the bottom of the stairs glaring at me.

"What?"

"Am I the only one who sees it?"

"Sees what?"

"The folded laundry at your feet."

I look down and, yep, sure enough, on the bottom step is a pile of clothes.

"So?"

"I left that there to see if you would pick it up. You never think to pick it up. Obviously it's my job. Leave that pile there. Mom will get to it. I'm sick of it. It's time you did more around here. I cook. I clean. I pay the rent. What the hell do you do? Besides eat, sleep, and grunt?"

"Why don't you get a maid?"

"Why should we get someone else to do it when with a little effort we can do it easily ourselves?"

"But you don't want to do it."

"I don't want to do *all* of it."

I was going to say Mrs. Porter doesn't complain but then I remembered that Mrs. Porter gets Charlene to do a lot of it. That's what we need. A sister. I've told Mom she should have another kid. Though I wanted a boy. Now I can see the advantages of girls.

"I don't think you should be getting an allowance if you're not going to help around the house."

"Fine. What do you want me to do?"

"We have this conversation every three months. Do you remember what I asked for last time?"

"No."

"Clean your room. Do your laundry . . ."

"I *do* do my laundry.

"Once every six months is not going to hack it. You never have enough underwear."

"Buy some more."

"I am not buying you a hundred and eighty pairs of boxers."

"Okay. Okay." And I salute her like she's some general.

"Don't you dare do that. I'm not asking something unreasonable."

"Whatever."

I turn to race up the stairs.

"Nic," she says.

I keep going.

"Nic!"

"What!"

"Well . . . what do you think about moving?"

I can't believe it. I can not friggin' believe it. All that praying worked! Dele is a genius. I do a victory dance on the stairs and end up on my ass. "Yes!" I shout.

She blinks in surprise. "Wow. That's great. I didn't think . . ."

"But can't Dad move back here?"

She blinks some more. "Oh. No. No, that's not . . . I mean for my work. To Boston. I've been offered—"

"No!"

I run back upstairs and slam my door. I lean against it just in case she tries to come in to talk some more. She's kidding, right? Move us farther away from Dad? Why is she so hell-bent on breaking up our family? It's like we're some roast turkey she's ripping apart with her hands, tearing the leg off, digging deep to rip out the wishbone. She's got to be stopped. I don't come out again all night. And she doesn't try to interfere. I guess she doesn't need to talk to me anymore. She got her answer.

The next morning, she doesn't say anything more about moving. Luckily she's got enough on her plate. The big enchilada? My science project. For the Maryland Middle School science fair. The fair isn't until next spring but you should see her freaking. Total meltdown. She can't get off my back. My project is about, you guessed it, Time.

Time is a freaky thing. It wasn't until clocks were invented that people started to worry about time passing. Suddenly time seemed to be going by too fast and they wanted to save it. But how can you measure something you can't see or feel?

Remember when I was telling you about the time thing

with the train? Well, there's this famous paradox that has to do with special relativity. It's about twins. One of them travels at near the speed of light to a far star and returns to earth. According to special relativity when he comes back, he is younger than his twin. Why? It's really easy when you think about it. The first twin, the guy going, and the twin staying—let's call them Goer and Slacker—both set their clocks at zero when Goer leaves earth for the star. When Goer reaches the star, his clock reads eight years. But when Slacker sees Goer reach the star, Slacker's clock reads sixteen years. Why sixteen years? Because, to Slacker, the spacecraft takes ten years to make it to the star, and the light takes six more years to come back to earth showing Goer at the star. So, viewed through Slacker's telescope, Goer's clock looks like it's running at half the speed of his clock.

Understand? Never mind.

On the trip back, Slacker views Goer's clock going from eight years to sixteen years in only four years' time, because his clock was at sixteen years when he saw Goer leave the star and will be at twenty years when Goer comes back home. So Slacker now sees Goer's clock advance eight years in four years of his time.

When Goer returns home he sees Slacker's clock advance from four to twenty years in eight years of his time. So he also sees his brother's clock advancing at twice the speed of his. They both agree that at the end of the trip Goer's clock reads sixteen years and Slacker's twenty years. So Goer is four years younger.

Moral of the story? Don't be a Slacker.

Anyway, it doesn't really matter because I can't do an experiment of a twin traveling at near the speed of light to a distant star and returning. I thought I'd scale it down a bit. Mom's idea, actually.

I've been thinking about how time is different for different people. Different cultures. How, if you're kept waiting in Brazil for a half hour and you're starting to get all steamed up, the guy who finally arrives isn't gonna know why you're so upset. He's gonna think you're a total nutcase when you start yelling. Because, in Brazil, a half hour isn't a big deal. When you study time in different cultures you find out what's important to them. Production or relationships.

There's this study where this scientist ranked countries by using three measures: walking speed on urban sidewalks, how quickly postal clerks could sell you a stamp, and the accuracy of public clocks. He figured the five fastest-paced countries are Switzerland, Ireland, Germany, Japan, and Italy. The five slowest are Syria, El Salvador, Brazil, Indonesia, and Mexico. You'd think fast-food U.S.A. would be right up there, but it ranked around the middle.

Mom says some cultures just want to go back to the past. It's like the future is not an option. There's this sect of Islam called Wahhabism, which Osama B. is into. They're trying to re-create the idyllic days of the prophet Muhammad. But people in the West, they think the future is going to be okay. They say "Progress? Bring it on." Most of them do anyway. Except Mom, who says the 1970s was where it was at. The Bee Gees? she says. End of an era.

So my project is going to determine if Virginians are slower than people who live in Maryland. I've been to Williamsburg to measure how long it takes them to get from point A to point B. I started the clicker when they passed point A and then shut it off at point B, then calculated the averages. Next week I'm going to do the same thing in Baltimore. I want to show which people rush more than others. Which people are led more by time than others.

Mom's been pushing me hard on it. She's breathing over my shoulder like a dragon.

"Will you get off my back?"

"This is important, Nic."

"Why is it so friggin' important?"

"It will help you get into the college of your choice."

Jeez, talk about light years away. Talk about time warp.

Kevin's lucky. He wants to be the CEO of a mega-church when he grows up. Where he lived before, they belonged to this church that had twenty thousand people. And they all met in a hall the size of a football stadium. They had a video room that was painted all black and was full of videos and games. They had their own football team and swim team. They had adult classes on everything: quitting smoking, drug addiction, how to become your own stockbroker. His mom was head of their life-coach section. They even had a bank and a little grocery store. He says he wants to start as a manager at one of their satellite churches and work himself up to become head honcho. He says they make good money. His parents are in the beginning stages of trying to organize a mega-church here.

They need a lot of signatures and a bunch of cash. But it'll happen, he says. And then he'll have an inside track.

"That's another reason for you to be saved," he tells me the other day.

"What do you mean?"

"Hello? It's a great job opportunity."

Whenever I sleep over at Kevin's house I like to check out his sister, Charlene. She's sixteen and she speaks in tongues. It's pretty wild. She's always holding impromptu Bible chats in the corner. She just plunks down and grabs whoever is around and starts babbling. It's like a foreign language. And then she pops out of it and grins and takes a swig of her Diet Pepsi.

Jim Butts says she's boy crazy. She's always dragging some guy downstairs into their rec room. I wouldn't mind being dragged downstairs but she doesn't seem to think I'm worthy. Maybe if I knew my Bible better. That seems to turn her on.

Then, one night when I'm staying over, right before bed, I open the door to the bathroom and Charlene is standing there looking at herself in the mirror. She turns and stares at me. She has on a tank top and panties. The tank top has a picture of two puppies on it playing with a string and it looks like they're jumping up and down on her boobs.

I say, "Excuse me," and start to close the door but she says, "That's okay. You can come in."

So I do. I stand there waiting. Because I'm not going to take a piss right in front of her. She goes back to looking at herself. We both stand there not saying anything. I really have to piss.

But she opens a jar of cream and starts spreading it on her chest. She's watching me through the mirror while she's doing it. I watch her back. We're *still* not saying anything.

She puts down the cream and turns around and looks me up and down.

"Hello," she says.

"Hi."

She stands there not saying anything more and it just pops into my head. I say, " 'When I became a man, I put childish ways behind me.' Corinthians 13."

She smiles. "Amen to that." Then she leans over and kisses me on the cheek. And, I don't know, I figure I've done what I need to do. Maybe the spirit takes over. I grab her and kiss her on the lips. She just stands there not responding, so I try to wedge my tongue between her teeth and touch one of the puppies at the same time.

"What the hell?" She pushes me away.

"I . . ."

But she doesn't wait. She shoves me out the door and closes it on my face.

"Nic."

I freeze. It's Mr. Porter, coming up from downstairs.

"You finding everything okay?" he says.

". . . Yes, sir."

"Good man." He pats me on the back and goes off to his bedroom.

See? I told you they're great with teenagers.

Kevin is asleep when I get to his room. He's an amazing

sleeper, just conks out the second he's near a pillow. So I take my jeans off and scoot into my sleeping bag. And I lay back, put my arms behind my back and think about heaven. Charlene is there. On a white couch with her cheerleading suit on, well some of it: her pom-poms. And I think, Life is gonna be just fine.

A lot people aren't so optimistic. My aunt Ruth won't let her kids play in the front yard because she's scared some whacko is going to drive by and steal them. Mom says everyone's scared of everything. And I started noticing how people use it to hook you. You ever watch the local news? It's always Death and Destruction—tune in at 6! They then promise to tell you how to save yourself. Last week the guy said, tune in at 3:30 and I'll tell you how to beat bird flu. So Mom tuned in and he didn't tell. He just spent ten minutes on how we're all gonna die. Mom finally turned it off and said, "Asshole."

Kevin says that bird flu and all these hurricanes are good because it means the Apocalypse is coming. It's what happens before the Rapture. And when the Rapture comes, all the saved people will start floating in the air and hanging out with God. And everybody else will burst open and spurt blood everywhere. Which is why he says I better get saved real soon. He says his family will be okay. And if I get baptised soon I'll be okay too. When I ask about my mom, he looks away and doesn't say anything.

So I ask again, "But what about my mom?"

And he shrugs.

"She'll get in with me, right?"

"Yeah, maybe they'll make an exception."

But Mrs. Porter doesn't think so. She says, "The Bible states quite clearly, 'All who die outside of Christ shall be confined in conscious torment for eternity.' "

"But my mom doesn't believe that."

"It doesn't exempt her."

"So what do I do?"

"Well," she says brightly, "you can always live with us."

There's a new senior pastor at the church. The old one got sent off after he tried to take down the American flag when someone hung it up at the back of the church. The congregation made a big stink. Then he got up in front of everybody and suggested that God wasn't a Republican.

"Can you believe this guy?" Mrs. Porter said.

So the new one is called William Stowe. He's got four daughters and a lot of plans. "We're going to grow this church. We are going to be a force. We are going to bring values and righteousness back to our neighborhoods."

And everybody hollered their heads off.

He says that what we need is not more knowledge and more tolerance but moral fiber. He talks about Nike's slogan. " 'Just do it.' Just do it? Just do what?" he asks. "Just do whatever you feel like? That's exactly what's wrong with this country right now. Just do whatever you feel like and hope somebody else will pick up the pieces. It's got to stop. And we've got to start praying together."

He wants to set up this huge Bible study master class so we can help re-Christianize America. "We're gonna need God's help and yours," he says. "So dig deep. God will provide but we need to prove that that's what we really want."

He's very friendly and everybody loves him. He played shortstop once for the Houston Astros. So he'll be a huge help in the league. His daughters are pretty hot. The two older ones, at least. Especially Faith. She's got long blonde hair and looks real friendly. Which is a good thing because everybody keeps coming up and hugging her like she's a doll.

After Sunday service, when it comes time for me to shake his hand, Mrs. Porter whispers something into his ear and he examines me and says, "Ah, yes." Up close his face looks like putty. His hair is the color of cornflakes. When he smiles, which he does after every sentence—sentence, smile, sentence, smile, sentence, smile—his teeth look like chalk. He invites me to visit him the next time I come to Bible class. Just to have a little chat.

So the next time we go to Bible class, Mrs. Porter nods at Pastor Stowe's office.

"Why don't you go in and say hello?"

He's at his desk, surrounded by papers and files, looking like an accountant. Behind his desk are a bunch of photos of his family. In one of them, his wife and daughters are spread out behind him like a peacock fan. Faith stands on the end, smiling, her hand on his shoulder.

"Have you met my daughters?" he says, seeing me stare at them.

"No."

"Well, we'll have to do something about that. Come in, sit yourself down. Have a muffin. Mrs. Stowe makes a mean pumpkin-bran muffin. Luckily she sprinkles them with lots of sugar, otherwise all that healthiness might put me off. Go on have one."

I take one and sit down. He grabs one too. I can see from the empty muffin cups on his desk that he's on his fourth. He takes a sip of coffee from a cup with I GOT HEAVEN written on it.

"So. Nic, you're new to our congregation, aren't you?"

"I guess."

"Not as new as I am, you old fart. Is that what you're thinking?"

And I have to laugh.

"We're glad to have you. Joanne Porter has been telling me about your special situation."

And I nod, not quite sure yet which situation he's talking about, I have so many of them: absent father, no iPod, sex-in-a-bottle babysitter . . .

"Your mother."

Ah.

"It's a credit to you that you have searched for the truth without any guidance. Save for the Lord, Jesus Christ, of course."

I take a bite of muffin. It's a damn good muffin. I slide my eyes over to see how many are left and wonder if he'll offer me another one.

"Do you get any religious instruction at home?"

I shake my head.

"Is she open to religious instruction?"

I hesitate, then shake my head again.

He leans back, puts his fingertips together thoughtfully. "You're not the first to be in this situation. Following Christ has never been easy. It cost the early Christians dearly. Sometimes their family, their careers, and even their lives."

"Their lives?"

"Those hungry lions in the arenas dispatched plenty. Other ones were covered with pitch and set on fire. They used them as human torches to light the streets of Rome."

"Wow."

"But here's the thing. Those trials never stopped their pursuit of the Lord. And eventually the Roman Empire surrendered. So you see, there is power in what you are doing."

"I never thought of it that way."

"Ask yourself this. Who would we follow if we didn't follow Him? Would we really want to ignore Him and follow our own instincts. Do you know what happens when we think for ourselves?"

". . . No."

"Moral decay. This nation is drunk on the wine of prosperity. And yet no one seems very happy. Is your mom happy?"

"She . . . I . . . I don't know . . ."

"Of course she's not. We were built for a relationship with Him. All of life is about searching to fill the void that sin and separation from Him have created within. Filling the emptiness with piles of things, earthly friendships, secular experiences, and sensual encounters ultimately proves to achieve less than what we had hoped for. Another muffin?"

This time I grab the one with the most sugar on top.

He leans back. "What does your mom believe in?"

"Herself?"

He nods his head sadly. "Self-management is not only the essence of the first sin, it is the very character of sin itself. We were designed to follow. The more we reach for autonomy the more we become enslaved as followers. Drugs, food, work, sensual pleasure, alcohol, self-centeredness. The greatest self-deceit is to tell ourselves that we can be self-sufficient."

We sit there a couple of seconds, chewing on our muffins until he swallows and says, "I think what's needed is a good example for her. I think it's time you proclaimed your faith."

"Proclaim my faith?"

"Get baptized. Make it official."

"Why?"

"*Why?*"

"I mean, why do I have to get baptized? Can't I just believe? Can't I just be nice to everybody?"

"You have to bear witness," he says. "You have to stand up and be counted for."

"Are your daughters baptized?"

"Faith has been called. And she has answered."

Now, that's interesting because the problem with me is I've never heard Jesus say anything to me directly. He's never called or anything. Not even e-mailed. So I ask, "How did she know she was called?"

"Simple. We were driving along one day when she suddenly said to me, 'Daddy, stop the car. The Lord is calling me,' and so I did, and we held hands and prayed together that he might enter her fully. I-95 it was."

"Right there."

"Right there, on the shoulder."

"Wow."

"Think about it."

"Mom won't like it."

"It is your decision." He leans back. "How's that Bible class going, by the way?"

"Yeah. Good."

He nods. "Can you understand a word he's saying?"

And I had to laugh again. He's a funny guy. "I like Dele."

"Oh, don't get me wrong. So do I. So do I. I just think he might be made better use of in another kind of ministry."

"I think he likes it here."

"I bet he does. Well, Nic, thanks for dropping by. And remember, you've got to jump in with both feet. That's what I tell my flock. I tell 'em, jump! The water's fine. It's more than fine." He opens his arms wide. "It's beautiful."

Later, when I drive home with Mrs. Porter, I think about how much I envy Kevin. I envy people who've believed all this Jesus stuff from the start. It's like it's no big deal to them. Me, I have to unlearn so much.

Chapter Thirteen

The next day there's no school so Mom takes me with her to work. Her building is right next to the university's fake farm. It's where they learn to be fake farmers, I guess. The barn's got horses in it. I go over once in a while and they seem to be real. One's called Dootsie and she's always on a diet. Kahlua's a biter. Cody's got a sign saying NO GRAINS AND NO TREATS like he's some naughty four-year-old, which maybe he is. Across the street from them are these long, low buildings labeled ANIMAL SCIENCE. You can smell the chickens and hear them calling. Poor suckers.

Mom's office is in the basement of her building. Which is pretty funny, seeing as she's studying the skies and she's stuck without a window. There's a board in the hall with all the staff's photos. Mom's picture is ten years old. She still has long hair with these bangs that flip back from her forehead and look like they could aerodynamically propel her into the sky. In fact, most of the staff, except for the new research students, have ancient photos. Nigel looks like Harry Potter. Harry Potter and the Small Penis. What a dork. Yeah, I read the Potter books.

Had to. Mom was gagging to read them to me. And, yeah, they were alright. But you know, I'm sorry, my school isn't anything like that. We don't wear uniforms and we don't have ancient headmasters. Our principal is called Ms. White. She's young, she's black, and she kicks ass. Without any magic.

Mom says that the life of a modern astronomer revolves around searching for money. She would love to be doing research the whole time. She wants to be on the last frontier, exploring new lands, new worlds. She talks about being in this relay race, being one of those runners who runs as fast as they can before handing off the baton to another runner—the baton being knowledge. Knowledge that will link one generation to the next, making it better and better. Instead she ends up cold-calling for dough and bludgeoning one research topic to death so that she's known as an expert and will get more money.

What I like is checking out the blackboards around Mom's department. They've got marks scribbled all over them. It's as if aliens are trying to communicate with each other. But they've got human costumes on so no one notices them walking around. One will saunter by, raise his human-gloved hand, and write $Vesc=sqrt(2*M*G/r)=sqrt(3)*Vc$, and leave it. Then another one, walking down the hall, will stop, get really excited, and start honking through his mask's proboscis and scratch out the 3 and write 2 and then add at the end: IDIOT! They go on for hours. And finally they fly home in their invisible stealth spaceships.

Mom insists I come with her to one of her lectures. I sit at the back and watch her go on and on about some obscure star and its mass. She stands like a tiny ant at the front of the huge lecture hall, the little red light of her laser pointer making waves on her white board. She must talk nonstop for a whole hour all about AGNs (that's active galactic nuclei to you) and black holes. Some of the students around me are scribbling their heads off. Some are just staring at her like she's speaking Bulgarian. I mean, I can see what she's getting at. It's not rocket science. Okay, maybe it is. She tells a couple of jokes and some people laugh. But you can tell they laugh because they think it might help their grade. Some bring in their laptops, supposedly for notes, but I'm sitting at the back and I can see them playing sudoku and solitaire through the whole thing. At the end Mom asks if there are any questions and there are so many, she has to stop them and say to e-mail her the rest. Then the students file out. One girl has serious high beams poking through her tank top. She glares at me when she walks past, like, What's your problem? And I want to say, Hey, I'm not the one who's so cold.

When I go back to Mom's office, she gives me a Coke while she makes some phone calls. She's got this tiny mess of a room. Posters of bursting stars, enough books to stock a supersized Borders, and her bike stashed in the corner. Plus all these pictures of me stuck to her bulletin board. It's like a shrine. It's kind of embarrassing.

It's not the first time I've been to her office. I come every year on Bring Your Kid to Work Day. It used to be called Take Your Daughter to Work Day but then they realized that all the girls were kicking boys' asses in the academic department and so they decided they were being sexist. Mom says they should have a Bring Your Kid to Watch Some Woman Give Birth Day. "That would focus them back on school."

I don't really know what the whole point of Bring a Kid to Work Day is. Is it to show that your parents are doing something constructive while you're at school? To show us that they're not all hanging out at the bar or the pool hall? I mean, probably not a lot of kids are going to follow in their parents footsteps, right? For one thing, anyone who's in the business of making VCRs is going be out of a job next week. There will always be insurance brokers, but who wants to be one of those? Wowwie, Dad, gee, that sounds fun, sign me up. And yeah, what my mom does sounds cool—stars and planets and everything—but really she spends a lot of time just fiddling with her computer. That's a lot of ultraviolet rays beaming into your eyes.

I have something more interesting in mind. Becoming an inventor, maybe. Mom says people used to get divorced over one of them leaving the top off the toothpaste tube. So think of all those marriages saved when they came up with attachable tube tops. Genius. Or maybe I could come up with a new political system. Like when the Greeks came up with democracy. Wouldn't that be cool? If while I was in college I came up with a whole new system for governments and nations that would solve everything and that would be the way everything was organized and in a thousand years they would read about me in the books and call it Nicoism or something. Or maybe I could come up with a new kind of musical instrument and start composing for it. Thinking outside the box. That's what I want to do. Or maybe I could come up with a robot that went to school for you and then at the end of the day just downloaded what he learned into your brain. God, I'd make a million.

"Hello, Nic."

And there he is. Dr. Jekyll. Nigel's got this muscle thing in his cheek that wobbles back and forth. I watch it.

"Following in your mother's footsteps?"

"No."

He laughs like I made a joke. But I'm as serious as a heart attack. You think I'm going to waste my time teaching ungrateful students all my life? No way.

Anyway, I don't like the way he laughs. He looks like an aardvark with that long skinny nose of his. Though I think aardvarks probably have a much better sense of humor.

Mom comes in. "Oh, hi, Nigel," she says real casually but then she stops and smiles at him and hooks her hair, what little of it there is, behind her ear. And they stand there beaming at each other.

And I think this might be a good time to tell her about my life decision.

"Mom?"

"Hmmm?" She's still grinning at him.

"I want to be baptised."

Eyes have never abandoned other eyes so quickly.

"You what?"

"I want to proclaim my faith in Jesus Christ, my Lord and Savior."

She stares at me, speechless.

"It's the first act of obedience to my new master," I add.

Nigel starts laughing. Why he thinks I'm such a joker, I don't know. So I look at him and say, "It's not nice to make fun of someone's religion." And he just keeps shaking his head like it's part of the act. Mom, though, she gets it right away and you'd think I punched her in the stomach.

"We'll talk about it when we get home."

Nigel makes a face like "Oh, boy, you've done it now," which pisses Mom off.

"Nigel, I'd appreciate it if you kept a neutral front on this. This is a family matter."

Oh, man, oh, man. Well, he kind of slinks out of her office after that.

And I say, Thank you, Jesus.

But I have to go stay with Aunt Ruth in Silver Spring after that. Mom drops me off so she can drive to Williamsburg and talk to Dad.

"Why can't I stay with Dele?" I ask.

"Because."

"Because why?"

"Because you can't.'"

"Why not?"

She sighs heavily and stares at her fingers. "Because he could be a pervert and I don't want you staying alone with him."

"You're just worrying about this *now*?"

So I'm at my Aunt Ruth's and Dele is living at our house. Call me crazy, but is that stupid or what?

Aunt Ruth is my dad's sister. Mom calls her a born-again Jew. She and Dad weren't raised very religious but she's become more so since she had kids. Five of them. Jessica, Rachel, Isaac, Nat, and Ben. Ben and Nat are twins and, man, are they spoiled. Jessica's cool. She wants to be a concert violinist someday. You know, one of those people who gets to stand up on stage and the rest of the orchestra shoots them dagger looks of envy from their sorry seats. That's her big goal in life. She already looks the part. With those long brown curls of hers, she'd be perfect on the cover of a CD, wearing a low-cut dress and pouting.

She practices five hours a day. No lie. An hour before school. Her younger sister and brothers wake up to her playing. Nice alarm clock. And then three hours when she comes back. Then an hour before bed. She never stops. She's studying with this maestro who thinks she has potential and he's always making her do endless scales. You can hear her from outside when you walk up the path. It sounds like the house is wailing. But when she's playing a real piece of music, you stand out on the stoop and forget to knock.

She says God gave her this ability, but I don't think she's giving herself enough credit. She says she just opens herself up and the music flows into her.

"I'm a vessel," she says.

"Like a boat?"

"No, like a person given amazing qualities. Look it up." Which I did. And now I always think of her overflowing with music pouring out of her ears.

When I come over I always ask her to play my favorite—Beethoven's violin concerto in D Major. Opus 61, whatever that means. Second movement. Jessica flips on the background CD. The orchestra starts slow, playing like they're all in agreement, but then, after the horns, Jessica begins, this lone dissenter telling her version. The orchestra answers back but she's insistent, like she's the last soul to tell the truth. And she's so convincing, so reasonable, so beautiful, you want to believe her. Even if you don't really know what the hell she's talking about.

Ruth says that Jessica's fingers move in her sleep. I asked Jessica what would be her biggest dream and she said, You mean after I married Brad Pitt? And I said yeah and she said to be the greatest violinist the world's ever seen, greater than Midori, Yehudi Menuhin, even Vanessa-Mae. "I want them to make movies about me. And I'm not going to be cheap, wearing miniskirts to get the attention. My music is going to grab 'em, hold 'em by the neck, and not let go."

Mom says Jessica's attention span is uncanny. She worries that Jessica's working herself too much.

"She needs to get out more. Have a life."

"But she doesn't want one. She wants to play."

Mom shrugs and says, "I hope it all works out."

Jessica's violin teacher seems to believe in her. I've been there when she's taking a lesson. He puts his hand on her stomach and says, I want it from here. Play to me from here. Like she's supposed to take everything inside her and turn it inside out. But it's not like she's some Darfur refugee or some Iraqi kid caught in the crossfire. What does a white girl from suburbia have inside her?

Kevin says she's got guilt. "She's Jewish. They killed Jesus. So they're full of guilt. She'll probably be great."

Kevin thinks she's hot but her being Jewish is a real deal breaker. Then there's the fact that she's three years older than him and wouldn't give him the time of day, which I don't mention. Kevin says that God is waiting for the Jews to get their land back from the Palestinians, so He can come down and kick butt. So God likes the Jews even though they did what they did. I told you, He's a merciful God. But then, when Jesus comes with his sword they're either going to have to convert or go to hell. And I wonder if Jessica will still think He's talking through her if He's a Christian god. I mean, it's the same guy. Isn't it?

When Mom picks me up the next day she isn't looking too happy. When we get to the house she parks the car and just sits there.

I look over at her. "So what did Dad say?"

"Your father thinks it could be a good cultural experience."

"Great!" I reach for the door handle.

"I don't," she says.

I slump back in my seat.

She shakes her head. "I just don't think I'd be doing my job as a mother if I let you do this. It means too much."

"But it doesn't mean anything to you."

"Oh, yes, it does. That's the problem. Look, I don't mind you checking out the Bible classes. But baptism. That's a big step. That means something."

"What does it mean?

She stops and thinks a second. "It means I have failed completely."

"Really? I just thought it means I love Jesus Christ."

She stares at me incredulously. "You do?"

"Sure."

"Why?"

"He was a nice guy."

"Was."

"And still is."

She shakes her head. "It means you are signing up for a religion that believes that women are inferior to men. That wants women to submit to men."

"Mrs. Porter says that that's not so bad. That somebody's got to be the boss. She says that men are better leaders and women better administrators. That women are good at taking care of kids and most women deep down prefer it that way."

There's silence in the car.

"Mom?"

"Look, I'm not going to argue with Mrs. Porter through you. But I'm saying no."

I don't say anything.

"You think I'm terrible, don't you?" she says.

"I don't see what's so wrong with religion if it makes people happy."

"I don't think it always makes people happy," she says. "I think it makes a lot of women very sad."

I wonder if that's why she's so pissed off about Him. Because He's not a woman. I mean, if He was a She and wore a WOMEN RULE T-shirt, would she let me believe in God?

She pats me on the hand. "How about this? We'll just have to agree to disagree on this one."

I pull my hand away. "We can't agree to disagree! One of us is seriously wrong!"

She sighs angrily. "Schizophrenics really hear the voices in their heads."

"Are you saying I'm mentally ill?"

"No, I'm saying you're young and impressionable."

"Okay, what about someone old like Pat Robertson?"

"He's mentally ill."

"Or Dele."

She cocks her head and thinks a second. "Dele is . . . how can I put this . . . is in the throws of an unrequited love. He's like a Shakespearean comedy character, misguided but good, for whom you only hope the best."

"Fine."

"Nic . . ."

But I've already gotten out of the car.

There's a box on the porch and an envelope addressed to me. I open it up and inside is a card from Mrs Porter. It says "Stay the course." In the box are a bunch of homemade cookies. In the shapes of fishes.

Mom says, "What's that?"

"When you've been to Bible class for two months you get cookies."

"How nice."

"Want one?"

She bites the fish in two.

Chapter Fourteen

When Carla finds out about my campaign to be baptized, she corrals me in the kitchen. "Do you have to push this? Don't you see it's upsetting your mother?"

"No."

"You are so selfish."

"I am not!"

"I don't get it. Why do you have to be baptised?"

I stare at her. How can she be so ignorant of the benefits of communal ritual?

She puts her finger up. "Presents," she says.

"Kevin got an all-terrain bike."

She crosses her arms. "Isn't Jesus present enough?"

And I raise my eyebrows, knowing that if I'd decided to become an atheist right now she would probably buy me a car.

Luckily Grandma Rose is on my side. I knew I could count on her. "Och, of course you should get baptized. Though it's a little late," she says when I call her. "Ah yes, a Christian boy. You'll be feeling the miracles of our blessed Lord Jesus. And once you get the hang of it you can become a Catholic. These Protestant religions . . . really, they're just to cut your teeth on."

So guess who gets invited over? Someone to pour some sense into me. It's been a while so I thought she'd lost interest but there he is again, at the damn door, ready for his American experience.

"Hi, Nigel." Mom gives him a peck on the cheek and takes his hand and leads him into the kitchen where Dele is reading his Bible.

"Dele, this is Nigel. Nigel, this is Dele."

Dele gets up, and though he's shorter than Nigel he still looks like he could kick Nigel's ass and not even mess up his shirt. He shakes Nigel's hand, breaking probably about ten bones. "Very pleased to meet you. Another star person. I love it!"

Nigel cradles his hand. "Star person. That's an interesting way of putting it."

Mom gets Nigel a Dos Equis and grabs one for herself. Even though it's only eleven o'clock in the morning.

"Dele?"

"Don't worry, I get my own." He grabs a Gatorade and follows them out to the backyard where they're kicking back, taking in the last rays of the fall sun.

Me, I just mosey out to take in the scene. Luckily I do because Mom and Nigel are ganging up on Dele, slugging away at him about all the bad stuff people do in the name of God. Like 9/11.

Dele says, " 'God is in control but the heart of man is deceitful above all things.' Jeremiah 17:9."

Nigel shakes his head and Mom rolls her eyes. "And what exactly is that supposed to mean?" she says.

"It is only the Lord who knows what is in the heart of man. It is only the Lord in Jesus Christ who can renew a right spirit within us—the spirit that sees others as people for whom Christ died. We continue to pray for God's mercies in a world that has chosen to do things in godless ways."

"But those men who crashed the planes. They believed in God."

"I do not believe their god asked them to do this. Men asked them to do this."

Mom raises her finger. "So you're saying He wasn't there when those men flew their planes into the Trade Center?"

"Oh, He was there," Dele says. "God was there telling the terrorists that taking other people's lives was against His will but the choice was theirs. He has given us free will."

Nigel snorts. "That's convenient."

"And He was there in the firemen and the paramedics and the police officers and all the people who tried to help."

"Yeah?" says Mom, leaning forward. "Well, what about for those poor people who jumped?"

Dele doesn't miss a beat. "He was holding their hand."

Nigel and Mom just stare at him.

"I must go," Dele finally says, standing up. "You've made me very hungry. I must pick up a hamburger before I go to service."

Nigel says, "Fast food. That's very American, isn't it?"

"Yes," says Dele enthusiastically. "McDonald's, Burger King, Wendy's. I love this country."

"McDonald's?" says Nigel, wrinkling his nose, like he's pronouncing the word "turd."

Dele cocks his head like he's agreeing. "I prefer Burger King. I like the mayonnaise." He sighs happily, patting his belly. "I'm getting fat."

Nigel says, "I have a problem with fast food."

Dele says, "Fast food for a fast country."

And I'm thinking of the times when I do go with Dele to Burger King, how he treats it like a fancy restaurant. He always sits up straight with tucked-in napkins at the top of his shirt and eats in slow motion, putting his burger down between bites, waiting until he's swallowed before taking a drink. And then we have to wait while he orders his coffee separately. Not exactly fast food.

Later, in the kitchen, Mom drops the bomb on me.

"Nigel is taking you out this afternoon."

"Why?"

"I just thought it would be nice."

"What am I, a dog?"

"What?"

"Dad can't do it, you're too busy, so you're getting Nigel to do it. Where's my leash?"

"Nic, I asked Nigel because I want you to get to know him. He's an interesting man."

"He's interesting to you because he thinks like you."

"He's an intelligent man."

"He's a dick."

"Just be nice."

I make him wait. I tell him I have to go upstairs to get my shoes, then spend a half hour reading *Bone*. When Mom finally drags me down he's standing in the hall dangling his keys. Outside a Stratus Grey BMW 630i, top down, shines in the cold sun. I can feel him looking at me, waiting for me to say, Nice car, but do you think I'm going to say that? Give me some credit. When we're strapped in, he slides his keys into the ignition. "So, where to?"

"The Bermuda triangle."

"Oh, ha, ha, ha," he erupts like Mount Vesuvius. I really tickle his funny bone. We settle on the latest Bond movie, which, according to his CrackBerry, isn't playing until three, which means we have two extra hours to kill. Which is how we end up zipping along to the Cheesecake Factory intending to scarf some bacon cheeseburgers and a couple of caramel latte cheesecakes.

So he's driving along, elbow popped out the window, other hand fiddling with the CD player, when he says, "This must all be very . . ." He stops.

"Very what?"

"Difficult."

"Why?"

He glances at me. "Let's just say I'm here if you need me. To talk."

"You're not my first choice."

He smiles. "That's what I told your mother."

I don't say anything and we drive along listening to Coldplay. What a loser. His eyes keep rotating over in my direction but I ignore him.

"Your mother has an elegant mind," he says.

I look over. In the intellectual world, is that like saying your mom has big tits?

"She sees things others don't," he adds. "She makes connections. I'm a bit of a workman in the field but she is an exception. Pretty soon she'll be able to call her own shots, decide where she wants to go."

I don't say anything.

"Harvard has expressed interest," he says.

"Do you know how cold Boston is?"

"I think you need to get your priorities in order."

"And they are?"

"Stop holding her back."

Just then, halfway down Wisconsin Avenue, where all those endless roadworks are, the back tire makes a popping sound and the car completely fishtails. We end up with the front of the car facing the traffic behind us and everyone slamming on their brakes and horns. Nigel scrambles out and sinks on his haunches to survey the damage. He sighs heavily and opens the trunk.

"Aren't you going to call triple-A?" I say.

"No, why would I call triple-A? Is that all your generation does? Something goes wrong, you call somebody. Don't deal with it yourself. Life is not at the end of a cell phone; it's right here, right now. In this space. Not on a screen."

"You forget to renew or something?"

He comes around, reaches over, and flicks open the glove compartment. He finds the manual and thumbs through.

"You don't know where your spare tire is, do you?"

He snaps it closed. "Of course I do."

I get out too. I don't want the assholes driving by flipping me off.

It takes a while but he finally finds the spare, which is hiding underneath the car. A truck squeezes by, blaring. Nigel takes out the jack. A half hour later he's finally figured out that you jack it up in front of, not behind the tire. I've never seen a man sweat so much. His sweat is sweating. I sit on the curb, an innocent bystander.

He looks over. "Don't strain yourself."

"I won't."

"You ever changed a flat tire?"

"No."

"Want to learn?"

"No."

About three hours later he's got the damn tire off and is just pushing the new one on. He looks over at me like he deserves applause or something. He stands up wiping his brow and is getting cocky.

"That should do it."

But then the lug nuts won't go back on. He spends another half hour trying them every which way, but it's like they belong to another make of car, one the size of a mouse. Finally he gives up and calls AAA.

So we both sit there, getting honked at. And to tell the truth I do want to talk to him. Because I've got a lot of questions, like why do people kill innocent children? Why are people not always happy for you when your life is good? Why do some people hate you when they've never even met you? Why do I feel so much and yet want to show so little? Why does chocolate seem to solve so many of women's problems? But I'm too embarrassed so I decide to tell him what I know.

"Did you know baby boomers have only a one-in-twenty-six chance of living to the age of one hundred?"

He pulls out a pack of cigarettes. "Yes."

"Did you know that in one minute the average person can speak about a hundred and fifty words?"

He lights up. "Yes."

"You did not."

"I did."

"Did you know the human heart beats about a hundred thousand times in a day?"

He smiles and shakes his head.

"Did you know the average lifetime of a hydrogen bond between water molecules at room temperature is three picoseconds?"

He doesn't answer. He takes a long drag. So I say, "A picosecond is . . ."

"I know what a picosecond is."

I shrug.

He blows a dragon snort of smoke into the air. "You know what Heidegger says about time?"

And I think, Heidi who?

"Heidegger said time is the basic category of existence. He said we live in its ever-shrinking shadow, and if we are to achieve anything in our brief being that lets us die without feeling we've wasted our time, we will have to go into heady conflict with the forces of scarcity that deny our desires."

And he takes another long drag of his cigarette.

It's six o'clock when AAA finally arrives. When we drive up to my house, Mom is waving at the window, just bursting to hear about our afternoon.

Chapter Fifteen

So I start thinking, What if I can prove Nigel wrong? What if I can prove there is a God? More important, that there is a heaven. Then I could show Mom and Nigel. I could say, Look, here it is. Check it out. They'd freak. And then maybe everyone would start behaving themselves around here.

Now, as I'm constantly reminded by Mom, a verifiable experiment is a a good science fair project. "Experiment" means it's a test to find an answer to a question. "Verifiable" means that it will have the same result no matter how many times you test it.

For example, say you notice ants move really slowly on cold days. You might want to find out if it's because it's cold out. Why do you want to know? No idea. But you'd get some ants, get a couple of containers, and make their environments different temperatures. Maybe put one next to the heater, one on the windowsill where it's cold, one outside where it's even colder. Then, measure what happens by taking a stopwatch and timing how fast it takes the ants to go from spot A to spot B. Do it a couple of times to make sure you're getting the same answer. Simple.

But how do you go about proving the existence of heaven? Not so different. You start again with a hypothesis. Then you do tests to support it. Scientifically. Like Copernicus did. He came up with the idea of a helio- (which means sun), as opposed to geo- (which means earth), centric system. Of course it had to wait for Galileo a century later with those telescopes of his to prove it. But Copernicus was the first one to make the suggestion. He noticed that the moons around Jupiter weren't remotely interested or affected by what was happening on earth.

So when Kepler came along and discovered that planets weren't cruising around the sun in a perfect round shape but were going around in ellipses, all the pieces fell into place. They passed batons of knowledge to one another across the generations until they had it all figured out.

So I'm gonna be the ideas man. I'm going to get things rolling and then I'll pass my baton on. I'll be part of the relay of knowledge too. And it's not going to be Mickey Mouse stuff, like when medieval people used to think stars were lights from heaven shining through pinholes in the sky. We're talking real science here.

I'm going to say that heaven is right outside the particle horizon. That's the maximum distance from which particles can have traveled to the observer over the course of the age of the universe. They used to think heaven was beyond the sun and stars. And hell used to be deep down in the center of earth. Now hell seems to be a lot of places you see on TV where bombs go off and kids are dying.

Anyway, I think maybe in a hundred years someone will come up with a Godscope, which they'll train on the edge of the universe and His face will be peeking in from heaven, watching us. Why not? If Mom can believe we were created from exploding stars why can't I believe that?

I tell Kevin all about it. He nods his head, impressed. "Dude," he says.

So I start work on it over the next week and by the time Mom gets home from work on Friday I have my hypothesis. When she walks in and takes a look at my project, she screeches.

"What the hell is that?"

"My project."

"What happened to Time?"

"Time can wait."

She reads out my title: "Twenty-first century: Movement from a Heliocentric World to a Heavencentric Outlook."

She turns her big eyes on me.

"I'm thinking outside the box here," I say.

"You're going to put that up in the science fair?"

"Yup."

"What does Mr. Vinay say?" Mr. Vinay is my science teacher. He and my mom play good cop/bad cop. One guess who's the bad cop.

"He says he's intrigued, sceptical, worried."

"Worried?"

"That I'll be disqualified."

Later that night, when I come back from Bible class, Mom is in the backyard, wearing her huge parka and smoking a clove cigarette. "Did you have fun?" she says.

"Religion is not fun, Mom, it's a commitment."

"You mean it's not just for Christmas?"

"Jesus loves you, Mom."

"Glad somebody does."

"What are you doing out here?"

"I'm looking at the stars."

I look up at the haze. "But you can't see them."

"Yup, but I know they're out there."

Mom made her own telescope once. She downloaded the info from the Internet. It looks like a cannon. It looks like it can shoot things at the moon but what it's really doing is shooting pictures down to us. It's not big, just about twenty-four inches, but you can see the mountains on the moon perfectly. And yeah, you feel like you could reach up and touch them.

Mom knows all the constellations: Pegasus, Pisces, Ursa Minor, you name it. Now, they don't really look like horses or fish or bears. You have to imagine it all. What you need to do is learn to spot their main stars and then branch out from there. Mom, she just stares up and recognizes them immediately.

"Oh, look, Nic. Taurus." She might say on a rare clear night.

"Where?"

"There, see? Below the Pleiades. See? Two feet over the top of the fir tree."

And yup, there it is. Right there to the left of Mars.

The funny thing is that not all astrophysicist professors know their constellations. I asked Nigel once and he looked down that long nose of his and said, "I'm an astronomer, not an astrologist."

Frankly, I'm always amazed Mom doesn't believe in astrology. I think she was born too late. She would have made a great druid.

When I was a kid I used to gaze out of my window and wish upon a star. For stupid stuff like more toys or Cocoa Puffs in the morning or a trip to McDonald's. That was before I knew how far away stars were. Centaurus Proxima is our closest star (apart from the sun) and it's four light years away. You know how far a light year is? It's 5.88 trillion miles. You know how many zeros there are in a trillion? Twelve. So I'm done believing that from 5,880,000,000,000 miles away, this star is gonna twinkle back at me and say, Yeah, you there in 2876 Darwin Road, N.W.—sure, I'll make sure your mom wakes up tomorrow and forgets it's not a weekend and fills your cereal bowl up to the brim with Cocoa Puffs.

It's weird when you're not allowed to believe in anything. I mean, who are you supposed to wish to? I've got a lot of things to wish for. Can't ask Santa, or fairies, or God. Not even stars. I guess if you're past the age of five, you're pretty much screwed in the wishing department. And you know, if there was someone or something you could wish to, you know what I'd wish for? Besides perfect hair? I'd wish little kids would stop dying in wars. I'd wish grownups, if they insist on fighting, would hire all these buses, get all the kids out, and put them in hotels until they're done. But then, when you think about it, they'd have to get the moms out too because little kids need their moms. And well, their dads too because little kids need to wrestle with their dads to get big and strong. Like little lions, you know? So maybe when governments get pissed off at each other they could skip the guns and the bombs and the missiles and just play chess. Just beat the shit out of each other on the board. And then, whoever wins can announce it on TV in the morning and everyone will nod, change their passport if they have to, and go about their business. Nobody gets hurt. Nobody has to bury anybody. And nobody has to cry. That's what I'd wish for. But who or what should I wish it to?

The thing is, the more I learn about life the more I realize grownups have no idea what they're talking about. I guess I'm just surprised how much they don't know. Until a couple of years ago I thought they knew everything and it turns out they can't agree on anything. How to raise kids, who to believe in, how many times a week you can go to McDonald's. Hell, they can't even agree on how to put the friggin' toilet paper onto the roller.

Later on, it happens like this: Dele is in bed. And so am I. Nigel must have come over after I went to sleep. And Mom must have let him in. We don't hear them at first because they must have tiptoed up the stairs and into her bedroom where he probably took off all her clothes and then his clothes before rubbing himself all over her. Anyway, Dele finally hears them. Well, no, he doesn't hear *them*, he hears *her*. Moaning and groaning and carrying on. So he sneaks out of his bedroom and picks up my baseball bat and charges into her bedroom to save her. And finds Nigel, naked and rubbing and so on. So Dele stands over the bed and pulls Nigel off Mom, and Nigel, get this, screams. And that's when I wake up and join the show. By the time I come running in, Nigel is curled in the corner by the nightstand and Mom is staring up at Dele furious, shouting, "What the hell are you doing?"

Dele says, "But you were in trouble."

And she says, "No, I was not in trouble."

"You were making that noise on purpose?"

Well, I just about bust a gut laughing. Mom makes us all leave. Even Nigel, who has to hop around and get his clothes. Dele and I walk Nigel down the stairs. And when the front door closes, Dele sits down at the kitchen table with his head in his hands and says, "A Christian woman doesn't get into so much trouble."

Chapter Sixteen

L ord, please help me to head off to Africa to be martyred. In
Jesus' name.

A woman missionary, Alison, came to our church and talked
about how she went to Afghanistan and converted people in
a café. She had to be totally undercover like James Bond because if they discover what you're doing they'll kill you. Do one
of those public beheading numbers. They are very particular
about the God they believe in and they don't want any free-
market competition.

Alison's given out a hundred copies of the Bible already. She's
very proud of that. Her secret, she says, is her happiness. She's
just so bubbly and nice. People start asking her why she's so
happy. Of course it doesn't hurt that she's got long blonde hair
that she covers with a scarf so she fits in, but the Afghanis can
still see bits of it. When people approach her she gives them the
good news. She wraps each Bible in old paper because if anyone is caught with the Bible they might be killed too. She just
came home to get her braces tightened.

"Were you scared?" I ask.

"Petrified," she says. "But this is the Lord's work. I don't have a choice, do I?" And everyone claps. I mean, this is what I'm talking about, making a difference, beating the infidels right in their own backyard, using Bibles instead of guns. What can be more honorable than that? Bomb 'em or Bible 'em? No contest.

I raise my hand again. "What if you knew a Muslim right here in this country?"

"Bring them a Bible," Alison says immediately. "Spread the good news, they'll thank you for it."

So I give Layla a Bible.

And she gives it right back. "Keep it to yourself, pal."

"I'm just trying to help here."

"One fifth of humanity is Muslim. Get used to it."

"You're not getting very good press now."

She sighs. "Did you know that scientific words like "chemistry" and "algebra" come from Arabic words, *kimia* and *al gabr*. Our culture is very rich."

"So what happened?"

She glances away. "I don't know. Some say we've lost our freedom to think."

"Give me a Koran," I demand.

We exchange books. The next time she comes over we pop open some Dr. Pepper and read aloud our favorite passages.

Layla stands up, clears her throat, and goes first. " 'If no proof of the girl's virginity can be found, she shall be brought to the door of her father's house and there the men of her town shall stone her to death.' Deuteronomy 22."

She sits back down with a satisfied smile.

I search for mine: " 'Those who resist Allah and His messenger will be crumbled to dust as were those before him: for we have already sent down Clear Signs and the Unbelievers will have a humiliating Penalty.' Koran 58.5"

I give her an eye waggle. "And you know what humiliating means."

Layla waves me away. "That's nothing. Listen to this: 'When you march up to attack a city, make its people an offer of peace. If they accept and open their gates, all the people in it shall be subject to forced labor and shall work for you. If they refuse to make peace and they engage you in battle, lay siege to that city. When the Lord your God delivers it into your hand, put to the sword all the men in it. As for the women, the children, the livestock, and everything else in the city, you may take these as plunder for yourselves.' "

She purses her lips. "Nice."

I find another passage. " 'Punishment for those who oppose Allah and His messenger is: Execution or Crucifixion or the cutting off of hands and feet from opposite sides.' Koran 5:33."

Layla flips through her book. " 'If anyone curses his father or mother, he must be put to death.' Leviticus 20:9"

She tosses the Bible on the coffee table where it slides and bumps into the Koran. We both stare. Layla finally blinks. "What do you think?" she says. "Are they just figures of speech?"

*   *   *

But I'm not going to worry about it today because today is the day I turn fourteen. November 11th. Same birthday as Henry IV, the Holy Roman Emperor, and Demi Moore. So I'm in good company. When I come down for breakfast, Mom has a couple of presents at my place. First thing I wonder is if any of them can be the iPod.

She says, "Go on, unwrap already."

Okay, a word of advice. If you ever get presents at our house, take it slow. When you unwrap, do it carefully. Don't just rip it open and scrunch up the wrapping paper like a normal person. Carefully go along the line that's been taped and ease it open with your thumb. Then lift the paper and lay it on the ground so it doesn't get messed up. When you're finished, Mom will go around and put the papers in a pile and fold each one neatly to reuse next year. Most of our paper has been used. It's all wrinkled and soft as toilet paper but Mom can't bear to waste it. Exxon is pouring gallons of pollutants into our seas and Mom is saving wrapping paper. It boggles the mind.

And no. It isn't there. The iPod is missing in action.

So I don't say anything. No thank-you, no nothing.

"What's wrong?" she asks. Like she doesn't know.

I still don't say anything.

"Come on. What's wrong?" Well, she's just asking for it.

"What's wrong? The one thing I ask you for is missing. That's what's wrong."

"You already have a Discman. I don't see what the big deal is."

"Do you know how heavy that is? I look like a complete friggin' dork carrying that thing around."

"Kids are getting mugged left and right for iPods."

"I'll carry a gun."

"Nic."

"And look at this stuff: a Light & Optics kit, an anatomy model, *100 Scientific Questions You've Always Wanted Answered.* Can't I just have something fun for once? Something that doesn't *expand* my brain. Doesn't add to my *vast* intelligence."

"But . . ."

"Thanks for nothing." And I leave her there, sitting alone in the kitchen, her mouth still hanging open.

Dele isn't much help. He gives me a Bible. Like that's supposed to make me feel better. I'm thinking, oh, yeah, that took a lot of thought. A lot of effort. He probably has some suitcase somewhere chock full of Bibles that he dives into for all occasions: birthdays, Christmas. Knocked up? Here, have a Bible.

When Dele gives it to me he gets all serious and says, "May the Lord, Jesus Christ, bless you on this day, your birthday." And I swear to God I think an iPod is going to appear out of thin air. He looks so serious and concentrated. Anyway, it doesn't. And then Mom comes in and says, "Well, that was nice of Dele, wasn't it?" And I look at her like, You are so lame. I go back to my room and let them stew in their shitty present-giving for a while.

What I really need is a ceremony. To show everyone that I'm fourteen. That I'm older. Because it's not obvious. No one takes a look at me and says, Okay, I get it. He's a man. He makes his own decisions now. Jacob Weinstein was bar mitzvahed last year. And he said his parents treated him differently afterward. Got off his back a little. Still did his laundry—which is key—but they sat him down and said, "Okay, your life is in your hands now. Think about the decisions you make. We have tried our best to steer you right up to now. And we wish you the best." Holy crappido. If my parents said that to me I'd be like, Gimme the keys to the car, I'm on my way to Vegas.

I keep asking Mom why atheists don't have any cool ceremonies to mark events. They don't do baptisms, or month-long fasts, or Friday-night Shabbat dinners. They can't even get excited anymore about Election Day because the polls are always such bad news. I keep telling her what they need are some good ol'-fashioned rituals. And Mom keeps saying, "Yeah, yeah, you're right. We'll have to come up with something." But so far, nothing.

Some of the girls at school get a Quinceañera party when they turn fifteen. And boy, do they live it up. I've never been to one but I've seen pictures. The girls get dressed up and look about thirty years old. Their parents spend real bucks on those things. Maria Garcia's father rented out the Hilton and flew in all his relatives from Peru. Or was it Venezuela? Anyway, they go to this big church thing where they declare her a woman and then they party until it's 1999. You ever hear that song? Talk about a sell-by date.

I just think I need something like that. To be able to say I'm making my own decisions now. To say, Okay, listen up everybody, I'm not thirteen anymore.

Maybe that's what I could do to make money. Run I'm-fourteen-don't-screw-with-me-anymore parties for everybody who doesn't get some sort of ceremony. I'd rent out hotels, fly in whatever the kids want: drugs, booze, starter hookers—you know, not too seasoned, young, who'd ease you in nicely. I guess it would be mainly a male thing. I could do it for girls too. But, really, they don't need it as bad. By the time they're fourteen it's real obvious they're women, know what I mean?

But I have to get over not having a ceremony because Sandra has agreed to come by. Yup, Sandra Miller. Kevin asked her. He said to me, "Have I got a present for you." And then he just texted her and she texted back: Okay, maybe. So Sandra Miller is going to be at my party. *My* party. And no, not that kind of party. No home bash for me. I wish. I can't with Mom living at my house. Kevin's parents would be fine. They'd be like, here's the pizza, probably no beer, but they'd leave us to it. Mom, though, she'd greet everyone at the door and then show them to their seats and then try and drum up conversation. Like "So Sandra, what are you planning to be when you grow up?" Like it's not obvious she's a shoe-in for *American Idol.* Nightmare. So when Mom asks what I want to do for my birthday, I tell her I want to go to Rock Creek Park, play some football, and have pizzas.

"That's it?"

"Yeah."

"What about a movie?"

"We did that last year." And I'm not doing that again. She insisted on coming with us. First she stood at the entrance of

Wisconsin Avenue Cineplex and handed out the tickets to everybody, looking them in the eye and saying, "Hello, nice to meet you. Welcome." Like she owned the place, like it was her own personal theater and she was inviting us in. And then she sat five rows behind us and laughed all the way through *The Matrix Revolutions*. If I could have afforded it, I would have put a contract out on her.

This year I have it figured out. We're going to hang out. Away from her. I'm going to have people meet me at Rock Creek Park so she can't get ahold of them. And then, when it's time, she can drop off some pizzas and leave.

"Isn't it a little cold?"

"It'll be fine."

I don't let her send out invitations. I just text everybody to meet me there on Sunday.

"Are you sure they'll remember?" Mom says.

"Of course, they'll remember. What do you think they are, morons?"

Sandra comes! Her dad drops her and her friend Melissa off. He slides down the dark window of his big black BMW to check me out. Sandra looks good in a BMW. She glides out and stands before me with her perfect face, not a thing out of place, an ad for the human race. I say hello but she doesn't say anything, just walks over to Kevin and gives him a big hug. Melissa steps out and gives me a wrapped present. Looks like a CD. She says, real formally, "Happy birthday, Nic." She's always polite. It's weird but I like that about her. She's always saying please and thank-you. Hello, good-bye. It's the only thing she's got going for her. She's not very pretty and she can be a real bitch when she wants to. Especially when she's around Sandra.

They both wear the same thing. Though it doesn't look anything on Melissa like it does on Sandra. Melissa is like a sleazy Kmart Special compared to Sandra's $400 Adidas. They've got heavy sweaters on because it's so cold, but they're cut off right below their boobs so you can see their freezing stomachs. I want to say, Hey, why don't you put on a real sweater, cover up. We *do* have imaginations, you know. Girls can be so weird.

They go and hang out by the tree. Sandra pulls out her cell and starts texting. Melissa leans over her shoulder to watch and they start laughing. Sandra runs her hand through her hair all the time. She's got the longest, prettiest hair.

When everybody's there, I look around and realize what a life-threatening mistake I've made.

Nobody's talking to each other. I have gathered people who have nothing to do with each other at school. So now Sandra is by the tree watching Kevin take down Iraqis on his Nintendo DS. And everybody else is standing around looking bored out of their minds and ready to bolt.

"Why don't we pray?" Melissa suggests.

She holds out her hand and I'm so surprised I take it. She yells to everyone else and they all come over like she's got some authority. Or maybe they're so bored they figure they'll give anything a shot. Suddenly I'm standing in a circle with Sandra and Kevin and seven others, with Melissa leading the show.

"Jesus, God, thank you for gathering us together today on

Nic's birthday. Help us to enjoy this day in your name. Help us have a rocking good time. And help Sandra win her Coty contract. Amen."

I can't believe it. Suddenly everybody's smiling at each other, talking, cracking jokes. Even Sandra grins at me from across the circle. I step forward to talk to her but Melissa grabs me in a big hug.

"Nic, Jesus is going to bless you today."

"Wow," I say when she finally lets go. "How long have you been a Christian?"

She smiles wide. "Since last Thursday."

Turns out her parents aren't too religious, either. Her mom's into chanting. She has a little shrine in her bedroom that she shouts at every morning.

"So, you know, I understand." Melissa puts her hand on my arm. "My mom is useless too."

Soon the guys are playing football. And because it's my party, I get to be quarterback.

At least for a while, until Kevin takes over. After that I'm just running around the field aimlessly. He tosses me a long ball and it's heading straight for Sandra. So I maneuver myself so that when I grab it, I can make a dive right next to her. When I take the fall, she runs her hand through her hair and laughs. She looks down at me, laughing, and I'm laughing and thinking what perfect lips she's got, what perfect eyes and skin, and I think it's just about the happiest moment of my life. But then Kevin comes over and jumps on me full force.

All the air goes out of me. Think of it, a ton of Kevin Porter right on my face.

He has my head shoved back into the grass and I can't breathe.

Sandra starts laughing even more.

"Hey, Kevin, let him up . . ." Melissa calls.

"Why? He looks good this way."

But he tips back and I come up punching. Jamming his neck with my fist. He loses his balance and falls back on the ground and I try to slug him. But he has his arms up and my fists keep glancing off. So I lean forward to keep him shoved down while my hand runs across the ground looking for something to smash him with, like a rock . . .

"Hey, isn't that your mom?" says Melissa.

And there she is, walking through the trees with a stack of pizzas. She can barely see where she's going the stacks are so high. I scramble up and start waving at the bench that's on her side of the field.

"Just leave them there," I yell. I don't want her near us.

But she keeps getting closer.

"Over there." I'm pointing frantically now.

But she keeps on coming with a grin plastered on her face.

"There!" I yell. "On the bench. There."

But she passes the bench and keeps walking toward us.

Kevin is laughing at this point and shaking his head.

"Hello." She arrives in front of us, holding the pizzas.

Everyone mumbles hello.

She says, "Did you have fun?"

"Yeah," I say. "Can you just put . . ."

"It's a beautiful day," she says.

"Is that pepperoni?" Kevin asks.

"Well, I don't know which one . . ." She sets them down on the grass. She opens them up and starts serving everyone and I want to scream.

As soon as they get their pizzas everybody wanders off and sits down on the grass. She stands there looking over them, smiling. I say, "Okay, okay . . ." I don't want to say, You can go now, but she's pushing it.

"Oh, the cake," she cries and runs back to the car. When she comes back she has the box balanced on one hand and is searching her pockets with the other.

"Where did I put the candles . . . ?"

"No candles. Just leave it, Mom." But it comes out too loud and everybody glances over.

Mom and I stare at each other a beat. Until she finally says. "Well . . . you have fun. See you later."

"Yeah."

"Say about"—she looks at her watch—"six?"

"Yeah."

"Alrighty." She walks off. Everybody's scarfing pizza and looking at the cake box.

"What is it?"

I have a sick feeling, but there's nothing I can do so I open it up and there it is: an ice cream cake from Carvel. HAPPY BIRTH-

DAY, NIC! scrawled on top in light blue. Kevin laughs again and whacks me on the arm. "Hey, birthday boy."

I whack him back. Hard.

But she forgets to leave a knife. Total lame-o.

Kevin grabs a stick and slices into it. It's still pretty hard, so he really has to saw but he finally gets through. He reaches in and grabs a piece.

"Want some?" He shoves it into my face.

This time my fists get lucky. He blinks at me and then jumps me. He catches me in the ribs but I dig into him, just let my arms shove back as hard as I can. I want him screaming with pain. I want to kick his ass all over that park.

"Stop!"

Suddenly Sandra's pulling at me and I'm so surprised I stop, thinking, Wow, she's actually touching me. But when I look into her eyes she gives me the dirtiest look and throws her arms around Kevin.

"Are you okay?" she says to him, leaning down, with her hair falling forward and her hands stroking his face.

I can't breathe.

"Come on, he's not worth it," she says, and I can tell Kevin is just as surprised as I am. She takes him by the hand and helps him limp over toward the tree, where they sit down. She leans forward and caresses his head. I can't help it, I just stare. I am staring so hard the entire universe could implode and I'd still be in the air, staring over at Sandra Miller stroking Kevin Porter's face. Even if they didn't exist anymore. Having been obliterated in ten-thousand-degree heat, I would be watching them, together, touching.

Sandra finally whispers something to Melissa, who comes up to me and says, "You okay?"

My consolation prize.

When the BMW glides back to pick up Sandra, I stand there like an idiot with ice cream on my face. She says, "Later," and climbs in. Melissa says, "Thanks for the party," and climbs in after her. The car slides out onto the road and I am certain I will never speak to Kevin Porter again as long as I live.

When Mom returns she can't believe the mess. But does she bring trash bags? No. She never has that kind of helpful mom stuff. I remember when I was a kid, she'd never have Kleenex in her bag. Ever. And I'd have snot running down my nose and she'd always act like she couldn't believe it was coming out *again.* So when she comes to the park, she just stands there moaning until Mrs. Porter rolls up in her Lexus. Mrs. Porter takes one look at the place and clicks open the back of her car. She reaches in and pulls out a roll of trash bags. She hands a bag to Kevin and another one to me. So we have to clean up the place with our moms standing next to each other, arms folded, chatting.

I don't talk to Kevin. I am so pissed off. And he's whistling while he works like we are still big buddies. Asshole.

Our moms are actually laughing together when we come back with our full bags.

"Thanks so much," Mom says to Mrs. Porter. "You're a life saver."

"Oh," Mrs. Porter says, "I'm obsessive-compulsive, what can I say?"

And they laugh again. Then Kevin says, "Later." I don't say anything. But Mom says, "Aren't you going to say good-bye?" So she calls out to Kevin, "Bye, Kevin," as if speaking for me. Like she's my own personal translator. Sorry my son can't speak, he's a deaf-mute, I'll speak for him like an idiot. My life sucks.

Chapter Seventeen

Two days later I'm still mad about Kevin and life still sucks. Which is why when I read on Born-Again.com, "If you would like to become born-again and reap the rewards of an exalted life, turn to our salvation page now," I do.

Luckily Mom's in her office so she doesn't see what I'm logged on to. But I keep looking over my shoulder just in case. When the Sinner's Prayer pops up, I read it out loud in a low voice. Then I click OK and it congratulates me in big, bright flashy colors: You are now genuinely born-again so be confident of your Salvation!!!!

It also offers me a special on Bibles but I don't have the $29.99.

When I tell Dele about it, he just about falls out of his chair, he's laughing so hard. I don't see what's so funny.

"But I thought this was what I was supposed to do."

"Oh, Nic, God is not in the computer."

"I thought He was everywhere."

"This is not a virtual religion."

"Fine."

"You must practice it in front of your peers and your pastor."

"Fine."

"Oh, do not be like that. . . . Look, look"—he pulls me back—"I think you need to call to Jesus. Ask Him to talk to you. Ask Him to show you the way."

"So you're not letting me in."

"I do not let you in. You let yourself in. If you feel joy and peace and love for Jesus Christ. But you have to ask yourself why you are interested in all of this. Do you love Jesus or do you like Kevin and his family? This is a journey and the first stop is being truthful to yourself."

I don't know what he thinks he's talking about. I'm not that lame. Deciding to join a religion just because of somebody's family. Selling my soul because of a pinball machine.

He really pisses me off sometimes. He thinks he knows everything. Do you know he cheats when he plays basketball? He hip-checks me and practically bumps me off the driveway. He's short but he's built like a truck. He plants his feet on the ground and that's it, he's not moving. And he likes to plant his feet on the ground right where I'm standing. Luckily my lay-ups are better than his. After our "chat" we play Horse and I can tell he can't believe I'm at S and he hasn't made O yet. So he plants himself right on top of me. And I am getting really pissed off and I end up yelling at him. Yelling at my pastor in the driveway for all the neighborhood to see.

I can tell he's pissed off too, but I guess he's a guy of God so he takes deep breaths and glares at me.

"Nic, you cannot push me out of the way."

"I didn't push you out of the way, you shoved me."

"I was in this spot first."

"The hell you were."

"Where I come from this is called no good."

"Where I come from this is called cheating."

"You are calling me cheating?"

"Yes! I was standing right there and you bashed into me."

"I did not."

"Yes, you did."

"What do you talk about? You were traveling."

"I was not, I was about to shoot."

And he waves his hand at me, dismissing me. He's just asking for it.

"What would you know about basketball anyway? It's an American game."

"You do not think we play it in Africa? We *began* the game."

"Yeah, right."

"There is so much you do not know."

"That's bullshit."

He sighs. "The language must go if you are to be an honorable player."

"Oh, that's good, coming from you!"

"Hey, what's going on out here?" It's Mom. She stands at the door.

"Dele is cheating," I say.

Dele just stands there, his hands hanging down by his sides.

Mom shakes her head, grinning. Like it's all fun. "I'm sure Dele doesn't cheat."

"I can't believe you're taking his side. You didn't even see anything. You don't know anything!"

"Will you stop screaming?"

"He's cheating!"

"Nic."

"Here, here's the damn ball." And I shove it at him.

He drops it, the loser.

I walk inside, banging the door as hard as I can. I'm so sick of being treated like a child. Like I have no soul yet. Like I don't have a clue. I decide to show them.

I shave my head.

It takes all afternoon and costs me a gallon of blood from all the nicks—never try to shave with your mother's leg razor. Especially one she's hasn't changed in a year. But it's time they start taking me seriously.

"So, Nic, how did you feel about your mutilation?"

Mr. Hautman, the school therapist for teens losing their minds, sits on his side of the desk. Mom is next to me and I have a lukewarm Coke in my hands. How do I feel? I don't know. What kind of stupid question is that? I feel great. Liberated. Fanfuckingtastic. But I'm pretty sure that's not what they were looking for here. So I take a sip of Coke.

"Don't you have any ice?"

"Nic," says Mom.

"Lucy," I say, "it's warm."

"No, we don't," Mr. Hautman says.

Mom clicks her tongue. Mr. Hautman is looking at us like some CCTV camera. Recording it all for the prosecution.

"Your mother is concerned about you. I am too."

"You don't even know who I am." Moron.

"Well, I'd like to get to know you."

"That's too bad, isn't it?"

Mom glares at me. "Will you just—"

"I don't want to be here. This is stupid."

Mr. Head Shrink butts in. "Your mother is worried that the lack of a father figure—"

"I still have a father. It's not that big of a deal."

"She just wants to make sure."

"It's fine."

"Do you think you see him enough?"

I shrug.

"Is this an appeal for more time with your father?"

I roll my eyes. He hands me a stack of papers.

"I'd like you to take these home and go through them. Answer them. Will you do that for me?"

I flip through them. Homework?

"Nic?"

"Can I go now?"

"Yes. See you next week."

When we get home, I go to my room and slam the door.

I'm never coming out again. She can send in the cops, the dogs, the troops, whatever. I'm not coming out again until it's time to leave home.

But I forget I don't have a refrigerator in my room and by seven o'clock I'm starving.

In the kitchen Mom is on the phone and she looks all white. She hangs up and puts her hand over her mouth.

"What's wrong?"

"It's Jessica."

"Yeah?"

"She was mugged."

"Shit."

And Mom starts crying. "They cut her hand."

Chapter Eighteen

The cops get them: two guys driving around in a stolen Corvette. Turns out they just wanted to hurt somebody, hurt them real bad. Jessica and her friend were walking back from her friend's house two blocks away. It was only 6 PM. Two guys came up, one had a knife, and after she handed over her purse he reached out and sliced her. No reason. Just out to mess somebody up. The cops found the guys at the deli where they'd gone to wolf down some subs and tell all their friends about their dirty deed.

Jessica has to stay at the hospital for a week even though normally she could have gone home right away. It's only her hand, it's not life threatening. Thing is, she's pretty upset. Mom mentions the word suicidal. Which is pretty heavy. They have to keep watch. Aunt Ruth and Uncle David sleep at the hospital the first couple of nights. My mom stays over at their place at night with the rest of the kids. I come too and end up sleeping with the twins because they sneak into my bed.

Jessica's better now, but the house is silent. She sits in the living room and stares blankly at the videos her mom puts on. I go over to keep her company.

"You okay?"

She looks at me.

"I mean, can I get you anything, a glass of water or something?"

She shakes her head, and I wouldn't really call it crying, but little tears just slide down her cheeks nonstop, making watery tracks. Her mouth sits in a long wobbly line.

I've brought my DVD collection of *24* and I slide one in.

"You seen this one?"

She doesn't answer so I sit down next to her, not too close but close enough just in case, I don't know, she wants to hold my hand.

She doesn't.

Mrs. Porter comes over to our house the next day with a huge tin of homemade chocolate chip cookies for us to give to Jessica. Mom opens the door and says thank you. "We were just on our way. We'll bring it over."

Mrs. Porter squeezes her own hands together and says, "It's just so awful. Please let her know we're praying for her."

"I will," Mom says.

"To think a thing like this could happen."

And they stand there shaking their heads at each other.

Mrs. Porter finally says again. "She's in our prayers."

"Thank you."

Mrs. Porter turns to go but then turns back to Mom. "This

must be such a difficult time for them. Are they. . . . Do they have someone to talk to . . . ?"

"They're Jewish."

"Oh, good. So they have someone to turn to."

"Yes, I suppose so."

Mrs. Porter nods. "Such a horrible thing."

"Thank you for the cookies," says Mom, and closes the door. She looks down at the tin. "For such a confused woman," she says, "Mrs. Porter really is a very nice person."

I wrote to my pen pal about it. Sergeant Roberto Aguilar of the 1st Marine Expeditionary Force. He's stationed in Iraq. I connected with him through this thing called Books for Soldiers. You send them books that they request. I guess they don't have much to do between shootings and get pretty bored staring at all that sand. Mrs. Hansen, our English teacher, got us started. Mom looked at the literature when it was time to shell out for the books and I needed her credit card. Those poor boys, she said. And girls, I pointed out. And she laughed at herself. Yes, absolutely, she said.

Sometimes we send my old books in a box and add toiletries. They want soaps and lotions, unscented so the bugs don't eat them alive. They also want toys that they can hand out to the Iraqi kids. I stick in a note that basically says I hope they're okay, thanks for being there, try not to get hurt.

A couple of them write back. Some are really good writers, some not so great. They put periods in the weirdest places. And the spelling. Man. Mom says that's because they're from poor backgrounds and live in places where the public schools aren't so hot. I feel sorry for them.

"Look at that," Mom says when I hand her another letter. "They're dying for their country and nobody bothered to teach them how to spell 'country.' "

We sent a package to a woman soldier, and she wrote back. She's got a two-year-old back home. Mom couldn't believe it. She was all indignatious about how the army could ship off a young mother to Iraq to maybe get killed, and I said they send dads all the time and she sort of sat down and sighed. "Yes, I suppose you're right."

Anyway, this woman airman—you're called an airman whether you're a woman or not—gave me her home address in Alabama and Mom and I sent her kid a doll and some stuff. We didn't know what race she was and didn't want to offend her so we sent her a mixed-race doll and hoped for the best.

Sergeant Aguilar, though, is my main pen pal. We started with letters but then switched to e-mails. He's a Packer fan too. He signed up for the military because he wanted money for college. But then they started enforcing this thing called Stop Loss and he can't get out. He's been there for two years. He's twenty. He gets real scared when he hears about other countries the president is pissed off at: Syria, Iran, North Korea, Venezuela. He wrote, "I'm gonna be an old man by the time I get to graduate." He's more scared of losing limbs than of dying. With dying it's sort of done and over with, but losing limbs . . . A guy from his platoon lost both his legs the second day there.

He's in some hospital now waiting for his house to be refitted for wheelchair access. The money's not available to do it so he's just hanging out, waiting. And he wanted to go to college too but now he's thinking, What's the use. He won't be able to get a job. Maybe if they could have saved his knees, but they had to cut right across his thighs and, well, he's scared of freaking out all the college kids.

When I told Sergeant Aguilar about Jessica, he wrote back and told me not to worry. He said if he comes back in one piece, he'll take care of those dirtbags personally. He always makes me feel better.

When I go to Shabbat dinner at Jessica's house a couple of weeks later, it seems okay. Even Jessica smiles every once in a while. She seems to really relax when her mom sings over the candles. Her mom's got this really nice voice, low and smoky. She'd be right at home in a rabbinical cabaret if they ever decide to open one, and Jessica just stares at her like she's holding on.

Her hand is less bandaged now. It doesn't look so much like a club anymore. Now there are just thin bandages over the part where the knife sliced through the tendons. Still, she can't feel much in her hand.

At dinner, Uncle David keeps leaning over to hug her and I can tell she's starting to get a little annoyed.

"I'm alright," she says and her mom warns him with her eyes. So he finally sits back and tucks into his chicken soup. Jessica made the soup. And the challah bread. Even the little cheese blintzes. Everybody makes a big fuss over her cooking skills until she rolls her eyes and says, "Okay, okay. Thanks a million, now enough already," just like our granddad would do, and everybody laughs.

I remember Uncle David once telling me of a Jewish sect where men lock themselves up in rooms to pray for humanity all day. They pray their hearts out. They pray that cars stay in their lanes, that rivers stay in their banks, that surgeons' hands stay steady. And even though tragedy sometimes slips through, he said, just think of all the possible chaos if it weren't for those men.

Jessica's mom and dad have decided that it's probably best if she stops violin altogether. She will never catch up now and it will always remind her of what could have been. She's going to go to cooking school instead. She's always liked cooking.

Chapter Nineteen

Pastor Stowe got out his guns today. He's going to defend Christmas.

"We're under siege, Nic. It's up to us to defend ourselves." He fishes around in his box for the right cartridge for his .45. "There are people who want to take away our religious rights."

We're guarding the nativity scene outside the church. It's all set up on the lawn: big white plastic statues of Mary and Joseph, the shepherds, and a couple of sheep.

It's a relay thing. Me and Kevin have the 12 to 2 AM slot. We also have hot cocoa in a thermos, angel food cake in Tupperware from Mrs. Porter, and sleeping bags. We are set. Mr. Porter even gave us these cool canvas chairs that you use on beaches so we can stretch out nice and comfy.

Kevin and I have sort of gotten over the whole Sandra thing. He says it wasn't his fault she liked him better. He was just trying to be nice. And besides, Sandra hasn't really talked to him since. It was just that day she was so friendly. Which makes it easier to forgive him.

Pastor Stowe sits back in his chair. He decided to start the whole security thing because last year the figure of the baby Jesus was stolen right out of the manger. People woke up one morning to find the baby gone, a beer bottle in its place. They got another doll, a supersized one, and tried putting a bike lock around the belly, but the lock kept slipping off. So Pastor Stowe came up with the personal protection program.

Now, if he'd just gone on to MySpace he'd know that it was Jim Butts and Brad Hornsby who stole the nativity baby. They got drunk after a home game and thought it would be funny as hell. They tried to melt the doll with a blowtorch, hoping for a fireball, but it just kind of fell apart into gooey pieces.

"I'm freezing," says Kevin.

The moon is full. The North Star bright. The baby's plastic face is glowing in the lights of the manger. Kevin is munching on the cake.

"Good to have you with us, Nic," says Pastor Stowe. "This is what this country needs more of, young men like you taking their responsibilities seriously."

"Yes, sir."

Across the street there's a house that's got giant candy canes glowing on the porch and electric reindeer with noses the size of stoplights on the roof. People drive by really slow and you can see the little kids in the backseats, their eyes big and wide, their mouths in the shape of "Ooooo!"

"We have to defend what's right," Pastor Stowe continues. "All these immigrants coming here and not assimilating. That's what the problem is. If they are going to come here they have to learn our language and worship our God. It's not asking much. And in return they get roads paved with gold and honey."

"Yes, sir."

"Have some more cocoa."

"Hey, look."

A bright white cop car sails down the dark road.

"Our men in blue." Pastor Stowe gives a big, friendly wave. But it's the hand with his gun. The cop car screeches to a halt. Two cops get out, their hands hovering at their hips.

"What are you doing, sir?"

"Just sitting here, officer. Taking in the cool air."

"Is that a gun you are holding?"

"It is, sir. I'm keeping it for protection. I'm just protecting my property."

"You own this church?"

"I am a warden."

"Do you have a license for that?"

"Yes, sir, I do." Pastor Stowe pulls out his wallet, hands the guy a slip.

The cop looks at it, both sides, and hands it back. You can see that he isn't too happy about it. But Pastor Stowe can hang out on the front lawn of a church with a gun in his hand if he has the license. It's the law.

After the cops have ambled back to their car and driven off, Pastor Stowe shakes his head. "You think they have to protect synagogues in Israel or mosques in Muslim countries? Hell, no. Because they're all Jews and Muslims. But when you get it all mixed up like in this country, that's when you get trouble.

They've got their countries, let us have our Christian country. It's only fair."

Kevin says, "What about people like Nic's mom?"

Pastor Stowe peers down at me and gives it a considered thought. "Well, son, I'm sure there's a country for her somewhere. Just don't know its name."

And because it is Christmastime Mom's being her usual weird self. She likes to take a picture of me doing something interesting and then send it to all her friends. But this year I won't let her near me with the camera, so she has to take a picture of our house instead. I don't understand Christmas cards. You don't talk to someone all year long and then you write this one-page Xerox bragging about all the cool things you did during the year and then, at the end, write Oh, by the way, have a Merry Christmas. Which, coming from an atheist, is pretty rich. So you know what Mom writes? She does the bragging bit and then at the end she writes *Have a Happy Winter Solstice!* I won't let her sign my name anymore because it's too moronic.

"Why do you write that?"

"Because not everybody believes in Christmas," she says.

"Meaning you."

"Meaning me and Jews and Muslims and Buddhists and Hindus and . . ."

"So how come it's so popular?"

"Excellent marketing."

Mom's a closet carol singer, though. She flips on Frank Sinatra and Elvis Presley and warbles along to their Christmas collections. There she is, chirping about the little town of Bethlehem and she doesn't believe a word of it. It's culture, she says. "You don't throw the baby out with the bathwater."

But I ask her, "How can you sing *Pa ra pa pa pum* if you don't think the little boy is playing for the king?"

"It's nice to play for a baby too," she says.

"It loses its majesty."

And she raises her eyebrows like she always does when she thinks I'm using a big word.

On Christmas Eve Mom makes us go into D.C. to help out at the So Others Might Eat soup kitchen. Mom serves up the turkey and rice and I go around and make sure everybody's got all their utensils and napkins. Everybody's pretty happy-clappy considering they're spending their Christmas in a gray basement. And the kids are wired. Some of them clutch toys from the Toys for Tots basket in the corner like they'll never let go. I saw this one little girl holding on to a monkey and she dropped it and her mom kept dragging her to the table. You'd think a siren went off the way she screamed. When I brought the monkey over to her she shoved it down her party dress to keep it safe and then stared at the roast turkey like it was talking to her.

This Christmas, in the middle of serving, Mom suddenly has to sit down. I'm sorry, she says, and she puts her head between her legs. Mrs. Clark goes over to her and tells me to take my mom's place, so I start ladling turkey and rice onto the plates. And this one old guy just looks at me and shakes his head, like he's seen everything now. I ask, Dark or white meat?

And he starts laughing. The guy next to him is muttering about how we should serve roast beef for once instead of turkey every year.

Mom feels better after a glass of water, but she spends the rest of the time sitting at the tables and talking to people. She's pretty good at that. She's not really very sociable normally but I can see she's making an effort. Most of them are chatty back, real "thank-yous" and "Merry Christmases." Some look at her like they'd rather she'd just go away, and she gets the hint quick.

By the end I'm pouring sweat even though it's below freezing outside. I've taken off my sweatshirt and long-sleeve shirt and just have on my Che Guevara T-shirt. Afterward, Mr. Clark walks us to our car and we drive back to our neck of the woods, as Mom calls it. It's so different. Gingerbread houses, twinkling white lights, big tall chimneys for Santa to slide down.

Mom says, "What are you thinking about?"

"Nothing." But I'm thinking about all those kids who think Santa leaves them presents in somebody else's basement.

"Gimme a kiss, it's Christmas," Mom says when we get home and are in the hallway upstairs. I open my mouth to say, Well, technically it's not yet, but I look at her and she looks so tired. She suddenly looks about a hundred years old. So I give her a peck on the cheek.

"Thanks," she says. She pats me on the shoulder and goes into her room.

Chapter Twenty

Mom got a call from a doctor today. When she's not home I'm the one who answers the phone. The doctor says, "Now be sure to give her the message." I hate it when adults do that. They are so lame on the phone. They are either super nice and act like we're exchanging bodily fluids daily, like "Hey, Nic, how's it going? It's soooo good to talk to you, man." Like I know who this person is? Or they act like I'm the biggest moron. They talk real slow and articulate like I just hopped off the boat and haven't met the English language yet. This doctor even says, "Look, why don't I call back and you don't pick up and I'll leave it on your answering machine." And I say, "It's okay, I'll give her the message." So he finally gives up and says okay but I can tell he isn't sure. He says Mom needs to call him as soon as possible.

When I give her the message she looks at it strangely.

"Dr. Bellow."

"Yeah. Who's he?"

"He's my doctor. That's weird."

"Are you sick?"

She shrugs. "Never felt better."

"You better call him."

"Hmmm."

Later I ask her, "Did you call him?"

"Yeah."

"And?"

"Oh, he just wants me to have some tests."

"Why?"

"Oh, that's what they do. More tests, more money for them."

"Are you sick?"

"Probably not."

"You're not sure."

"I'm sure I'm fine. Time for school."

"Do you want me to pray for you?"

"If that will make you feel better. Mostly I want you to find your shoes."

"Do you want me to pray out loud or in my head?"

She thinks a second. "Why don't you do it silently? That way I'll be surprised."

I read somewhere that kids in the olden days didn't go to school. They became apprentices. They followed someone around who knew how to do something and learned a trade that way. Like a blacksmith or a butcher.

Nowadays, though, they just round up all the kids and put them into schools to keep them off the streets. And then, when they turn eighteen, they let them out again. Because a lot of them don't seem to learn much. There doesn't even seem to be anyone in charge. The teachers are supposed to be, but tell me another one. They've got this thing going on where they humor the obnoxious kids. They joke with them, laugh at their jokes. They try to look like they're in control but they're so not. If they didn't joke, they'd be ignored. And the class would dissolve into a free-for-all. So they pretend it's their idea, but it's not.

The sad truth is, school is run by the popular kids. You ever notice how much energy it takes to be popular? Well, for the average populars. Not the top cream. The top cream seem to sail through effortlessly. There's maybe six or seven of them in the whole school. And they seem sort of clueless. It's weird, all these people talking about them all the time, voting them on to the homecoming courts, trying to sit next to them, trying to talk to them, act like them, dress like them, *be* them. You wonder what it is that they've got that everybody else doesn't. I mean, they're all good-looking. But not *People* magazine good-looking. More ordinary, clean. Like Mary Wallnot. Long brown hair, nice face. Not too fat, not too thin. Makes good grades. Not perfect ones but up there. She seems like a nice girl. She even looks kinda shy. But man, it's like she's a goddess or something. And don't get me wrong, I'd sell one of my testicles to hook up with Mary Wallnot. But why her?

No, it's the second rung that does all the work. They're clawing up the sides of the ladder, desperate not to fall into the pit of unpopular people. You know it took them five hours to get dressed. You know they've been on the phone with each other twelve times before they see each other every morning. You know that being popular is a full-time job for them. They are never off. They are never not being popular. And I think maybe it's something their parents teach them. Because I don't know how to do it. Wouldn't even know where to start. I blame my mom. I think that if she'd raised me right I'd have gotten some popularity skills. She was so busy making sure I knew everything. Didn't she know that admitting to intelligence is social death?

And then there's Tanner. He's top dog of the second rung at our school. He owns the place. Along with his court jesters who make you want to puke. I used to be friends with Tanner. We did everything together—eat worms, piss on ants—and then suddenly last year he grew. In two months he went from an eleven-year-old kid to looking like a fifty-year-old man with zits. And his voice is so low he sounds like a humvee. My voice hasn't broken yet. Mom says I sound angelic. Like it's a compliment, like I don't want to stab her in the eyes when she says that. When Tanner grew he dropped me like a hot potato. He just stopped talking to me, told me to fuck off. So I did.

I still see him around at school, in the hall. He's got this gang of cyberborgs now who follow him around. You'd think he'd leave me alone but it doesn't work that way. When I see him in the hall I have a fifty-percent chance of getting away. If I'm lucky he acts like he doesn't know me, like my mom never had to take him home early from a sleepover because he wanted *his mommy.*

But then he'll just turn on me. He'll crack some joke and his goons jump all over me. And Tanner keeps walking like he had nothing to do with it. Once he said, "Nice hair," and his goons shoved me against the wall and ruffled it all up. And the girls, they are the worst. They laugh. They laugh like machine guns. And then they move on, leaving you picking up your guts from the floor.

Yesterday when I saw the pack coming down the hall, I could see Tanner looking straight at me and I knew I was in for it. He tricked me, though. Walked right on by and I relaxed. But then I heard it.

"Hey, you."

I'm looking in the other direction wondering if I can reach fourth period.

But his main goon, Jerry Clark, is in my face.

"Got a problem with your hearing?"

So I turn to face the music. Best thing to do is go all blank on the outside, try not to move a muscle.

That's when I notice Sandra is with them. I've never seen her look so happy. She has this huge grin on her face. She looks kind of dorky, to tell you the truth. You could push her with one hand and she'd fall over because she isn't paying attention to anything else but walking with Tanner and his gang.

He shakes his head. "Your mom, man. She needs to be eliminated."

Clark goes, "Yeah, yeah, man." Like we asked him.

Tanner laughs and says, "And you know what? She'd understand. Survival of the fittest."

And they all just start howling like that has got to be the funniest thing said by man in the last one hundred thousand years. Then Tanner grabs my book and throws it down the hall. "Don't want you thinking too hard. You might bust a screw loose. And then you wouldn't be able to think at all. And your mom, she'd have to put you down."

A teacher walks by. Tanner flashes a smile.

"Nic here dropped his book. Just telling him it's not nice to litter the halls."

And the teacher nods. They're not too thrilled about walking along the halls, either. You'd have to be bleeding from the ears and missing one shoe for them to slow down.

He leans close. "I'd bash your head in, but Melissa likes you." And he looks back at Sandra, who grins. She looks like a wolf with those front teeth of hers. They all high-five each other like that's the saddest thing they've ever heard. I want to kill every one of them. Especially Sandra. Her, I want to stick up on a cross and crucify. Drill nails straight into her palms, slice her with a butcher knife, and let her fry. Those Romans really knew how to treat people.

The next thing I know, Mrs. Porter is taking Kevin out of school. She says there is not enough God in school and at home he would get a better Christian upbringing, so she's going to home-school him.

I don't think that's such a good idea. The kid still doesn't know his hypotenuse from the hole in his ass. And frankly, I don't know if Mrs. Porter is going to be much help.

"Poor Kevin," Mom says when she hears about it.

"Why poor?"

"His world is getting smaller and smaller."

But when I visit he's grinning from ear to ear. He had a pretty easy morning. They did some math problems and then he had to log into this Bible course on the Internet, where he had to read a passage from the New Testament and comment on it. And that's it. He and his mom ended up going to a special viewing of Mel Gibson's *The Passion of the Christ.* Kevin said there was so much blood he almost barfed. When they came back his sister, Charlene, was sitting on the front porch in her cheerleading outfit freezing to death because Mrs. Porter forgot she didn't have a key.

Mrs. Porter says that next year, when she's got more experience she's going to home-school Kevin's little brother too. I guess she figures it's too late for Charlene. She's a junior already. Her mind has been corrupted. Jack is only six. He's a funny little dude. Full of the weirdest information. He likes to go on and on about Cain and Abel. Knows exactly how Cain did the dirty deed. What the mark looked like that God put on Cain's forehead. What the place was called that he banished Cain to. But the kid doesn't know the name of the third planet from the sun.

Mrs. Porter says he knows how to pray. And I'm hoping he'll pray for some answers.

So I ask him, "Why is the sky blue?"

"Because God made it so," he says.

"That's right, dear," says Mrs. Porter from where she's chopping up onions and tomatoes. Since I want to hang around and see if I'll be invited for dinner I decide to tell him. "It has to do with light particles. The sunlight is made up of different colors, all the colors of the rainbow. You know, like Roy G. Biv: Red, Orange, Yellow, Green, Blue, Indigo, Violet. And they have different properties, which makes them travel from the sun in different ways. Red is heavy and just thunks down to the ground. So do green and yellow and orange. But blue is pretty zany and light and so it bounces all over the place. Bumping into particles before it hits earth and so we see the color coming from all directions. Which is why we see the sky as blue."

Jack cocks his head a moment and I can see Mrs. Porter watching us.

Jack finally says, "Wow, that's a pretty neat trick of God's."

I glance at Mrs. Porter. "Yup," I say, "God's probably pretty proud of it."

Mrs. Porter wants Kevin to grow up and change all the laws of the country. She wants abortion wiped from the planet. "All those unborn babies," she says, "it just makes me cry."

She glances at me, then back to her sautéing. "Your mother probably doesn't agree with me on this one, does she?"

I shrug. I know Mom wants to keep abortion legal, but I don't think she's itching to take down unborn children everywhere. I've done everything in my power, she once told me, so that I don't have to make that choice.

"A baby is not a choice," says Mrs. Porter.

Personally, I think all girls who get pregnant should be forced to have their babies. Just think of the excellent business opportunity. Everyone is always going on about not being able to adopt grade-A babies. But if you had a constant supply, entrepreneurs could set up baby banks where wannabe parents could just drive up and place an order, like "I'll have one of your Superdeluxe with big brown eyes and a side of diapers to go." You could call it McBabies. Of course people would have to be cool with half the schoolgirl population waddling down to homeroom and getting exemptions from Phys. Ed. But just think about the boost to our gross national product.

Another bunch of marines get it today. A road bomb incinerated their humvee. I thought the whole point of these big humvees is that you can't destroy them. But I guess you can. Four of them burned to death. Mom's reading the paper and shaking her head, saying, "Well done, George."

There's also an article about how they want to drill in the Arctic and destroy what's left of the natural world. I don't know why Mom reads the papers. They put her in such a bad mood. I wish there was a newspaper that just reported what went right the day before. Like, Hey, listen up! Yesterday, 6 billion people managed to stay alive. Or we didn't destroy 9 billion acres of the world. Or little Johnny Doe didn't get run over by a car, die in a fire, or get pummeled to death by his mom's boyfriend. And there would be pictures of people from countries not at war, just going about their boring business: grabbing a trolley at the supermarket, looking for their shoes, taking out the garbage. But all with smiles on their faces.

The antidepressant companies might try to stop it. It would make too many people happy and they wouldn't buy their products anymore. God, I'm sounding just like Mom, aren't

I? But you could spend the whole time dwelling on the bad stuff.

Mom says, How can you possibly believe in God with all this misery going on?

And I think, Well, if I was God I probably wouldn't give my humans a perfect world, either. How else are they going to learn to be good? Sometimes I think I want to be a good person just so my mom will love me.

Chapter Twenty-one

"Hey kid, got any Jesus jokes for me?"

Skye's at Dad's when I get there. I'm at Dad's because Mom has to go to an astronomy conference and I get to skip school and stay in Williamsburg for four days. Mom drives me downtown to the Greyhound bus terminal and stands at the side of the bus waving to me when it pulls away. I pretend not to know her. I say to the guy next to me who's watching her jump up and down, "Maybe she's one of those psychos they let out of St. Elizabeth's."

Skye's been at Dad's the last two times I've visited on weekends. Dad calls her a poor little rich kid even though she's twenty-eight. She just about punches him. I think her dad ran some oil company or something. She didn't graduate from college. She waited until three weeks before graduation, then dropped out. Turns out she completely skipped senior-year classes because she was living in trees, smoking a lot of dope. She stayed with one of her old professors for a couple of months, but then her parents threatened to come after him so he threw her out. When Dad met her she was working in one of those restaurants where you have to wear a colonial costume. By the time he was tucking into the Queen's Mince Pie she had his phone number.

She just sort of hangs out at Dad's place until he tells her to go away and get a life, and she finally leaves. She never takes her eyes off my dad. If he disappears into the kitchen, she'll hop up and go in too. He gets grumpy if she gets too close when I'm around.

When I arrive this time he calls upstairs and yells, "Skye, Nic's here, we're gonna spend sometime together." She comes stumbling down, rubbing sleep from her eyes. "Alright, alright, I'm going." She grabs her coat and gooses me on the way out.

"See ya. Wouldn't want to be ya," she calls to my dad.

The first night I'm there, Dad makes spaghetti. When he cooks, he likes to wear his green DANGER, MEN COOKING! apron Mom bought him eons ago. But he likes to wear it with no shirt on so he won't splash anything on his sleeves. And sometimes when he's just wearing shorts he looks like this naked gorilla stirring away at a pot with a glass of red wine in one hand.

At dinner he tries to have a talk.

"How's life?"

Oh, brother.

"It treating you okay?"

"Yeah."

"What's up with school?"

"It's, you know, there."

"You happy there?"

"I guess."

"You're not sure?"

"It's okay."

"Just okay."

"It's fine."

"You don't want to talk about it."

"What do you mean? I am talking about it."

He stares at me. Then puts down his fork and leans close.

"I know this is a tough time for you, Nic. But just hang in there. In five years you'll be out. School is a funny thing. It squeezes you and then, just when you think you're going to die, it lets up and you walk free."

He thumps me on the shoulder. "Just try not to do anything stupid. I know you'll find this hard to believe but I remember junior high like it was yesterday. The angst, the fear, the horror."

I don't know what he's talking about. It's just school. The way he makes it sound it's like he had Freddy Krueger for a homeroom teacher. No wonder he's so weird. I mean, it's not great but I'm not seeing any tunnel with lights at the end yet. Maybe that'll come.

Then afterward, just when we're settling down to a mean game of chess—I've got his queen and castle forked and Dad is squirming—Skye comes back. As if she lives there. She schlumps back in, no knocking, and tosses her bag on the couch.

"You done bonding yet?"

"For the moment," says Dad.

And I think, Wait a minute, it's still our time. What the hell is she doing back?

But he doesn't say anything when she comes over and gives him a back rub. He looks like he even likes it.

I stare at her fingers moving all over his body.

"So, champ," he says to me, "ready to hit the hay?" What is he, a pseudo farmer now? Sure, Pops, I'll mosey on over to the barn.

I try to grab his eyes with mine, but he's looking at Skye and she takes his hand and starts to drag him away. "Beddybies time," she chants.

"I'll be there in a sec." When she finally saunters away, making kissy faces at him all the way up the stairs, he says, "You okay with this?"

And I mumble, "Sure."

"Okay, then," he says, "I'll see you in the morning." And off he goes. I can hear a toilet flushing down the hall. So I sit there by myself, staring at the chess board, turning up the music pretty loud. I don't want to hear anything.

The next day, I have to do my homework at the college library while Dad gives a lecture. Some of the students do double takes when they see me, then nudge each other and laugh. Like I'm some moron who's walked into the wrong library by mistake.

When I get home Skye is in the kitchen making herself a sandwich. Doesn't she ever go home?

"Do you live here?"

"Sometimes."

"You know my parents aren't divorced yet."

"So?"

"That means you're an adulteress."

She laughs. "What you gonna do? Stone me?"

And I try to think, What would Jesus do? But since nothing comes to mind immediately I go for that old standby: a poorly thought-out revenge plan.

"I'm bored," I say.

"Don't you know that only boring people are bored?" She shoves the sandwich into her backpack and heads for the door.

I follow her. "You going to just leave me here?"

"I stopped babysitting years ago. Lost too many kids."

"That's too bad because I could have told you some things my dad likes."

She laughs. "Kid, I know exactly what your father likes." And she pulls open the front door.

I race after her. "Oh, come on, let me just go with you, hang out. We should get to know each other, don't you think? Family-like."

When she pauses on the front steps, I know I have her.

She checks me out and then smiles. "Okay, then, come on."

We end up picking up a couple of her friends at the corner of Lafayette and Richmond Streets. Two guys with rusty beards and a girl named Ruge or Root or something. They all look like they stepped straight out of Robin Hood, but without the green tights. Root's got Rastafarian braids—you know, where they put dung on their hair? Weird. It probably stinks too.

Though I make sure I don't get close enough to find out. In the car, Skye nods at me and she says, "This is Robert's kid."

The guys, they nod their heads and say, "Cool."

But Root says, "What did you do? Kidnap him?"

We end up driving to Jamestown Island, the site of the first permanent English colony in America. About a hundred guys came over in 1607 and then, in between getting attacked by the local Algonquins and dying of hunger and disease, they managed to set up the first New World government. Then they arranged almost immediately to bring slaves over from Africa. I know this because I've been there a couple of times. Mom's got a thing about Pocahontas. She married the Englishmen's leader, John Smith. You know the story. About her raccoon friend and all the colors in the wind.

The island's also got this loop that you can drive around and admire all the scenery. But instead of driving along like a good citizen, Skye suddenly turns a hard right and we go flying into the bushes and down this hill where she finally stops the car and barks, "Hop out." We all scramble out and walk even farther down the hill until we can sit on rocks and look out at the James River.

You ever listen to a bird sing? Really listen. They talk to each other. There are two gray tits high up in the trees just talking away. Having a conversation. The one in the right tree starting off and the one in the left tree, I can't see him, answering him. It goes something like this: tweet tweet *tweeeeet?* And the other one goes, twit, twit, *twit-twit.* Real fast. It goes on forever, back and forth between them, and then they must have decided on

something because suddenly the bird in the left tree hauls out
at about five hundred miles an hour and the one in the right
just goes back to sleep.

I like birds. I like their hollow bones. I remember being
into archaeopteryxes when I was a kid. They were my favorite
dinosaur. Other kids were hot about t-rexes and stegosauruses,
but me, I thought archaeopteryxes were the coolest things ever.
Turns out they were the first birds and could be a transitional
fossil. At least that's what some people say. Mrs. Porter thinks
they might be a left-wing hoax. I told her once about meeting
someone who tree-sat. I didn't say it was my dad's girlfriend,
because, man, Mrs. Porter would have thrown me out of Bible
class. So I told her somebody I knew knew somebody who
knew somebody who sat up in trees trying to save them. She
said, "That's the strangest thing I've ever heard. Those trees
were put there to serve you. God is perfect. He knows what
he's doing. You don't have to spend the night in a tree. There
will always be enough. You must trust Him." Dele is a little
different. He's more like, let's feed the hungry and then worry
about the trees later.

I can tell Skye and her friends come to this place a lot because one of the guys checks under a rock and comes up with
a small metal box, which he shakes with a huge grin. He opens
it up and starts rolling a joint. He takes a toke then passes it to
me. Luckily I don't cough.

Skye takes a long hit and holds her breath. She says out of
the corner of her mouth, "Now, this is what your dad likes."

"The view?"

"The view, the company." She smiles.

"Sure beats working," I say.

Root laughs.

Skye shakes her head. "I'm never getting a real job."

"What are you going to do, then?"

"What do you mean, what am I going to do? I'm going to live and leave this place better than I found it."

"How?"

"I'm not going to have kids, for one thing. I'm not going to produce any more gas guzzlers, no more tree cutters, no more consumers."

Root takes a hit. "Humans are rotten, man."

They all nod at that. One of the guys says, "We need to die out."

"Then maybe the earth can heal," Skye says.

"Good thing the Rapture's coming," I say.

All four pairs of red eyes swing over to me.

"Because all the people will disappear," I explain.

Root smiles. "God. I didn't think of that."

It brightens them right up. "When's it supposed to happen?"

"Pastor Stowe says it could be in fifty, sixty years."

Skye nods and takes another hit. "He'd better hurry up."

And we all nod and watch the water. Which by now is turning this amazing salmon color with a huge streak of deep purple underneath, and I think about a world with no humans. I wonder how long it would take for our footsteps to disappear. All the buildings to crumble. Everything to get moldy and to rot away. When the Rapture comes, the earth will grow dark almost immediately because there'll be no one to keep the fuel burning for electricity. So just think. No more light pollution. The earth will spin round and round with just animals blinking at each other. And all that noise humans make, all those radio waves we emit that float out into space, will stop. And the sound waves we've already made will be the last trace of our existence.

But I don't say any of this because I can't move my mouth. My tongue feels like an elephant in jeans three sizes too small.

"Wow," says Skye.

"Yeah," says one of the guys, shaking his head. "Good shit."

"Well, I'm not driving anywhere." Skye fumbles for her phone. "Call your dad, tell him where you are. Tell him to pick you up." She hands me her cell.

"You're going to sleep out here in the cold?"

"I've got sleeping bags in the back of the car. Even one for you if you weren't such a wimp."

And finally, I see my chance.

"Dad," I say to the pizza delivery guy, "I'm with Skye. It's really fun, we're going to sleep out here. I'll see you in the morning. Alright?" I hang up, betting the guy isn't going to call back, he's got too many pizzas to make.

"Okay?" says Skye when I hand her back her phone.

"Yup. He was all for me staying."

She nods her head. "You better piss now because I don't want you pissing in the sleeping bag tonight."

She's about to give me another toke when she reaches around

me and gives it to Root instead. She says, "Don't want you puking on it, either."

Luckily one of the guys brought some granola bars and we tear into those and Skye's one sandwich like starved mountain lions. Then we drink some plum-apple juice. But not too much. Skye's really obsessed with not having to piss. We roll out the sleeping bags and then we just hang there, shooting the shit until finally Skye says, "Okay, you can shut up now. Go to sleep."

She makes a pillow of her knapsack and rolls over. She doesn't move. Of course I have to pee almost immediately. Luckily I'm able to unzip the bag, maneuver myself, and let it fly all over the bark in front of me.

So I just manage to fall asleep when Skye's cell rings. She doesn't wake up. None of them do. I scramble around and find it in her bag. I can see it's Dad's number calling. I turn the cell off.

In the morning Skye stops off at McDonalds and loads me up with a pound of trans fats before heading to my dad's to drop me off. When she drives up to his condo, Dad comes flying down the steps, charges up to the car, and tears open the door. "Where the hell have you been?"

"What?"

"I said where the hell have you been?"

Skye turns her head to see me slipping out of the car and figures it all out in one second. She pulls the door shut and locks it, then opens the window a crack. "Now, Robert, you know how I am with authority."

He smacks the door with his palm. "Get the hell out of the car. I want to talk to you. You can't just run off with my son like that. Are you crazy?"

She crosses her eyes at him. Dad leans forward and shouts through the crack. "Don't you ever come near me or my son again!"

Skye shoves the car into reverse and barrels backward down the driveway. She flips him the finger before squealing off.

Dad barks at me, "Get in the house." Which I do, pretty quick.

Inside he paces around like a panther. I tuck into a double-sized bowl of Wheaties. I'm still starved. He finally stops in front of the kitchen table. "I'd prefer it if you don't mention this to your mother."

Chapter Twenty-two

When I get back from Dad's, I find Mom slumped in the kitchen. She's sitting in a kitchen chair with her head down between her legs.

"What's the matter?"

"I'm okay, just a little dizzy. I'm fine."

She puts her head up and she looks so white. And sweaty. She takes a deep breath. "Just a panic attack."

"What are you panicking about?"

She laughs. "Oh, everything." And then she puts her head back between her legs and we both listen to the Elvis clock on the wall ticking. Finally she comes up for air.

"Come, talk to me," she says. "Be a good son and come talk to me. Here," she pats the chair next to her. And because she's acting so weird I figure I better do it.

She sighs again. "There, that's better." She looks around the kitchen. "Let's order pizza tonight."

"Okay." I jump up again.

She laughs.

"What?"

"I had you sitting for, oh, two seconds."

"I'm getting the menus."

"Then come back."

"Fine."

I like the crust of Domino's, but the cheese on the Papa John's is better, plus they've got this special going on. And if you spend twenty bucks they throw in ice cream. But we never make it to twenty bucks. Mom always says no, we don't need a large, medium will do. But a medium is only $17 and I try to explain that if she just paid $3 more, she'd get a free four-buck ice cream. And we get into this real thing about it.

But tonight she says, "Fine. Large it is.'

I pick New York Chunk ice cream because I know she likes chocolate. And, well, so do I.

Later, when we're sitting there staring at all the leftover pizza, she says, "Let's look at the stars." I laugh because Mr. Adams next door has got his terrorism lights on and you couldn't see a star out if it was shooting straight at your head. He put them up last year. Mom yelled at him but he just said he was making the neighborhood safer. They've stopped speaking to each other. It's weird, they'll both be out in the front yard searching for their newspaper in the bushes and not say one word. Mom talked to a lawyer about it and was told Mr. Adams had rights. She said, "What about my rights to a clear sky?" And he said, "Your rights end at your fence."

My mom stands up. "He's out."

"Who's out?"

"Mr. Adams."

"Yeah, but he's got his light on."

"I know. But I've got a ladder and you can climb up and unscrew it."

I look at her and she's smiling. I'm wondering how many glasses of wine she's drunk. But I only notice one.

"It's freezing out," I try.

"But no clouds."

So before I know it we're outside in the backyard, checking out the opposition. Mr. Adams's front yard has this really tall metal fence around it, but, lucky for us, he didn't bother to do it in the back because the yards are separated by tall holly bushes that will shred you to pieces. In the back, way back, right next to the boundary with the people behind us, you can just squeeze through. So I do. Mom slides me the ladder. And a screwdriver. And I'm standing in his backyard, completely shined on by all that light.

"What if he's got a camera or something? Like a surveillance thing."

I can tell from Mom's face she hadn't thought of that. What an amateur.

"Wait a minute." She runs off and comes back with the George Bush mask she wore for Halloween.

"Here."

So I'm wearing a Bush mask, lugging a ladder down Mr. Adams's yard. I can barely see. I put the ladder against the house and lift up the mask to look. The light is so bright I'm blinded a second. It's hard to climb. At the top, I can't find where to unscrew the lamp so I give it a couple of whacks with the screwdriver. The glass cracks and the light blacks out immediately. Real terrorist-proof.

"Nic, look!" Over the hedge I can see her staring up at the stars, which are just shining through the yellow orange haze. I stay up at the top of the ladder because I feel closer to them, until Mom says, "Nic, quick! Get back here."

By the time I drag everything back through the hedge, Mom's hauled out her telescope and is trying to focus it toward Saturn. But when it finally finds the right spot the lens points at nothing. The haze has gotten the better of old Saturn. So we lie back on the metal slats of our sun loungers. It isn't so bad with our big coats on. We stare up at the sky and don't talk. This is what I like, when we're together and not talking. It's the best.

Mr. Adams shows up the next day. Turns out there was a camera connected to the light and it got someone in a bright green anorak and a Bush mask whacking the light to death. Mom is pretending to look all innocent and confused when I walk in and it's all over. The problem is, I'm wearing my coat because I'm heading out and it's real green and real obvious.

Mr. Adams settles for $1,000 in damages. Dad calls and yells at Mom for getting me involved and maybe screwing up my chances for college. Guess he doesn't think so much of her juvenile-delinquent upbringing skills, either. Mom puts down the phone, goes over to a chair, and leans her head down through her knees.

"You okay?"

"Just fine," she says, "Everything is just fine."

*   *   *

Kevin told me today he doesn't want to hang out with me anymore. He says I'm a loser. He says he and Jim Butts have been talking. They're sick and tired of waiting for me to make up my mind. If I'm not going to commit to Jesus I can go to hell and they won't care. At Bible class they sit together. It's not a big thing but . . .

Now it's like I don't exist. When I try to talk to Kevin within hearing distance of Jim Butts he ignores me. Just stares straight ahead like I'm some fly buzzing at the window. I don't know what I've done that's so wrong. And Jesus doesn't have much to say about it. I keep asking him for a sign that I'm okay. That I'm not a complete loser. But he's keeping his cards close to his chest on this one.

So I try to catch Kevin after Bible class. Before we have to get in the car, because it's impossible to talk about it with Mrs. Porter there in the front seat. But the second Dele wraps it up, Kevin hauls out of the room.

"Hey, Kevin, wait up . . ."

I rush after him. He's practically running.

"Kevin." I grab his arm.

He whirls around. "What?"

"I just wanted to talk—"

He pushes my arm away. "Will you leave me alone?"

"But—"

"Just get the hell away from me!"

"Ready to go, boys?" It's Mrs. Porter coming down the hall dangling her car keys. "Nic's got another ride home," Kevin says.

"Really?" She turns her eyes to me. "Is that true?"

". . . Uh, yeah."

"Alright, then." She smiles. "See you later."

I watch them walk off together. Mrs. Porter's skirt swishes back and forth. I remember Kevin asking me once what would be the worst thing that could happen to me. I said I didn't know, maybe get hit by a car or something, but not die—just lose my arms and legs. And then lie in a bed watching everybody go on with their lives and be so helpless I couldn't even kill myself. He agreed, that would pretty much suck. And I asked him what would be his worst thing and he said, Disappointing God. I thought, wow. So maybe he's right. Maybe I'm just not good enough.

But I want to make it okay with Kevin again. I want to say, Look, I'm tempted, I'm really tempted. I mean, it sounds great. And yeah, some days, absolutely I feel Him. Other days, nope. Not a sign. I guess it's that leap of faith they're talking about. The problem is, I'm used to being told I should know things for certain. Then some things I think I know turn out to be wrong. Like the nine planets they told me existed. Turns out there's only eight or, depending on which astronomy magazine you're reading, maybe eleven or more.

Mom says that's the beauty of life. There is always more to learn.

So I don't know. I just don't know. I just don't know who to believe anymore.

I figure I'll catch Kevin at the Teen Meet that Pastor Stowe has planned at the church. It's a new thing, every month, in the auditorium. When I get there a band is setting up. The American flag is back, a supersized one, hanging behind the stage.

About a hundred kids mill around, many of them wearing the I GOT HEAVEN T-shirts Pastor Stowe sells in the new church gift shop. The girls look hot. They run up to each other, hug and squeal. The guys walk around in packs pretending to ignore them. Parents smile and talk on the sidelines. In the back, at a long table, Mrs. Porter pours juice.

"Having a good time, Nic?" she says.

"Where's Kevin?"

"Oh, he's around here somewhere."

Then I see him. Giving Sandra a squeeze. She's looking up at him with adoring eyes and he's wearing baggy jeans and a leather necklace around his neck, acting like Joe Jesus. I'm just about to go over to him when guess who shows up right in front of me? Melissa. The stage lights reflect off her new braces and she's got a pimple bang in the middle of her forehead. She looks like she's been shot.

"Nic!"

She gives me a big hug, squeezing five seconds longer than I find completely necessary.

"Hello, Melissa."

"Isn't this just the greatest?"

"Yeah."

"I'm pumped." And she leans forward to grab me again.

Luckily, that's when Pastor Stowe jumps on stage and starts clapping with his arms above his head. Everybody cheers and claps back.

He walks to the middle and stops with his legs spread out. He shouts, "Who do we love?"

We yell, "Jesus!" Who else?

"Who do we want?"

"Jesus!"

"When do we want him?"

"Now!"

"WHEN DO WE WANT HIM?"

"NOW!!"

"Yeah, alright, amen!" He raises his fist in the air and we all start chanting "Je-sus, Je-sus, Je-sus!"

The place goes wild when the band digs in. And I've got to say they've got all the tricks: punchy trumpet, low-slung funk, a persistent drum. The singer, she's got yellow spiky hair and a torn T-shirt and black goo around her eyes, and I swear she's singing right to me:

Is everybody letting you down?
I can see your sad frown.
But I've got news for you.
You're gonna like it.
Yeah, yeah, yeah.
He's gonna help ya, yeah.
He's gonna be there, yeah.
Yeah, yeah, yeah,

Yeah, yeah,
Yeah, yeah, yeah,
Yeah, yeah.

Okay, so they're not Superchick but they're all right. I just stand there with the biggest lump in my throat because, well, it says so much. Everybody is waving their hands above their heads. We're all singing along, smiling at each other, feeling the same thing, feeling we're all in this together. Feeling that even if we're not allowed to talk to each other in the school halls because some of us might not be cool or popular enough, we have something in common. We have Jesus.

It must go on for about an hour. I never stop. I'm singing and jumping and so heated up you could probably fry a burger on my head.

Until Pastor Stowe appears again and motions to the band. They crank it down to a slow, peaceful tune. He moves to the front of the stage again. He raises one hand and croons into the microphone, "Are you lonely? Are you misunderstood?"

And it's like he's looking right at me.

He reaches out his hand toward us. He says, "I understand. And I'm gonna tell you what to do. Come on down. Give your life to Jesus. He understands. He will comfort you. He is the way. Lift your burdens and place them on His shoulder."

Then he gets down on his knees and bows his head.

When the lights suddenly go up, everyone blinks. There is silence, then *boom*, like Mach 5, everyone starts crying. People all around me going down like mowed grass. Girls mostly, sobbing their hearts out, hanging on to each other. Sandra hyper-ventilating in the corner, blue eye shadow all down her face. Parents fan out, offering cups of water.

Pastor Stowe has hopped up again and is handing out cards to kids. "Sign up, commit yourself to Jesus, and let all your pain go."

And they do. Wouldn't call it a stampede but definitely a full movement toward the front of the room.

I stand there, the sweat drying on my back, my heart still pounding. I look over to see Kevin on the sideline. Sandra has thrown her arms around his neck, sobbing. He's busy comforting her. He's also busy watching me.

And I think, Why not? Why not go up, grab the card, and sign my life away? Maybe Kevin knows something I don't. Maybe that's why he's so pissed off. Because he knows it will be good for me. And then maybe Sandra will let me get busy comforting her too.

"Nic?"

I turn to see Mrs. Porter. She's not two feet away, offering me a card.

I stare at it a second, then lift my eyes to hers.

Suddenly a door opens behind me and a hand hooks me around my neck and pulls me in. I land against the back wall of a small closet. Melissa locks the door. A lone bulb shines above us.

"What are you doing?"

Melissa rolls her eyes like it's so obvious what she's doing.

She raises her arms over her head and strips off her shirt. She wears a light green bra and the cups are overflowing.

My mouth drops open. She pulls me to her and starts kissing me. I'm so surprised I start kissing her back. She seems to know what she's doing. And I think, it's too bad about her face because her tongue is fantastic. She pulls away after a bit. I stare down at her boobs.

There is a sharp knock at the door. And a rattle of the doorknob.

"Nic. Nic. Are you in there?" It's Mrs. Porter.

Melissa puts her fingers to her lips.

"Are you okay in there?"

Melissa clicks off the light.

Mrs. Porter rattles the doorknob again. "Nic? Do you need help? Nic . . . Nic?"

I know she's not going to let it go so I have to answer. I call out, "No, thank you . . . ma'am," as politely as I can. Then I turn back to Melissa and get busy myself, praising the Lord for his infinite gifts.

Melissa comes over the next Tuesday, which is one of the days Layla doesn't come because Mom doesn't work very late. But there's still about two hours between me getting home and Mom getting home. So it's just me alone in the house and I have to let Melissa in. I mean, she's just standing there on my doorstep. What am I supposed to do? Let her freeze to death?

Inside she pulls me down on the couch and explores my

mouth with her tongue. I'm trying to keep up when suddenly she loses interest and pushes me off her. She wanders over to my science project.

"Is that it?" She checks out my cardboard presentation on Time.

"Yup."

"Kevin said you were doing something on heaven."

"Yeah, I had to stop."

"Why?"

"Mom didn't think much of my baton."

She nods to the door. "That her office?"

"Yeah, but . . ."

She walks right in and turns on the light.

"Is this where she does her work?"

"Yeah."

"Her godless work?"

I shrug. I reach for her again but she sidesteps me. She walks over to Mom's desk and starts fiddling with her books.

"She doesn't like people touching her stuff," I say.

"Don't you think it's unforgivable the way she brought you up? Not letting you know about Jesus?"

"But your mom didn't—"

"Oh, she sent me to Sunday school when I was younger. I just didn't pay much attention. Your mom didn't even tell you about Bible class. You had to find it all by yourself. I mean, we're talking child abuse here."

I look around. I never thought of that.

"Just think about it. Your mom could be an instrument of the devil. He's pretty sneaky."

When she sees my face, she strokes the back of my neck. "Oh, don't worry, I bet she doesn't even know what she's doing. She's just a puppet, doing it against her will. He does that. He takes prisoners." And she gives me another long, involved tongue waggle.

On Mom's computer screen, a gold planet twirls slowly. Melissa must be kissing with her eyes open because she suddenly breaks free and leans forward. "What is that?"

"It's a computer-generated image of a planet orbiting Upsilon Andromedae. She's trying to find out its mass."

"God will reveal it to her when He's ready."

"She's worried she might miss her deadline."

"Nic," she says, putting her arms around me, "what do you think He'd make of this room?"

I look around. The computer is bleeping and flashing bright red lights like it's keeping the planet on life support.

Melissa shakes her head. "Poor God. Don't you think He has enough problems without people nitpicking the details. Trying to refute His story. Coming up with wacky theories of their own. He's exhausted. Here He is trying to conquer Satan and your mom is quibbling about how old His universe is. *His* universe. Don't you think He knows how old it is?"

"Yeah, I don't know. Maybe."

"Maybe? Well, look at it this way. So your mom's looking

for her planet. What if she finds it? What if it's full of strange viruses that would make smallpox look like a sniffle?"

"Her planet is too far way. We'll never reach it." I pucker up and try to land on her lips but she pulls away.

"I'm sure Christopher Columbus never thought we'd reach the moon."

She has a point. That's when she drops to her knees and starts messing with the computer wires.

"Hey!"

"Do you want her to prove there is no God?"

"Finding life on another planet is not going to prove there is no God."

"There are no other planets in my Bible."

"You're saying my mom's the enemy?"

She pops her head up. "Let's just call her collateral damage."

And with one last yank she rips out the entire electrical circuit.

When Mom comes home, she finds me sitting in the dark next to her computer with its guts hanging out.

"Nic?" She turns on the lights. "What are you doing?"

She's so busy looking at me she hasn't noticed the computer yet. "Nic?"

And then she sees it. The gasp she makes sounds like a rake across her throat.

I stare straight ahead, not moving a muscle when she bends at her knees and screams. The force is like a wave pounding on the sand, over and over, until I'm crushed to shell.

"This is turning into a problem," she says, her eyes still red, when Dele comes home a half hour later.

"No, it isn't," I say. After all, it turned out she was connected to the university server and she didn't lose anything. She might not believe in God but she's no dummy.

She talks to Dele. "I'd appreciate it if you could speak with us tonight."

"I will be right down," he says, heading upstairs to deposit his bag of Bibles and slide into something more comfortable.

"Thank you."

I know what she's gonna do. She's gonna ask him to leave because she thinks he's poisoning my mind. Making me believe stuff she doesn't want me believing. And I say screw that. I can believe whatever I want. She doesn't own me. She doesn't own my mind. Talk about thought control, thought police. So I'm making sure I am ready for the talk. I have all my arguments. She isn't going to push me around. She isn't going to get rid of Dele without a fight. A crusade. That's what it's going to be.

So when Dele comes down, she's sitting in the living room in the big armchair like a queen. I'm expecting her to raise her sceptre.

"Would you like a glass of water?" she asks. And Dele can see that she's only being polite, so he says no. But I say, "Hell, yeah," just to make her get up and do it. I sit down next to Dele and smile at him like we're gonna win this thing.

But she ignores me and says, "I need my space back."

Dele says, "Of course."

She says, "Thank you."

He says, "No, thank you for letting me stay as long as you have."

She starts to say . . . but I jump in with, "Hey! What about me?" And they both look at me like, Yeah, this has something to do with you. Not.

So I say, "He's not going."

Dele says, "Now, Nic . . ."

I say, "No, no way. I like you here." And I pull my ace out. "It's like having a dad here."

But Mom has her own ace. "Your father is coming home, Nic. And we need the space."

Chapter Twenty-three

So Dad's coming home. I can't believe it. All that praying and look what happens. You just can't knock it. But there is something wrong with the picture. I don't like the way Dele pats Mom's shoulder when he leaves the room. I don't like the way she smiles at him like they know something I don't.

So as soon as Dele slinks off to his room I follow Mom into the kitchen. Mom takes out the mop from the closet. It's showtime.

I lean against the kitchen counter. "When you went to your astronomy conference, you weren't going to an astronomy conference, were you?"

She puts the mop back again. "No."

I wait.

"I went to a doctor in New York to see about my dizziness."

"Why didn't you tell me?"

"I didn't want to worry you."

"I'm fourteen."

"I thought I'd get better."

"You mean you're not?"

"Not as quickly as I thought."

"But you'll get better."

"I should. It's amazing the drugs they have these days. Good ol' science."

She tries to leave it at that. She even heads for the door. But I catch her. "But you lied to me. You said you'd never lie to me."

It's a big thing for her to be reliable. To keep her word. She's always said I could depend on her to tell me the truth as she knows it.

She turns around. "You're right. I'm sorry. It was the one thing you could count on and I blew it."

"So is it serious?"

She nods her head. "Yes, it's serious. It seems to have no sense of humor at all." So she explains what she has. It's a head thing. I look it up on the Internet and it isn't pretty. Your head can explode and all your thoughts will be obliterated. Of course she doesn't see it that way. She sees it as a minor setback, a blip in her radar screen, something she can outrun, outthink. Time will tell.

Next morning, Dele is ready to go. He stands at our door with his big suitcase and extra stuff shoved into a couple of plastic bags. He's stripped his bed and shoved his sheets into the washing machine. He's hired a taxi to take him away. Mom stumbles down the stairs in her ratty pink bathrobe. They're really polite about it.

"Thank you very much, Lucy, for taking me into your home."

"No problem, Reverend." She pulls her robe belt tighter.

"I am very much obliged."

"It was my pleasure," she says, and they both smile.

When the door closes behind him I look at her and she says, "Don't you look at me like that."

I shake my head.

"Don't you shake your head at me."

"He has no place to go."

"The church has other accommodations. He can stay there."

"Really?"

"Of course."

"But why—"

"He wanted to work on you. Did he succeed?"

I don't know what to say. And I sure don't know if I should be pissed off or flattered.

"You mean Dele lied too?"

She defends him. "No. I wouldn't say he lied exactly. I'd say he overstated the truth."

She stretches and blows out her cheeks. "Boy, it's nice to have my house back." She saunters to the kitchen. "You hungry?"

Mom's skin is so pale these days you can see all her veins sometimes. On the side of her head right next to her temple, it's all blue. Talk about thin skin. She's like an alien. I don't know where she comes from. Luckily I've got my dad's darker skin.

My life is hard enough without having pale skin and red hair. Tom Bradshaw has red hair and Gina Kosta told me it gives her the creeps. Better to have a normal-color hair when you're a guy. One that doesn't make you stand out. Kevin says the devil had red hair. That one I didn't know. But somehow I'm not surprised. I should tell my mom. Knowing her, she'd take it as a compliment.

She's been too quiet lately. Not her usual mouthy self. The other morning I spilled some Gatorade and she said to clean it up. I told her to clean it up herself and usually she'd hand me my ass on a platter, but she just looked at me with these big, sad eyes and said, "Nic." And, well, I felt about as big as a cockroach and I scooted over real quick to grab the paper towels. Shoot me before I have to see that look again.

I can tell she's not feeling so great. She sort of shuffles around. She's more absentminded than ever. The other day she forgot to move the trolley from behind the car in the supermarket parking lot and backed right into it.

And then she gives me an iPod. Just like that.

I'm in the kitchen wolfing down a couple of Pop-Tarts before school and she wanders in and sits down. She slides over a box to me. I stare at it. "What's this for?"

"It's because I love you."

I look at her. Yeah. Right.

She says, "Really."

And I say okay. I hesitate a second before I reach out and take it.

"Thanks, Mom."

"You're welcome."

She sits there, hands in her lap, watching my face. I'm not sure what she wants so I nod again and race out the door.

Have you ever noticed how smooth the world becomes when it's accompanied to music? Ever hear "What a Wonderful World," by Louis Armstrong? Put that on and everyone walking along looks happy. Everything is golden even if it's raining. Like on a video. Put on "Skin o' my Teeth" by Megadeth and everyone is walking toward their doom. I wish I had a sound track to my life. Everything I did would suddenly be in rhythm. All the sad bits wouldn't be stupid, but they'd take on this weight. I think what's so sad about sad is that it often happens for a stupid reason. Like Brad Hornsby's brother. He got drunk and smashed his car into a lamppost. Sad but really stupid. But can you imagine if U2 was playing in the background? The squeal, the screech of the brakes, his drunken eyes opening in horror, his body propelling forward, smashing into the windshield, pan down to his seat belt, which was not buckled, the rising steam from the crushed engine. Majestic. Not stupid. A real tour de force.

I was thinking I'd like to go out to Nirvana. And on that third bar when he goes ningningning . . . That's when it happens. It's all in the music score. If you arrange it right, your life becomes like a really excellent video clip.

When Dad comes home to stay, he and Mom act too polite. He's a stranger in his own house. When he first walks in she offers him a beer and shakes potato chips into a bowl and we all sit in the living room like dorks. I ask him why he can take so much time off and he tells me he's on sabbatical. He's writing a book.

"On what?"

"On the gods of death. I'm writing about the correlation between a culture's belief in death gods and its propensity toward violence."

"You get a sabbatical to write that?"

"Yep."

"But why do it here?"

He leans back as comfortably as you can in a Shaker chair. "What better place?" he answers, and he looks at Mom and they smile some secret smile. And it makes me really happy. A hopeful happy. The kind that makes a flip in your stomach.

The weird thing, though, is he's not sleeping in their bedroom, Mom and Dad's. He's camping in the guest room where Dele used to be. He's shoved his suitcase in the corner like he's in a motel.

"Why are you in here?" I ask while he's getting dressed in the morning. He's tearing through his bags, looking for his underwear. His watch and change are on the nightstand. His tan suit hangs on the back of the door.

"We have to move slowly."

"Why?

"Because."

"Because why?"

He says, "You know, Nic, there are some questions I'd rather not answer."

"Why?"

And he looks at me.

"Okay, okay."

So Dad's living back with Mom now. They're not really married; they're not anything. I'm not sure what their point is. Maybe they'll let me know.

The next night we sit down to a fancy roast beef dinner that Mom cooked. We end up having the potatoes after the ice cream because they take longer than she expects, but, hey, I think it's her best yet. After forking it all down, Dad sits back and pats his flab. "Now, this is nice."

Mom swirls her red wine in her glass. "Ah, you missed this, didn't you?"

"More than you know."

It's nice being a family again. Having them on both sides of me, gazing across the table at each other and smiling. It's a good night: Dad watching TV in the living room, Mom checking her e-mails in her office, me catching up with the MySpace gang in the kitchen. All back under the same roof. It's a good feeling.

Later they both come in and kiss me good night when I'm in bed. Then they just stand there while I'm trying to read, until I say, "Can I have a little privacy, please?" And they both stumble out, giggling. Then they go into their separate rooms. I can hear two doors closing. And I shake my head and think, modern families, man.

But now my dad acts like he owns me. He acts like he can tell me what to do. He says, What the hell is this mess? He says,

Clean up your room. He says, Don't you have anything better to do than lie around all day? He wants to do *projects* together. Mom asks Dad to mow the lawn and he says, Doesn't Nic have any chores? I want to say, Yeah, living with you, pal. I miss Dele who, I now realize, was seriously singing for his supper.

Guess who's dancing for his dinner now?

Dad says, "That patio needs cleaning. There's moss all over it."

I say, "The rain will wash it away."

He yells, "Nic, get out there!"

"Make me." I walk away, waiting for him to come after me. But he doesn't. I can hear the car door slam and the engine roar. I think, hey, hey, hey, who's the boss now? But when I come home from science club my PlayStation is gone.

Mom's pretending she knows nothing about it. Dad is being Homer at the table, reading the newspaper like he's God or something. So I have to—get this—*apologize*. Four times, because he doesn't like my tone. I'm not groveling enough.

Luckily, in the future, parents are going to be obsolete. Women are going to leave their eggs in pods, pay for superior sperm to fertilize them, and then rent incubators to bake them into babies. Then, after nine months, they'll just make an appointment to pick them up, maybe in the evening after they've come back from the gym but before *Desperate Housewives*. And then they'll just bring them home, stash them in the baby wing, and buy some robot to take care of them. Maybe visit them on weekends. There will be none of the "But I'm your father" crap because they won't know who the hell he is. He'll be, like, donor #435-49547. And even if they did know who he is he'll have so many kids he won't be that obsessive about what you're doing. How can you keep track of a thousand kids? They'll all be really good-looking too, with perfect hair so they'll have it easy when it comes to middle school. Me, I was just born too soon.

On Sunday I decide to mosey over to see how Dele is doing. I find him in a section of the church I've never noticed before. It's got a couple of bedrooms and a small kitchen with a microwave and a broken coffee maker. Dele's in one of the bedrooms, winding his tie around his neck, getting ready for the service. But he stops when he sees me and gives me the biggest thump on the back like I've been lost in the Arctic.

"Nic! How are you?"

"Fine. Yeah. Good."

"It is good to see you." He holds me by the shoulders.

"Uh, I just thought I'd stop by."

"Good. Good. I am glad you are here."

But I want to know. "Why didn't you just stay here before?"

He smiles. "Jesus asked me to look in on you. How is your mother?"

"Okay."

"You must say hello to her for me."

"Sure."

He turns to go.

"Was it a number thing?" I say.

"What do you mean?"

"I mean, did you try to save me to add to your portfolio?"

He blinks, then smiles. "Something like that. It is good to see you, Nic."

I notice a new photo by his bedside. It's a small kid wrapped in a bright red shawl. "Who's that?"

"That is Lolo." He tells me Lolo's mom died of AIDS and Dele's church back home is looking after him. They've started a tiny orphanage with the money Dele sends over. Lolo looks pretty pitiful.

"He is blind," Dele says.

"Wow, that sucks."

He gazes at the photo then blinks away. "I must get these leaflets distributed. I see you later."

I'm just about to leave when Kevin and his family come in. They have some tall, really blond exchange student from Bosnia with them. Kevin's sister is eyeing him up big time. So I decide to watch them and see what happens. Turns out his name is Jans and he's Catholic, and at the part when Pastor asks if anyone wants to be saved the guy thinks it's time for communion so he jumps up and practically runs down the aisle. Maybe he's trying to get away from Charlene. He doesn't notice that it's only him until he's too close to Pastor Stowe to get away. Everybody's clapping and Pastor Stowe is waving his arms, yelling, "Thank you, Jesus, thank you, Jesus," and practically headlocks the guy. The best part is when Pastor Stowe shushes everybody up so we can hear his answer and he asks him, "Do you accept Jesus Christ as your personal savior?"

And Jans says, "Well, actually . . ."

But Pastor Stowe isn't listening too hard because he clamps him on his head with his hands and prays like crazy. When Jans stumbles back to his seat I can tell he's going to be on the next plane out of here.

Hey, what can I say? We're a friendly country.

The next Sunday Pastor Stowe announces that he wants our church to grow. Like a corporation. He wants to attract more people and build even bigger facilities. He's hired a couple of consultants. When he introduces them, these two guys in black jeans and turtlenecks stand up and wave. He now wants the congregation to dig even deeper in their pockets and make the Lord proud. He says all the dough will reflect God's power and love. Enough of us living on scraps. It is time we proclaim our faith.

Kevin gets ahold of a blueprint. Pastor Stowe is planning a media room with black leather couches. He's going to incorporate the latest multimedia technologies into Sunday services. There's even talk of starting up our own TV channel. He's dragging us into the twenty-first century, he says.

The thing is, Dele's against it. He thinks we're spending too much on redecorating, which could go to charity and helping out the local community. Pastor Stowe says he appreciates Dele's sentiments but the Lord calls us to different ministries, Dele to help the poor and Pastor Stowe to make sure we are not obliterated in this day of decadence. We have our orders. May we work together to praise His word.

But Dele isn't letting it go.

They have a big meeting about it. Most people are really excited about the new designs. Most people except for Dele and Mrs. Vogler whose kid got run over. Dele keeps saying, "Is this the right direction?" Until finally Pastor Stowe says, "Dele, I would appreciate it if you would stop interfering."

Dele looks pissed off. "You call it interfering?"

Pastor Stowe opens his arms wide. "We want a church that is thinking about success. We are bound for glory. Self-actualization. That's what I like to call it. God wants us to be successful. Success is not a bad word. It is a good word. The best."

"What about helping people?" cries Mrs. Vogler.

"You know, there are different churches for different kinds of people. One of God's many miracles. I like to call our church a CDC—a Can-Do Church. Not a gimme church. Not always putting our hand out all the time, asking for money for this orphan or that. People get tired. It makes them feel guilty. God doesn't want us to feel guilty. He wants us to enjoy what we have. He wants us to be happy."

"But . . ." Dele starts.

Pastor Stowe raises his hand. "I am the head of this church. I will make decisions as I see fit. Though we welcome you as a brother, it is time now for you to shut your mouth."

And I have to tell you that a lot of the congregation cheers.

Dele's eyes get so small and black it sends a shiver up my back.

Then, maybe to soften it all Pastor Stowe adds, "I have prayed and Jesus has told me he wants this."

That's when Mrs. Vogler calls out, "Jesus doesn't want this. Jesus thinks you're an asshole." Then she waddles out the back door.

Well, I don't know what Jesus thinks but I can tell you the rest of the congregation is pretty shocked.

Within a week, my parents start fighting. About stupid stuff. It's mostly my mom. It's like she's got this hot poker and she's jamming it into all my dad's soft spots. She's so happy he's back that she's hellbent on his applying for a job in town so he can stay permanently. But he doesn't want to. He says he likes it down in Williamsburg. She rolls her eyes. "Ah, yes, all those sexy tree huggers."

"I don't have the choices you do, Lucy."

"Write three more articles a year, Robert, and you'd have your pick."

He stands up without a word and walks out.

The problem is, Mom has trouble understanding people who don't want to be the best at something. She probably considers it an evolutionary malfunction. Her genes have got their orders and are marching forward.

After that, Dad starts doing his writing at our local library. Then, one night after I'm in bed, he starts shouting.

"Will you just stop! For the love of God, will you just stop!" My stomach feels sick because it sounds like he's crying. A grown man crying.

Then I hear the front door slam. I race downstairs and swing open the door and find him sitting in the driver's seat of his car. He's staring at me through the windshield like he knew I would appear. He signals me with his hand to come with him but I can't move. My feet are stuck to the ground, my mind is paralyzed. The only thing moving is my heart, which beats like a bat touring hell. It seems an hour goes by in that stare. I feel like an amoeba breaking in two. Finally he turns his head and backs down the driveway.

"Nic?" Mom calls from the kitchen.

I watch Dad shift gears once he's on the street. He takes one last look at me and disappears down the road.

"Nic!"

"Yeah?" I almost whisper it.

"I just wanted to know if you're still here."

"Yeah, I'm still here."

Chapter Twenty-four

When Dr. Rajid calls, I take the message.

"Another doctor?" I say when Mom comes home. She nods like she's expecting it. When she disappears into her room to call back Dr. Rajid, she closes the door. I can just hear her voice but not the words. And then I don't hear anything. I want to know what's happening, but the door has "Don't you dare come in" written all over it. So I go downstairs and dig into a bowl of ice cream. She doesn't come downstairs for an hour and when she does she is all smiles and real efficient. But her eyes are cherries from crying.

"What did he say?"

"Who?"

"The doctor."

"Oh, him. He said, um, just that I need to take more tests . . ."

"Why?"

"Well, um, the first ones weren't great . . ."

Mom has to stay in the hospital for a couple of days. So Dad comes back. He'd been staying with Aunt Ruth. He walks in, drops his bags at the door, and leads me to the kitchen. He sits in Mom's place at the kitchen table.

"Sit down, Nic."

He tells me the doctor's found something. And it isn't good.

"How much not good?"

He sighs deeply. "It's going to be challenging."

When I look up at him I see that look. That look which reminds me that grownups are just as clueless as I am. It scares the shit out of me.

"Challenging?" I say. "You mean if she tries really, really hard she'll get better?"

He looks at me like he's laying eyes on me for the first time. "I mean, if we try really, really hard we might get through this."

So I've been reading on the Internet everything about brain tumors. Did you know that each year about 190,000 people in the United States are diagnosed with primary or metastatic brain tumors? They're the third-leading cause of cancer death in people aged twenty to thirty-nine. You can get headaches, seizures, personality changes, eye weakness, nausea, speech disturbances, or memory loss. And there's like over 120 different types of brain tumors, which means they're hard to treat. All doctors have is radiation therapy, chemotherapy, and surgery. In the end only 30 percent of women survive five years. Not to mention the complicated fact that the brain is the control center for just about everything.

It's amazing how many people you've heard of who have

died of brain tumors. Pete Sampras's tennis coach, Tim Gullik-son. Bob Marley. Astronaut Deke Slayton. Lyle Alzado. Gene Siskel. Lee Atwater, who Mom says was this real bad guy from the Republican National Committee. Once Mom would prob-ably have said, Isn't that appropriate? Though I don't think she'd say that now.

What she's saying now is, "Don't worry. We're going to beat this thing. It's amazing what medicine can do."

Kevin says, "God's attacking her brain. Think about it."

After school Dad drives me over to visit Mom in the hospital. But instead of driving into the underground parking lot, he drops me off in front.

"Aren't you coming?" I say.

"I talked to her on the phone."

"Don't you want to see her?"

"She wants to see you."

I must be staring at him like an idiot because he says, "It's okay. Go. I'll pick you up at five."

When I walk into Mom's room, she's tucked in bed like a child with sheets up to her chest. She's lying back, staring at the ceiling.

"In the end we're all alone," she says.

I swipe some chocolates from the box of Whitman candies someone's left her.

"I'm not alone," I say. "I've got you and Dad and Dele and Mrs. Porter."

Mom smiles. "Ah, yes, I forgot about Mrs. Porter."

I spit the chocolate with the strawberry filling into a Kleenex. "And the people at church."

She scratches at the bandages taping down her IV. "That's nice. I'm just saying that when we go, we go by ourselves."

"Not if someone's holding your hand."

She looks down at her blue veiny hand. "Well, I suppose that's technically true . . ."

"I don't want to talk about it."

"I'm sorry. I don't know why I go on like that."

"You're not going to die."

"You know, I wasn't even thinking of me. I was thinking in general. In the abstract. It's a bad habit I've got."

"Yeah."

A TV laugh track blasts in from the hall outside. A nurse passes Mom's door and gives her a friendly wave.

Mom bellows at her. "Will someone please turn off that goddamn TV?"

The nurse retreats.

"Nic."

I don't answer. I'm staring at her chart trying to figure out what it all means.

"Nic. Look at me."

I peer closer. What the hell does "meningioma" mean?

"Nic. It's going to be okay."

"Who said it wasn't?"

Mom settles back against her pillow. "When I get out of here I'm going to do something good. Something good for people."

"What people?"

She waves her hand in the air. "You know, people. All those poor sick children wandering around homeless. Think of the house we live in. It's huge. They could have all stayed with us."

I don't say anything because she's right. The rec room alone could house fifty little kids.

"I guess I thought I was too busy. I guess I thought I wouldn't be able to do what was important to me. And then you realize what's important."

"You can get some kids now."

She laughs.

"Really. You could fly someplace, pick up a couple of kids, and fly back."

"I'm a coward, Nic. I couldn't even go to a dog pound. I would never be able to choose. No, I've been very lucky in my life and I've wasted it."

"What were you supposed to do, save everybody?"

"One would have been a good start."

"The church has a sponsor-a-child program."

"Yes, Joanne Porter told me."

I look up from where I'm poking at the buttons on her bed to see what moves. "She did? When?"

"She came by this morning. We got to talking."

"She came here?"

"Yes."

"To the hospital?"

"It was very nice of her."

"She bring cookies?"

"Yup. Peanut swirl."

"Where are they?"

"I ate them."

"*All* of them?"

She shrugs. "I gave them to the nurses. They were like vultures around a carcass."

"What did she say?"

"Joanne? She was very good, actually. Very restrained. Her brother had cancer. So she knew all the lingo. She nursed him until he died. That part I didn't like."

After pressing all the buttons on Mom's bed, I have run out of things to do. She's too tired to play any games. Pretty soon she stops talking and just stares at the wall. It's like she's run out of batteries. So I go in search of Dr. Rajid. The nurse at the main station says he's not available.

"Why?"

"He's busy."

"Doing what?"

She looks up. "Taking care of people. It's what doctors *do.*"

Really, it's pretty low when a nurse is sarcastic.

"Well, find him," I say. "I need to talk to him."

She returns to staring at her computer screen.

"It's important," I say, trying to sound threatening, like she should listen to me, like the possibility that I have an Uzi and three grenades in my pocket isn't remote.

She looks over at the other nurse and rolls her eyes.

So I have to walk around, open doors to linen closets, offices, even a staff toilet. I peek through the window of an operating room. Let me tell you, that's not a great place to spend your working hours in—bright lights, blinking machines, the Grim Reaper checking his watch in the corner. There's a doctor in there, a tall guy with a green shower cap on his head, standing over some poor sucker's body. He's not even looking into the man's skull where his brain is, he's looking at these screens laid out in front of him. The nurse has blood on her gloves. The doctor's are immaculate.

I finally find Dr. Rajid in some staff room looking at somebody's brain scan. He's pointing at a dark spot and talking up a storm. Three other doctors stand around him, hanging on his every word. I step up behind him. "You're Dr. Rajid, aren't you?"

Dr. Rajid takes one look at me and says, "Get this child out of here."

Child?

I get closer, right at his shoulder, and say "Do you believe in God?" Because, really, that's all I want to know. See if he's got some kind of inside track. Though Dad says Dr. Rajid thinks he's God himself.

And boy, everybody suddenly gets real quiet.

But he ignores me and keeps pointing to the spot on the scan and talking. Two seconds later the security guard shows up, a big black guy with a big black gun at his hip and an assortment of other take-down goodies hanging from his belt. When he says, "Let's go," there aren't many options besides agreeing.

He turns out to be a pretty nice guy, though. He doesn't

shove me around or stun me with a laser. Though that would be pretty interesting. No, he just leads me by the arm right back to my mom's room.

At her door, I figure I might as well ask him. "Do *you* believe in God?"

He looks over at my mom sleeping, her eyes halfway shut, her mouth open and snoring. He says, "This must be mighty difficult for you."

I wish people would stop saying that. It isn't so difficult for me. I'm not the one being drained of blood every two seconds. I'm not the one barfing into our mixing bowl.

"Do you?" I ask again.

He cocks his head. "Well, I guess you could say I believe in a . . . spiritual essence. I don't know if it's a god exactly but there seems to me to be something around us or maybe in us . . ."

And I nod quickly to speed him up because I've heard this one before. I need something more specific.

"Yeah, yeah. But do you think there is someone out there you can talk to?"

He peers down at me. "Do *you* need someone to talk to?"

"No, I mean, do you ever talk to anyone?"

"Oh. Um, sure. Sometimes. In a more kind of spatial sense. A transcendental conversation, if you will . . ."

"What about Jesus?"

"Jesus." He smiles. "Now, he's certainly captured people's imagination."

"Do you believe in Him?"

"Believe in him? Well, he certainly was a hi—"

"Historical figure. Yeah, I know that. But do you think He's still around?"

He scratches his smooth chin. "As in the sky?"

"I guess."

"No, I must say I've never fully gone down that road."

I nod.

He looks over. "Do you?"

"I'd like to."

He nods. "It's an attractive option. . . . Can I get you a soda?"

Chapter Twenty-five

Mom's at home now. Taking a bucket of pills and doing chemo. She's even back at the university part-time, still working on her baton. And she's working as quickly as she can. Right now it's hard to find an earth-sized planet, they're just too small to detect. But she can look for Jupiter-sized ones and study them. She's got one that's wobbled into her sights near Gliese 876 and she's studying the hell out of it.

But after awhile, her hair falls out. Even though she wore this skull cap that was supposed to keep it in place. When she took it off all her hair stuck to the inside. Carla went out and bought her a couple of scarves and helped her wind them around her head. She looks like a pirate.

"I'd kill for a drink. Champagne, Black Russian, Manhattan, martini with three olives, Sea Breeze . . ." She's been listing all the drinks she's looking forward to drinking once her doctor gives her the all-clear.

And though she doesn't tell me, I know she's been on the Internet looking for miracle cures. I check out her history and there it is: cancer cures. Do you know how many sites there are? A zillion. And you wouldn't believe the stuff they're trying to sell you. There's a place in Mexico that offers a complete brain transplant. It's cheap but you'll come out with an uncontrollable taste for burritos.

Ask for another one, I'm full of them.

Look, I'm just trying to be cheerful, like they want me to be. Like they're trying to be and not doing a very good job at it. It's like a morgue around here. All anybody can think about, talk about, try not to talk about, is the tumor growing inside Mom's brain. It's like another member of the family.

And I can see it's affected her brain already because some days she works on a scrapbook. Let me say that again. My mom— you know my mom by now—sits on the couch, wrapped in a blanket, with this huge baby-blue book with empty pages on her lap. She goes through a huge box of old photos, snipping and pasting away. I don't think you realize what a thing this is. When Mom first heard about scrapbooking, she said these women obviously have too much time and too little brains. And here she is playing Mrs. Betty Scrapbook.

"Where did you get that?"

She makes a precise snip, her tongue clenched between her teeth. "Joanne brought it over."

"Mrs. Porter brought over a scrapbook?"

"Yeah. I hadn't thought of it but it's a great idea. If a bit ghoulish."

"You hate scrapbooks."

"Well, they're not so bad. They give you lots of memories.

I can see why they're so addictive. You really relive your whole life doing one."

"Why are *you* doing one?"

She looks up at me, then down at the photo she's snipping. "You know, I've wanted to do a photo album ever since you were born and I just never found the time. So here I am. What do you think of that?"

"Is that me?"

"Yup. Three months old. Aren't you just the cutest-wutest wittle thing?"

"Ugh."

Occasionally she'll have an angry day. Usually she keeps a lid on it but then she'll become a raving lunatic. Once when I come down in the morning I find her sitting at the kitchen table, staring at nothing. When I walk by and don't say anything, she just about rips me a new one.

"Can't you say hello?"

"Huh?

"Hello. I'm a person in the room. You have come in. The polite thing to do is say hello."

"Hi."

"Hi."

"We don't have any milk," I say, staring into the refrigerator. Wrong move.

"Well, why don't you get your lazy ass out of the door and get some?"

"I can't drive."

"You can walk, can't you?"

I reach for the juice. She covers her head with her hands. "I can't believe this awful person I've become."

And I don't correct her because, you know what? She *is* awful sometimes. She can be such a bitch it's unbelievable. She always apologizes, which is one thing for her, but she still does it. I head for the door.

"Where are you going?"

"Back to my room."

"Why? Is it too awful to stay here?"

I stare at her like, duh.

"Fine, get the hell out." She puts her head down and starts bawling.

I roll my eyes because I don't need this. Good day bad day good day bad day, come on. We all have bad days but she just loses it.

So I start for the door again and she swings her head up and growls, "Don't you dare leave me."

"I was going to get some milk."

The change is incredible. "Were you? I'm sorry, dear. You're so good sometimes. And I'm so awful. I don't know what comes over me. I'm sorry. I'm sorry." And she holds out her hand and I take it, mumbling, It's alright, thinking, Damn, now I have to walk all the way to Calvert to find milk.

When I get back she's dressed and her scarf is wound around her head. Her face is still splotchy but she's got lipstick on and it glows against her pale skin. She's acting all efficient like she has a clue where anything is. She looks over at the laundry basket and I can see she's fighting the urge to just tear off all her clothes and crawl back into bed.

"Okay, now," she says and reaches for the detergent.

I can't tell anyone at school. I'm an outcast enough as it is. Adding a mother with serious cancer would bump me down to the zone of zit-picking, dandruff-flaking bottom feeders. Besides, it's nobody's business. It's private. But my parents must have called the school to inform the administration because one day Mr. Branden grabs me on the way out.

"I'm sorry to hear about your mother," he says.

"I don't know what you mean."

"About her being sick."

"She's fine."

"But I—"

"I don't know what she's been telling you but she's completely healthy."

He opens his mouth, then closes it. He pats me on the arm. "You're the expert," he says and turns away.

Some days after school I'll tiptoe in and up the stairs and sit on my bed, listening to my iPod. But I feel weird just sitting there while she's lying in the next room, waiting for I don't know what. So I'll get up sometimes and go stand at her door and she'll smile like I'm a bunch of daisies.

Mom better not die. I feel guilty even thinking about it. I've never been here before. It's not something they teach you at school. Maybe they should have a class in it. Called Death and How to Survive It. The first thing they'd have to teach you is to never go to an atheist funeral. I've been to two. They are not a

hell of a lot of fun. They try to be cheery because they're supposed to be celebrating a person's life, but there's no MC like
a pastor or anything so people just wander around with huge
craters in their hearts. They read the dead person's favorite po-
ems, play their favorite music, and serve organic wine and beer.
Then, at the end, instead of saying, See you later, you have to
say good-bye. Take it from me. Stay away from them.

Carla starts coming around a lot, trying in her weird way
to cheer us up. She brings over books and toys for a kid way
younger than I am, but Mom gives me the warning look and
says, "Isn't that nice of Carla?" and I've got to say, "Yeah, Carla,
thanks. Thanks a bunch." Luckily she's stopped bringing
around her tofu salad because Mom finally told her she hates
it. Now she brings double-chocolate brownies instead. She's
the one who brought up maybe getting a priest to come over if
Mom wants. And Mom just started laughing her head off. She
had tears rolling down her eyes. And Carla got all huffy and
said, "Well, I don't know . . . I just thought, you know, some
people return to their roots . . ."

And Mom reached out her hand to her and said, "Carla,
you are a dear, dear friend."

Dad suggested finding a Buddhist monk but Mom said, "I
wouldn't know a Buddhist belief if it bit me in the head." And
when Dad started to tell her about one she put up her hand
and said, "Stop. I'm not shopping now."

He said, "Last suggestion: How about a Humanist?"

Mom said, "I'm sure they are nice people but I have my own

humans already around me." And that was the end of all that stuff.

"You sure you're not tempted?" I ask her one morning, offering her my Bible.

She looks up from her paperback. "Is that what you expected? That when the going got tough I'd change my mind?"

I shrug.

"You hear that?" she says.

"What?"

"That."

A bird is chirping away outside, singing its pea-sized heart out. Mom sits there smiling. "Beautiful, isn't it?"

It sounds all nice and gooey and understanding, doesn't it? But it isn't really. Carla yells at me when she sees the kitchen sink full of dishes and crap everywhere. One day, she walks in, sees me tossing my empty Mountain Dew can at the overflowing garbage, and screams, "Are you kidding me?"

And I'm like, What?

She grabs me and marches me to the garbage can and tells me to take it out. "It's time you start taking responsibility for yourself!"

I tell her to go to hell.

I'm not going to go into what they all call me after that.

Mom asks me up to her room. It smells of sick.

"You know, you do survive it," she says.

"What?"

"Your adolescence."

"Maybe you did." And I stare out the window at the car she hasn't driven lately.

"Maybe you should take a page from Dele's book."

"The Bible?"

"Well, not specifically. But maybe think of others, help others, look around. See someone unhappier than yourself and concentrate on helping them. It'll make you feel better."

"Is that why he does it?"

"Maybe not, but it sure seems to work. Besides"—she smiles—"just think how nice it will look on your college application." She laughs, then puts her hand to her head. "Ouch."

So I try turning over a new leaf. Try to help Mom out. I do the laundry. I pile it on the stairs where it's probably going to stay until I have to bring it upstairs myself. Am I the only one who sees it? I mop the floor and take out the garbage. Soon the house is immaculate. And nothing. Nada. Not a peep. I'm not expecting applause or anything but a thank-you would be nice.

No, Mom comes down, takes one look at the microwaved scrambled eggs I cooked for her, makes a face, and retreats back upstairs. Then Dad stomps in with some groceries. He deposits the bags on the counter, pours a glass of OJ, drinks it down, and lets out a burp. He then prowls around the kitchen looking for something to eat.

I say, "Don't you walk on that floor with your boots."

He looks at me like I've got three heads.

"I just washed it."

He looks down. "You did?"

"Yeah, and those grapes you're demolishing? I washed those too."

And you know what he does? He comes up and gives me the biggest bear hug. "You are a good son," he says, his voice all choked up, and then he walks out the door into the backyard where I can hear him crying, trying to muffle it with his hands, and I think, That's more like it.

The next day Sergeant Roberto Aguilar e-mails me. He writes: "I'm sorry to hear about your mom. She sounds like a nice lady. Tell her you love her. I speak from experience. If my kid grew up to tell me he loved me, I'd leave this earth a happy man."

But I haven't told my mom I love her since I was six years old. It's not something you go around saying. If you went around saying it all the time, she might think there's something wrong. Like maybe it's not true. Or I've screwed up or I want something. And anyway, how do you start a conversation like that? Oh, by the way . . . in case you're wondering . . . So I just come out with it. We're playing chess and I'm winning. Of course. I scoop up her queen and say, I love you, Mom. And she laughs because she thinks I'm saying it because she's given up her queen but then she sees my face. And I say it again.

"I love you, Mom."

It's the hardest thing to say, isn't it? I mean, it seems so obvious but to say it. Get it out there. It's like you're dropping a bomb.

She doesn't say anything, just takes my hands and kisses them over and over, getting them all slobbery and snotty. Then she laughs and tries to wipe them off with the blanket. She holds them so tight they hurt.

"I don't know how long I have with you, Nic."

"I know."

And then she hugs me. She tries to pull me close but I'm too big, so I lean over her lap awkwardly. She's all skin and bones. And that's when I start to cry.

Chapter Twenty-six

B ut I know there is one thing I can do to cheer up my damsel in distress. I pick up my jousting lance, click shut my helmet, and ride to battle. I compete in the Maryland Middle School science fair.

I arrive at the arena and stride through the crowds to my allotted spot. The place is crawling with GOSes. Geeks on Steroids. I try to avoid the whole crew on the sidelines who are frothing at the mouth—their parents.

"Good afternoon, Mr. Delano-Coen. I'm glad you could join us."

It's Mr. Vinay. He's got on red-and-black check pants and a matching jacket. It's enough to make a kid ditch science forever. He nods at my board and title: TIME—WHAT TO MAKE OF IT.

"I see you've returned to your senses."

My competition is fierce but I am unbowed. My board has so many charts and graphs and fancy words it boggles all minds who stop by to contemplate it. I talk my heart out. I talk so much the judges are practically running down the aisles to get away from me. I've got it all—the hypothesis that I prove wrong. Did you know that Virginians are actually faster than Marylanders by two seconds? I got the proof. Above all I've got the will. My genes are jumping.

I even include the testimonials of some of the people I timed walking. I asked them about their thoughts on time. One forty-five-year-old lady, when I told her that, statistically, she probably has 519,200,000 seconds left to live, said, "I don't know whether to jump for joy or go back to bed."

When I ride back and lay the gold medal on Mom's lap, the reception I get is pretty damn magnificent. We're talking screeches, tears, an upper body disco dance. She insists I break out a can of root beer, which we share at her bedside. The way she acts you'd think my life was set forever. That you can now just take a look at my life chart and see its trajectory shoot into the sky: Ivy League, Nobel Prize, girls in tight jeans. Well, the last one she doesn't mention. But we both know it's part of the equation.

When I rush over to tell Dele about my victory, I find him sitting in the church's new media room looking like someone has punched him in the gut.

"What's the matter?"

"I've been fired."

It is the first time I've seen Dele not smile for a whole minute. He looks like a different person. An angry man. Turns out Pastor Stowe not only fired him but called the INS to inform them that if he didn't find another employer willing to extend his visa he'd be in the country illegally.

Mrs. Vogler is hopping mad. She's talking about circulating a petition.

"People have been very kind," says Dele.

"But I don't get it. You wanted to stay here. You prayed every day, all the time. How can this happen?"

"Sometimes God says no."

I sit down beside him. I haven't thought too much about that part. That No-you-can't-have-what-you-want part.

"He has another plan for me," Dele says.

"You really believe that?"

"I try to. There are times when I must try very hard not to hate."

My mouth falls open. "Hate? But you love everybody."

"I am human, Nic. I do not love everybody."

"But . . ."

"There are men I do not love. About whom I must pray every day not to hate."

"Pastor Stowe?"

He laughs and shakes his head. "You asked me once how my father died. I tell you. He was killed by Muslims. I found him next to his best friend, their faces sliced through."

"So you hate them. I would."

He is silent.

"I mean, they're seriously vicious, aren't they?"

He shakes his head sadly. "It was a retaliation. Two weeks

earlier, the Muslims, the Hausas, had declared Sharia law in the north. The Christians were upset. It did not apply to them but they were worried that someday it would. This is the sort of thing that festers, that turns a man's soul to hate. The Christians demonstrated. They yelled, they shook their fists, they destroyed property. The Muslims came to my town and killed many people, many friends."

"Your dad?"

"No, not then. When they had seen what the Muslims had done, my father and others went out one night. I saw him go. My mother cried. She tried to stop him. He carried a machete.

"I did not see him for three days. But I saw what he had done. In the market in the north section lay the dead, burned, mutilated. Muslim women chopped, their babies crawling over their bodies, wailing for milk.

"My father was killed a week later. And it goes on. And on. And on."

Dele leans forward and covers his eyes. "I think you know by now, Nic, monsters do exist."

We sit there for a long time in silence. Dele finally wipes his eyes with the back of his hand. He puts his smile back on. "But please," he says, "tell me your good news."

"I got gold."

Dele smiles and takes my hands. "Well, you see? God is good. Happy, happy day."

I help Dele pack. He doesn't have much but the sum is refusing to fit into his suitcase and duffle bag. We finally have to go

out and buy another two suitcases for all his gifts. Piles of batteries, razors, lotions, electronic toys, a dozen FBI sweatshirts.
His mom's air conditioner—the thing is heavier than a Moses
tablet—sits in the middle of his bedroom.

About six of us drive to the airport to see Dele off. He's hugging everybody like crazy and pushing his mountain of suitcases through the check-in line. We all watch as those suitcases
slide through the shoot and pray like crazy that they don't get
lost. And before you know it, it's time to say good-bye.

He takes my hands in his. "When Jesus was on the cross he
was terrified but he said to God, I trust you know what you are
doing. And he did."

"But he died."

"And he rose again."

I don't say anything.

"You have trouble with that one, don't you?" he says.

"Does it make me a bad person?"

"No, it makes you human. Jesus loves you, Nic. He wouldn't
want you to be afraid."

"And my mom?"

"Jesus loves your mother very much. He loves his black
sheep. They are very dear to him. He will look after her."

"My mother does not love God." Like Dele hadn't figured
out that one yet.

"Who does she love?"

". . . Herself?"

"You, Nic. She loves you. And there is her love and service
to God. In her love and service to you."

"What will happen to my mom?"

"I am sure she's getting the best care." He picks up his bag.

"What if she dies?"

He slides his passport out of his pocket. "Do not talk like that."

"Where will she go?"

"I believe she will burn in hell for all eternity."

He watches me gasp, with that small smile of his.

We stand there staring at each other in silence, the noise of the airport barreling all around us. And I pull out the only argument I can think of.

"But all those people in Africa who've never heard of Him, all those people you haven't reached yet, are they all going to hell when they die too?"

He doesn't say anything. He looks down at his shoes.

Which just pisses me off. "You don't like the difficult questions, do you, Dele?"

"On the contrary, Nic, I welcome the debate. But I do not think you like the answers."

He leans close. "Do you think I would waste all my time trying to save a man's soul if I did not believe with all my heart that I am saving him from damnation? It is not a game."

He puts his hand on my shoulder. "But this I can tell you. Remember, it is her decision. And while breath still remains in her body, there is still time. Miracles do happen."

"Do you think that's true?"

Dele doesn't answer. He just places his hand on his heart, then on mine. Then he slaps me on my cheeks, squeezes me tight, and turns away. Mrs. Vogler's singing "Onward, Christian Soldiers" as he makes his way through the security line. She's practically shouting it when the security guys take him aside to frisk him. And then he's gone. Just like that. Back to Africa.

The conversation I need to have with Mom isn't easy. I realize that from the beginning. But I can't put it off any longer. She isn't too happy. She doesn't actually *say* "Over my dead body," but you get the idea. She knows she's lost the battle. What can I say? She's weakened. I take advantage of it.

"It's a done deal," I tell her.

She laughs and bows her head like a defeated general. "Alright. Go ahead."

When I grin in victory she raises her finger. "But remember, Nic, you're going to have to grow up someday. And realize it's just you. You're going to have to find something else to make sense of this world. You're going to have to be brave. It's hard. I won't deny that. Some days it's overwhelming, listening to all the horror in the world. Some days it's better. You see strangers bumping into each other and laugh and reach out to each other to make sure each other's all right. Other days everything is so desperately sad."

"How do you live like that?"

She shrugs. "I try and concentrate on the things I can do. Look at stars, pay the mortgage, love you."

I turn to go.

"Nic."

"What?"

"Come here." She holds out her hand.

I walk over reluctantly. She grabs my hand and puts her other one over it so I can't escape. "Just promise me this. Promise me you won't become the other."

"What are you talking about?"

"It scares me. It scares me so much. I don't want to become the other for you. I don't want your heaven to be closed to me. Because my heaven is here now on earth with you."

"But for how long?" I say.

She lets go of my hand. She turns her head away. "Well, at least when an atheist has bad things happen to her, she knows it's nothing personal."

I leave the room pretty quick after that. Doesn't she know I'm doing it for her? That I'm believing my hardest because if I believe maybe God will let her in. Like they do with immigration. You're born in this country, great, no problem, you get to stay. Your mom? Well, I guess she is your closest relative. Okay, fine, she gets to come in too. Mom thinks I'm believing to drive her nuts. But I'm only trying to make sure she goes someplace nice. And I'm believing as fast as I can.

The next morning I hop out of bed early. I'd like to say the sun is shining, the clouds are pink, but the sky looks like asphalt and the clouds are pissing rain. Under my sweats I wear a dark T-shirt and shorts so that when I get wet no one will see anything they're not supposed to. When I brush my teeth in front of the bathroom mirror I wonder if the next time I look, I'll seem different. Better.

I sneak downstairs so I don't wake Mom. I want to feel free and clear and focused. I don't want any negativism today. The house is so quiet it practically echoes when I open and close the refrigerator door. There's no milk so I douse my Frosties with Mountain Dew. Then just when I open the front door I hear her calling.

"Nic. Nic! Wait!"

I ignore her and run down to the curb where Mrs. Porter's car is waiting.

At the church it's a party. Everybody is running around getting things ready. Because it isn't only going to be me. There are going to be five of us, one after the other. The tiled pool is open and ready. The water is hip-deep. Last year some minister in Arizona got electrocuted and keeled over dead when he grabbed the mic while he was still in the pool. So Pastor Stowe is going to stand next to the pool and say the prayers while two dads swing us back into the water.

Everybody treats me like a king, giving me hugs and grabbing my hands for quick impromptu prayers. I barely have time to shove a couple of danishes down my throat. Even Kevin says hello and good luck. Jim Butts comes over and shakes my hand. Mrs. Porter keeps hugging me, messing with my hair. You'd think it would behave on a day like this but it's being a heathen.

Then, just when it's all about to start I see her at the back. Standing by herself, wearing her special-occasion dress and looking nervous. Mrs. Porter gives her a huge wave and Mom sort of finger waves her back.

And then it's time. Just like an assembly: step into the pool, say your bit after Pastor Stowe says his, hold your breath, close your nose, and back you go, supported by the two dads dressed in rubber waders. People are hollering and clapping. While I'm waiting in line I keep looking over at Mom. She's staring at the pool with her mouth open. Then she looks up at me with the biggest eyes I've ever seen and she's forgetting to smile.

"Nic?" Sweat is running down Pastor Stowe's face.

I step into the pool. "Yeah, I'm ready."

Pastor Stowe places his hand on my head and closes his eyes. "Oh, Heavenly Father, oh, Heavenly Father, it is by Your grace that Nic is counted worthy to be called Your child. Help him to keep Your commandments. Renew his strength every day that he may be strong in faith and increase in zeal. Preserve him for the glorious day of Your coming. We ask this of You in Your precious name."

He pops open his eyes.

"OK, Nic, we're going to dunk you, and you'll rise up with Christ."

And there in the bright lights I am born-again. It happens so fast. I remember the dads pushing me back and the water rushing up my nose and then it's over and the camera flashes are going off. I am wading to the other side of the pool when I hear the yelling. And suddenly the singing stops and I can see everyone staring at something on the floor. And I hear Mrs. Porter yell, "Call an ambulance!"

Chapter Twenty-seven

"Alright, Mrs. Delano." The nurse comes in all crisp and bossy. "We're ready for you." She takes one look at me and stops. "I'll give you a few minutes and then we'll be on our way." She walks out again.

Mom needs to have an operation. The tumor is pressing against something serious in her brain. Which is why she passed out at church. When they got her to the hospital they were able to revive her with drugs. Now, in her room, it's just the two of us. She's lying back with her eyes closed, crushing my hand.

"Mom?"

"Yes, Nic."

"Are you scared?"

She opens her eyes and all these tears spill out. And she nods her head.

"Don't worry," I say. "It'll be okay. I'll be right outside."

She pulls my hand to her cheek. "You're going to grow up to be such a good man, Nic."

"How do you know?"

"Because I have faith too."

"Lucy Delano?" It's the nurse at the door again.

Mom pulls me close and breathes me in. "You smell of chlorine." She kisses my forehead. "Do you remember what I told you about love?"

"Yeah."

"Good. Because there'll be a quiz when I get out."

When I get to the waiting room Aunt Ruth and Jessica are there already. Dad leans against the wall with his hands over his face. Mrs. Porter is patting him on the shoulder. Kevin is staring out the window into the hospital parking lot. Grandma Rose sits clutching her big handbag on her lap.

It's nice of everyone to be there but it makes me more scared too. Like they know something I don't. Like they're getting ready to help me through the wailing part.

The operation is supposed to finish at five. At five-thirty the nurse comes in and says to my dad, "Can I talk to you a minute?" Dad looks over at me and I stand up to go with him. The nurse opens her mouth but he says, "It's okay, he should hear this." So the three of us walk outside and stand in front of the men's bathroom. She says, "It's been a little more complicated than the doctor expected. A lot of bleeding. But her vitals are still steady. It could be another hour or so."

Dad stares at her, waiting for more. But she says, "That's all I can tell you," and walks away.

Instead of following Dad back into the waiting room, I wander down the hall in search of a soda machine. I remember Cathy Meyer telling me about how her mom died of cancer when she was ten. It happens. The night before she died, Cathy noticed the sign on the grief counselor's door on the way to the bathroom. Like it was already decided. So I'm trying not to look at any signs on any doors.

Instead I see Carla rushing down the hall, a basket case on two legs. Her face is streaked with mascara, her hair all frizzed out, her hands wringing the hell out of each other. She practically collapses in front of me.

"How is she?" she pants.

"She's gone in."

"I came as soon as I could."

"It'll be a couple of hours."

She nods and wipes her face with her hand. "I got lost. And this neighborhood . . ." Her voice trails off.

"Yeah."

"Nice hospital."

"Hope so."

"I hear it's one of the finest in this field and Dr. Rajid, I looked him up on the Internet, he's . . ."

"Yeah. She might not make it."

Carla nods.

"So, what do you do now?" I ask her.

"Now?"

"Yeah. When you can't pray. And you need to."

She glances up at the ceiling, then back at me. "Well, I guess I stand around and hope like the dickens."

"Come on, then," I say, and lead her to the waiting room.

*   *   *

Mom makes it. When she wakes up, she's the same color as her sheet and talks like a duck because her tongue keeps sticking to the roof of her mouth. But the doctors say they got everything.

"Thank God," Dad says.

Mom smiles. "Let's not forget the doctor."

When squeezed, Dr. Rajid admits that she might get better or she might not. Depends, he says. On what? Dad asks. Not sure, Dr. Rajid answers. So I guess that means she's got fifty-percent chance of living. Mom says that's not so bad. It's about what everybody's got.

But she won't be able to go back to her old job. She might be alive but the tumor has done its damage. She probably won't regain all her faculties, as the doctor calls them. But every day, with drugs and lots of therapy, if we're lucky, she might again become a little more of who she is.

So she's passed on her research to Nigel and is back at home, trying not to wait for him to call or e-mail her about every little detail.

She likes to pat me on the knee. "We'll take it slow," she says. "We've got all the time in the world." And believe me, an afternoon with someone with impaired memory *is* endless. Monopoly is too advanced for her right now so we play a lot of checkers. When she wipes the board with me, she laughs so hard, you'd think she'd found her earth-sized planet.

One night, to give her a workout, I set up my star planetarium in her room. What else do you do with a woman who thinks she's stardust? But it's a good thing, I guess. Because stardust, like love, seems to last forever.

I turn out the lights and then flick on the bulb inside the machine. In the darkness all the stars are projected onto the ceiling and shine like pinpricks from heaven. Then I sit down next to her bed and point to a cluster of stars about a foot from the closet door.

"Okay, Einstein. What constellation is that?"

She looks up and concentrates with all her might.

"Crux," she says.

"No, that's in the southern hemisphere." I wave my pointer over Orion. "This is obviously northern. Try again."

"Lyra?"

"Lyra? Does that look like a lyre to you?"

"Cassiopeia?"

I glance over at her in disbelief but then see she's about to cry.

"Woof woof," I say.

"Canis Major!"

And I say "Attagirl."

"Hope is a privilege," Grandma Rose tells me the next morning. "Hang on to it with all your might." Which I guess means that unless you're a blind homeless orphan you still can have hope. And even if you are a blind homeless orphan, you just might have someone like Dele.

I haven't been to church since my mom's operation. It's been pretty busy at home. They've sent over a ton of food and Pastor Stowe has called a couple of times to see how we're doing. Which is nice of him. But to tell you the truth, I'm not sure who I'm talking to there anymore. There are times when God seems to be on my side. When the good things happen. But that would mean He had a hand in making my mom so sick and even hurting Jessica, and I don't see the point of that. I'm not sure I'm going to break up with Him, though. Because it's nice to have someone to talk to.

Which is why I go over to Kevin's house to see how he's doing. I miss him. I want to talk like we used to—before it got all weird and stressed and angry.

But he isn't there. He's gone to some Moral Leaders of the Future camp in Arizona. Mrs. Porter asks me in and sits me down with a plate of chocolate chip cookies.

"I'm so sorry, Nic," she says.

"Yeah. Me too."

"Milk?"

"Sure . . . please . . . ma'am."

She pours me a tall glass and then goes back over to the kitchen sink where she's drying dishes. Neither of us says anything. We just listen to the quiet and the clinking of plates. Until she says to me, "Nic, tell me about Time again." And I know she's asking me this to take my mind off things because I'm not sure she understands what I'm talking about. She's just being nice. So I start:

"We're always at a single moment called the present, with the past behind us and the future to come. And we're here only for a very short time. All together. So what does that all mean? . . . I don't know."

And I lay my head down on the table. Mrs. Porter puts

down the pot she's drying and comes over and hugs me. She just leans over like that for a little while and doesn't say anything. Because maybe the truth is like that lone violin in Beethoven's piece. Beautiful even if it ends up breaking your heart. And maybe when we're all gone, that music will be the last thing heard floating through space, telling of a time when we lived on earth and had so many opinions.

At the end of the summer, Dad goes back to Williamsburg for good. Not a surprise, I guess. So there isn't the happy ending I was hoping for. You know, my parents running toward each other and hugging the hell out of each other and living happily ever after. Nope, it's more of a "Thanks a bunch, I'll always be there for ya, have a nice life."

Mom and Dad hire a lady to come help out full-time. She turns out to be one of those young Slovakian numbers whose picture you find on beer mugs. She arrives the day Dad is leaving. She walks in, drops her bags, and grabs me into tight hug. Her breasts are like activated airbags. She says, "Oh, Neek, we have goot time, you and me. Okay?"

And you should see Dad's face.

When it's time for Dad to leave, Mom stays upstairs while I go out to his car to say good-bye.

"So . . . Nic," he says.

"So . . . Robert," I say.

He laughs and hugs me close and I notice that in the past six months I've grown half a foot taller than him. He thumps me three times on the back.

"I'll be up every couple of weeks."

"Yeah. Okay."

I stare down at the overgrown grass that neither of us ever got around to mowing.

"Good-bye, Nic."

"Good-bye, Dad."

When I start high school in the fall, I see that the lockers are the same: cold metal stinking of old socks and jockstraps. The students are the same too: con artists in designer jeans and a few rough diamonds with bad hair. Even the teachers are the same. Except for Mr. Peck in chemistry. He seems different right away. He's got straight hair in a bowl cut and a thin goatee that looks like a question mark. He points to his eyes. He says, "What are these?" After a couple of confused seconds he gets what he wants. "Eyes. Good. I can see I've got a couple of geniuses here."

He reaches up and in noisy chalk writes OBSERVE straight across the board. And he underlines it three times.

He says, "Listen up, people. I'm not going to tell you what I hope is so. Or what I wish is so. I'm going to tell you what I can observe or what others have observed, because I don't have the instruments." He says, "Today we are going to observe what happens when we mix calcium chloride and phenolphthalein."

He looks around the class, then zeroes in on me. "We'll start with you." Then he hands me a graduated cylinder.

It's long and sleek like a baton.

And I remember how Mom likes to tell me she believes in the universe. She believes in its wonder. In its ability to confound us. Which is why she wants me to know everything. Why the leaves on the trees change colors. Why the sky is blue. How the wings of a bird make it fly.

And I asked her once, "Why do I have to know it all?"

"Because it will save you," she said.

I sit there a long time, staring at the glass, seeing my mom's face reflected in it.

"Nic?" Mr. Peck says.

"Yeah, all right."

And I reach out and take it.